Lovers' Leap

Rikki Goodwin

Cover Art Design by: Kelly Moran/Rowan Prose Publishing

Photo Credit: Adobe Images/Deposit Photos

First Edition

ISBN: 978-1-961967-64-9

Rowan Prose Publishing, LLC

www.RowanProsePublishing.com

Published in the United States of America

GONE, BUT NOT FORGOTTEN
GHOST
GLASSES
Rikki Goodwin

Acknowledgments

I didn't realize what *Lovers' Leap* was really "about" until my eightieth read-through during the editing process: Obsessive love and the damage it causes. So, my first thank you is to Paul Simon for writing "Slip-Sliding Away." This story might have been inspired by Delores's unnamed husband and his lost identity.

I know people like that—people who insist they are no one without the distinction of partners, their children, their careers. So, my second thank you is to my husband, Patrick, for all of the hobbies and interests that we share, but especially the ones we do not. Thank you for always giving me time and space to be my own person. Thank you for being yours.

Thanks to the body piercing community and all the friends I've made at my "real" job, especially Rachael for reminding me that we are always more than our careers.

Thanks to my new writing friends! It's a lonely endeavor and that's why I love it, but it's always good to have community. Thanks to my brother-in-law Craig for being literally the only person to read this before I got a publisher for it. Huge thanks to Kelly for believing in me and the rest of the Rowan Prose team I've gotten to know over the last few months. Thanks to everyone in the Books of Horror group for introducing me to a whole world of indie authors (and making me buy a new bookcase, sheesh!).

Finally, my family. My blood family (Mom and Dad, Jon and Ian, Barbie and Lennon, David and Amber), Patrick's family (There are too many of you to list, but Connie is my favorite), and my shop family (Christian, Melissa, Xander, Michael, Aldo, and all of our friends who don't technically work with us, but are always ready to help). You're all a mess and I love you.

Now

Dimitri doesn't know where we keep our dishes.

We've lived in this constricting, dated apartment together for over a year, skinning our elbows on its tired walls, searching for a magic portal in the too small closets for our meager wardrobes. He's the one that unpacked and organized the kitchen when we moved in, paring down our combined collections of cooking contraptions to almost nothing, filling up every available space. He cooks dinner more than I do, intimately familiar with the home for every pan, every spice, every knife and yet, here he is, opening the second wrong cabinet in a row hunting for our plates.

My body is on autopilot, but cold sweat trickles down the small of my back, tickling each knob of my spine with the caress of a spider feeling its way along a thread. My internal monologue is a very unhelpful repetition, *oh shit oh shit oh,* but instead of clawing my way out of my own tickling skin, the pasta gets removed from the stovetop and drained in the sink, then I dump some margarine in there and start stirring. *Oh shit.*

Thankfully, he's finally found the plates and set the table. He got the silverware drawer right on the first try, but that's an easy guess. We only have the three drawers and one stands ajar from my removal of a wooden spoon. An open book test he's still failing. A chair scrapes as he takes a place at the table and when I turn, pasta in hand, I'm not even surprised to see he's decided to sit in a different chair than usual. He's in *my* chair. I don't comment, I just ladle.

"This looks wonderful," he says.

It does not look wonderful.

Taking my (*his*) seat, I try so hard to think of a good explanation. What could cause a person to abruptly change their mannerisms and suddenly not know where their own dishes live? Some kind of medical thing? Could "some kind of medical thing" also be the cause of his transgression earlier today? I take a bite and chew. The noodles aren't even cooked all the way, and I forgot salt.

I can't do this.

"Where are you going?" he asks.

I'm already halfway across the room, heart thudding unhelpfully loud in my ears, turning the apartment into a drum circle. "I. Uh. I need my phone charger." I might be screaming over my heartbeat. "I think it's in the car."

"Hm." His mouth sounds full.

He's suddenly the monster under the bed that I'd never dare to look at. My neck won't turn to see, and my legs won't cooperate, either. I'm staring, frozen, towards the door. What if he tries to stop me from leaving? Would he do that? Do I even know what he'd do? My hands slide down my thighs, searching for the little square lifeline I'll need if I leave this place, but I only feel cheap material, damp with sweat. *Oh, shit.* Dimitri's fork scrapes his plate behind me and I turn back, scan the kitchen. My phone is plugged in on the kitchen counter, the little battery icon on the screen a cheerful green. I do the quickest calculations I've ever done in my life. I've never been a math girlie. Should I run back for it and sprint out the door, leave all pretense behind? Could he catch me? Should I just head towards the car and abandon the phone?

My eyes are darting around, imagining escape routes, and they accidentally fall on him. He's staring right at me, a tiny smirk on his face. A knowing smirk. He's aware that I am not fooled by whatever is going on here.

That's not Dimitri.

I grit my teeth, force my legs to walk straight past him, (I notice in my peripheral that he unbelievably takes another bite of noodles) yank my phone from its cable, and head right back toward the door in the most confident, brisk walk I can muster.

"Your charger is plugged in on the counter," he says to my back.

I'm at the door, pawing for my keys on the little hook. No more pretense, I guess.

The door slams behind me as I scramble down the apartment steps. My breath is coming in little weird gasps now. What if he follows me? What might he do? Where should I go?

The neighbors wouldn't help. Some kind of incident goes down in this apartment complex most nights of the week. We all just draw our shades and lock our doors, mind our own business. One time, I called the police, worried about one of my neighbors who had a man pushing her around in the parking lot. They had screamed at each other for close to an hour before I called. After the cops had come and gone, the neighbor beat on my door. I didn't answer her, which might be embarrassing to admit, but I was terrified. She screamed at my closed door that under no circumstances should I ever dare to nose into her affairs again. I didn't. I don't expect anyone to do so for me now.

I feel stupid just imagining that I might need help against Dimitri. I know him. I love him. He'd never hurt me. *Dimitri* would never hurt me, but I really don't think it's Dimitri sitting at our dining room table eating my shitty pasta.

I press the car's unlock button four or five times as I run down the short sidewalk. I will not be caught fumbling to unlock a door. I don't look back. I don't hear our door open and shut, but it's difficult to hear anything over my wheezing breaths, my thunderous heart. I lock the car from inside before I even turn it on. I don't know if I've ever done that before. This is a day of firsts, I guess. I chance a glance up at our living room window.

He's standing there, looking out at me.

He's back lit from the light over our dining room table. The entirety of our apartment shines through the glass. I cringe and think, *we really need to get some curtains,* before I remember that we might not ever do anything together again. *We* might not exist after this night. Dimitri might already not exist.

I can't see his face though. He's all shadow though the dingy glass, a halo of the dining room light (one bulb burnt out) only showing me his edges. Maybe he has no face. He might be swaying from foot to foot or maybe I'm hyperventilating, making myself dizzy, making the world turn back and forth, a spinning top nearing its end, ready to collapse. He holds up a hand and gives his arm a weird little shake. He's waving at me?

Shaking away the image of him, I let my world collapse until it's only the interior of the car, nothing more. I only have to get the car started. I only have to get away. It takes my shaking hand a few seconds to get the key in the ignition, but the car has no fear and purrs easily to life. Its world is not crumbling around it. It has a job to do, and it will do it. Person starts the car and it goes where it's told. As I throw it into reverse, there's no stopping myself from looking up one more time.

Dimitri is gone.

Focus. I turn to back out of my parking space. *Drive carefully, don't be stupid. It'll be okay.* I back out slowly, spin halfway around in my seat, then twist forward again to begin my escape. He's standing at the driver's side window.

I gasp but don't scream. I don't slam my foot down on the accelerator, don't peel away into the night. I look at him. He looks the same as he always has. He looks exactly like the man I've been dating for two years and have been friends with for longer. I know his freckles and his dark hair hanging down and touching his eyelashes (*how can he stand that, doesn't it tickle?*). I have my foot on the brake. Am *I* suffering from some kind of episode? Maybe I'm hurting more from what happened than I initially realized. Maybe I'm in shock, or *was* in shock and now things are crystal clear and forever changed.

Is it me?

He raises a hand slowly again and the motion, so minuscule, is so foreign to the man I know, that panic claws its way back through my chest, digging its little prickly nails through my lungs, slamming against my heart as it thrashes. Something is definitely wrong, I'm not crazy. Something is wrong with him. I can't pin it, it's an aversion crawling over my skin. It's a tickle on my neck that might be a hair or might be a bug. I shudder. He isn't Dimitri. He's someone else. He's something else. He *is* swaying a little. He could be caught in a breeze, like he's no more than a leaf. He makes a fist and I cringe, but he then he rotates his wrist in a tiny circle. *Roll down the window.*

I know I shouldn't, but I hit the button, roll it down a two inch crack.

"If you're going to the store," the thing who is not Dimitri says, "can you pick up some eggs? I thought I might make us cake." It smiled a smile that was such a good imitation of Dimitri's that I felt my lips turn up, too, the traitors. "I remember that you like cake."

My mouth is dry. Why would he say such a weird thing? Why is he being so weird? Do I like cake? I don't even know right now. "I'll grab some." And then I slowly, oh so slowly, drive out of the parking lot, rolling my window up as I go.

I wait until I'm out of sight of the apartment complex before I grab my phone off the passenger seat and dial with shaking fingers. I put it on speaker and set it in the cup holder, like I always do when I'm about to drive and talk. Like I'm just running to the store so Dimitri can make us a cake and want to chat with my friend on the way.

Finn answers in a half a ring. "Hazel? Jesus, Hazel, is that you?"

He's whispering. The "s" noises are harsh playing through the car speakers.

"Something's wrong. Something's wrong with D." As soon as I say it out loud, the panic beast bubbles from my throat, and I burst into hysteric tears. I'm going to have to pull over, I'm shaking so much. I can't see, I can't breathe. Am I far enough away from the apartment to pull over?

"Thank fuck," Finn says, completely ignoring my sobs. Why is he whispering? Where is he? "I'm hiding in my own god-damned basement. Lucy is being weird as hell. I thought maybe I was going crazy."

"I'm coming to get you," I manage, my voice thick and not my own. "I'm in the car, I'll come get you and we'll figure this out, okay?" I realize as I say this that I'm already calming down a little bit. Finn is scared, so that means I have to take care of him, I have to be in control. I can't be in control if I can't even breathe properly.

"Maybe they got sick or something up there," he whispers. "Maybe we should get them both to a doctor?"

My stomach clenches. Up there. The bed and breakfast. He just so casually mentioned it, like it didn't turn all four of our lives into a waking nightmare. Like he isn't afraid to glance at his own reflection in the bathroom. Like he doesn't see the place straight through his eyelids, like they're nothing more than tinted glass every time he closes them. Up there. But he doesn't mention what Dimitri and Lucy told us just an hour ago. Has it only been an hour? *It was like a possession,* they'd said. *It wasn't us.*

"I want to come get you first," I say as I'm speeding. I let off the accelerator. "We need to talk."

The speakers produce nothing but crackling silence for a moment and I worry that the connection might be lost. Does anyone have good cell reception in their basements? But then he hisses, "I'm afraid of her, Hazel. I'm afraid to go upstairs." He confesses like it's a dirty secret. I hear the shame oozing through the line.

"I..." I don't know how to say it. I haven't even seen Lucy, what if there's nothing wrong with her? "Dimitri let me leave. He didn't try to stop me," I finally answered.

"Do you think it's Dimitri?"

The question is a punch to my sanity. I wasn't going to say it, not out loud. It's obviously Dimitri, how could it not be him? It looks like him, it sounds like him.

"No," I answer.

"Thank fuck," Finn says again, and I am soothed in the knowledge that I'm absolutely talking to Finn. No other could impersonate him so perfectly.

"Look," I say and put on my turn signal. Finn and Lucy's exit is approaching. "I'll be there in like two minutes. Just meet me out front. She'll let you go. D didn't ask any questions. Just meet me out front."

"Don't hang up. Just stay on the phone with me, okay?" His voice is cracking. I tell myself it's just from him whispering so much, but I think he must be crying, or at least trying not to cry. Finn is crying. Finn doesn't cry. Finn didn't cry at his own parents' funeral. If Finn is crying now, it'll be the second time today he's done so, maybe even the third, and I probably can't handle whatever is going on. It must just be from the whispering.

"I'll stay with you." My own voice is trembling again. My new courage is already leaving. "Just get out now and start walking down the street. Don't wait."

"Okay. Okay, Okay." There's a rustling noise and I picture him standing up. Was he like me, trying desperately to be casual, sitting on the old loveseat down there that we used to make out on, back when we were teenagers, and the house was still his parents'? Or was he maybe wedged between the washing machine and the wall, hidden in the dark and out of sight, with his hand up to quieten his breath? Like Lucy was some apex predator, stalking the house, and not the shy little redhead that's afraid to ask for cream for her coffee? I shake my head. Lucy would never hurt anyone, especially not Finn. At least, that's what I had thought until today.

"You still there, Finn?" I ask.

"*Shh.*" I hear more rustling. I think maybe I've just been placed in a pocket. It's the middle of the night and there are literally zero other cars at the intersection where I sit, waiting for a green light to grant me permission. I tap my fingers against the wheel impatiently, crane my head to see the stoplights facing the other direction. They aren't changing.

"Hey," says Finn in his normal voice. I jump at how much louder it is, scramble to dial the volume down, terrified of feedback playing through his phone, of alerting Lucy.

I hear her then and her small voice is much further away and so quiet that I almost turn the volume back up again. Would I be able to hear a difference in her voice? "Hey! Where have you been?"

"Just...just downstairs." Finn isn't great at sounding casual. "Hey, I'm going to, uh. Go run down to the gas station. I need a Red Bull or something, I'm beat."

Another crackly pause. I lean forward, not wanting to miss Lucy's response. My light is still red. Their house is only a few blocks away.

"It's so late," she says. "Why don't you just go to bed?"

My fingers are tapping as fast as my heart rate. *Just go*, I'm pleading. *Just run.*

The pocket I'm in scrapes against the speaker again. "Nah, I don't think I could actually sleep. It'll probably be a late night. You can go to bed though, you don't have to wait up for me. We can talk more tomorrow?"

"Oh, I don't sleep anymore," Lucy says casually, as though discussing a bad habit. I imagine her little upturned nose crinkling with distaste.

I slam my foot on the gas and blow through the red light. "Go!" I scream as loud as I can. I feel like my throat is tearing. I wonder if he can even tell what I'm saying. "Run! Now! I'm almost there."

There's only the scratching of fabric against the speaker in response. I can only hope he's running. I strain to hear the squeak of their big oak door, a sound even more familiar to me that my own apartment door, begging to hear it. He'll get to me. He'll get out. I hit a speed bump in their neighborhood going about sixty miles an hour and actually feel the car leave the ground for a second before making a horrible grinding sound as it returns to the pavement.

There. The door, I hear it opening. I also can barely hear Finn's breath over the static. I just have to get to him. I just have to get to him and we'll figure everything out together. It's going to be okay as long as I'm not alone.

I slow down as I approach the house. Finn could be running toward me now and I don't want to miss him in the dark. I don't see him yet, but I can hear him.

"Lucy, please. I think there's something—" His words cut off in a strangled yell and I hear it twice. Once, from their front yard and then repeated a second later through my speakers. I think I might hear it repeated in my head forever after.

With presence of mind I never would have thought I would possess in a situation like this (if I, ever, in my wildest dreams could imagine a situation like this), I back the car up and turn so that my headlights illuminate their yard like winter sunshine.

They both stand on the expertly landscaped lawn. Finn looks very much like a deer would look, his face haggard in the cold light, his usually carefully groomed beard going a little wild with the day's neglect, his steely eyes almost comical in their terror, but Lucy seems to not notice me. I study her. She's in a nightdress, white, with lacy sleeves and trim. I wonder, as I have a million times in the past, how she could possibly sleep in those get ups. It looks itchy. My brain is refusing to take in anything more.

She is completely motionless except for the tiniest sway back and forth. Am I dizzy? No. She is rocking, like she is trying to keep steady on a moving boat. Like there is music playing, but only she can hear it.

She has her delicate hand clasped tightly around Finn's wrist. I know he could twist and get away from her. She's so small. She has to climb on the counters to reach things in the kitchen cabinets. She sits so close to the steering wheel when she drives that she has to turn backward to look at me in the passenger seat. She can't hurt Finn. She wouldn't hurt him.

"Where are you going, really?" she asks, and it's like she's with me in the car, thanks to the phone. It's in Finn's sweatpants pocket, hanging out and dangerously near falling to the ground. I stifle a scream or a sob, I can't tell which it was trying to be.

Alarm bells are ringing in my head. Blaring sirens. They are screaming, *look at her.*

I look at her nightdress. Her bare feet in the dewy soft grass. Her hair, newly brushed, fanning around her face like a porcelain doll's. Her fingernails digging into Finn's wrist. Her right hand holding a long, wide kitchen knife, reflecting white light into my eyes.

I throw my door open, forgetting to put the car in park. It rolls forward and bumps against the curb. I'm screaming. I'm screaming Finn's name. He's staring at the woman who is his wife, but is not his wife, and I don't think he can move at all. I think he's completely shut down somehow. I get out of the car, leave the door hanging open, and trip over the curb. My palms slip across the cold dewy grass, and I end up with my chin in the dirt and my shins scraped raw on the concrete.

"Lucy," I say from the ground. My voice sounds much calmer than it has any right to sound. I say her name like she's a dog holding something it shouldn't have in its mouth. "Lucy. What are you doing?"

Her head turns to me, so, so slowly. Her eyes show mostly whites. She forgot to turn her eyes with her head. They're still staring at Finn in front of her. They snap to me and catch the headlights' glow, flare in the night like an animal's. My heart is in my throat.

"Finn, *move!*" I beg, pushing myself from the ground. His head shakes like there's a mosquito near his ear. He finally begins to pull away from her grasp.

Lucy yanks him towards her, and he stumbles. I don't know if she is stronger than usual or if he is just caught off guard. She is still staring directly at me.

She digs the kitchen knife deep into his stomach. It happens so fast. She doesn't hesitate, doesn't even turn to look at him. The knife is just suddenly gone, only a handle buried in his t-shirt. She still has his wrist in one hand, the knife handle in the other. He screams and then a second later, the car screams in his voice, too. Maybe the car is afraid after all.

"Stay home tonight," she says, and she might be talking to me. Her eyes are locked with mine and her face shows no hints.

Finn sinks to his knees, screaming endlessly into the quiet night. I think I see lights turning on in the surrounding houses in my peripheral. This isn't the kind of neighborhood where people scream outside after dark.

Lucy doesn't bend with him, and the knife reappears at the end of the handle she's holding. She drops his wrist, lets him fall, a discarded toy.

I decide I'm going to kill her. I think nothing else.

Still crouched in a half standing position at the curb, I dig my heels in and sprint towards her. I might be yelling, I don't know. *I'm going to kill her.*

She watches me approach with something I imagine as disdain, but it might just be utter indifference. "You should go home," she says, her voice bored.

I intend to slam into her and knock her to the ground, I think. That's as far as my mind had worked out a plan. She waits until I am close enough to almost touch her, then steps to the side. She *must* have stepped, but it was so fast, she is suddenly just further to the left than I calculated. She sticks out a bare foot and I go sprawling into the grass again. It probably was hilarious to watch from any of the neighbors' windows. I hope someone has called the cops. I hope some suburban dad comes out here with his baseball bat, hoping to be a hero on the news tomorrow.

I'm lying on my stomach, about to push myself up again, when white hot pain sears through my right hand. I'm stuck to the ground. I really, really don't want to, but I look. The knife handle is planted in the middle of my hand. Crazily, I realize that I chopped vegetables at their kitchen island with this knife only a few nights ago. *How far you've come, little knife.* I finally remember to scream, but it's immediately muffled by a hand being placed over my mouth.

I stare around wildly, a trapped animal. Lucy has abandoned me. The hand on my face is large and rough. It's covered in tiny scars from years spent working in kitchens, little burns and nicks, and smells strongly of burning tobacco, of tar and death and nicotine. It's the hand I know best and a stranger is controlling it.

"Hey, I thought you were going to get eggs," Dimitri's voice says jovially. "What happened?"

My face breaks apart, all of me breaks apart. My sobs pierce the night that was settling back into silence. Dimitri (*this is not Dimitri)* cups his hand to deaden my racket, but seems to take care not to stop my breath. He pulls the knife slowly out of the ground. "Shh." He yanks the handle, and it comes free of my hand, also freeing a shriek from my throat. The air brightens around me with the vivid ferocity of the pain, giving everything white edges. It's literally too much to bear, I've never felt anything close to it, not even my IUD. Dimitri lets the knife thud to the ground beside me. "Let's get you home."

He picks me up and puts me over his shoulder, starts walking back to our car (we only have one car, how did he get here? Finn's car, I remember dimly. I borrowed Finn's car earlier today, a lifetime ago.), I try to kick, but shock is setting in. Everything is in slow motion.

Lucy is dragging Finn into the house by his ankles, his shirt hitched up around his armpits, his phone shines in the grass, having abandoned the pocket during his fall. His soft flesh glows in the moonlight, except where it doesn't. Except where it's dark, dark blood, the patch of darkness growing as I watch. He is completely still.

"Finn? Finn!" The sight jars me back to life and I start screaming, kicking, scratching.

"Hey, now." The man who is not my partner coos like I'm only a fussy child. He opens the passenger door, flips me into the seat, and my head thrashes and knocks against the roof of the car on the way down. I think it might hurt more than my hand for some reason. "Careful." He leans in to buckle my seatbelt and smells like Dimitri. My brain is snapping like a rubber band. It's all too much. He closes the car door.

I hammer on the window, still calling for Finn. I just want him to look back at me, is that too much to ask? I'm too late. His head is being dragged through the front door and Lucy's little arm reaches out and pulls the door back into the frame. I hear the squeak of it and the familiarity in this nightmare makes me sick. I stop slapping the glass, leaving blood smeared all over it. My head and hand now both have angry heartbeats.

The car rocks as someone sits in the driver's seat. The driver side door closes with a gentle clunk. I can't make myself turn away from the closed oak door of Finn and Lucy's house, and it starts receding into darkness as the car's headlights leave it.

"Who are you?" I ask, and it's barely a whisper.

"You know me!" He laughs with my boyfriend's laugh. He stole it. "Don't worry about Finn. You'll see him soon. We were going to keep it a surprise from you two, but—" the car rolls gently over the speed bump "—we're going to start this weekend over! The last few days were such a mess."

I finally drag my eyes away from the window, but I can't make myself look at him. I stare straight ahead. We're coming up to the stoplight. It's red again, or maybe still. I eye the door handle.

As the car slows down, the thing that is not Dimitri moves and I jump, startled. But he isn't reaching for me, he is casually reaching down to his own door handle. He engages the child safety lock. The car comes to a stop and he waits patiently for the light to change. "We're going to go back up to Lovers' Leap, all four of us. We'll make things right."

Finally, blissfully, the blood loss, pain, and horror is too much and my vision starts to tunnel. I hope I don't wake up.

Chapter 1

Three days earlier

"Do you think you could get the weekend off?" Finn asked, like an idiot. I was driving to work and my phone was sitting in my cup holder, on speaker.

My frustrated sigh vibrated the air, and my eyes rolled back, putting me and everyone else on the road in danger. "Yeah, if I would have requested it two months ago. The schedule for this weekend is already out. Have you really *never* worked a real job?"

He laughed. "You know perfectly well I haven't. Well, listen..." His voice was choppy, his breath loud.

He must have been jogging. I hated when he talked to me while jogging. Not only was it annoying, but it was a reminder that he'd grown into the kind of person who jogged, and I should have probably also been doing something healthy. At least something productive? Instead, I reached over and cracked open the first of what would probably be many canned energy drinks for the day, shielding its carbonated spray from my phone screen with a cupped palm.

"Call off. I've got a proposition for you. Dimitri, too," he said.

I gulped the soda instead of responding right away. I was running late, again. They should have given up scheduling me opening shifts long ago, but a coffee shop really only *has* opening shifts. I sped up and passed the car ahead of me that was already going ten over the speed limit. "I can't just call off, Finn. I have rent to pay. Weekends are good tips."

"I'll pay you."

"What the fuck?" I slammed the can back down, and it sloshed onto my hand. Now I could show up both late *and* sticky, wonderful. "You'll *pay* me? You haven't even told me what this is about. You are *so* oblivious sometimes, you know that?" I squeezed through a yellow light. Orange, maybe. "What if I lose my job, are you going to pay me then?"

My face burned with embarrassment, small blessing he couldn't see. I'd had to borrow money from Finn more times than I would have liked to admit. Probably more times than he'd ever admit to anyone, too. I *thought* I'd mostly paid him back. Sometimes, when I remembered that I owed him money and brought it up ("I'll get you the rest of it next payday!" seemed like a perpetual phrase I'd utter), he'd insist that it was a gift and not to worry about it and just be ready if he ever needs a favor. He'd never needed a favor. He never seemed to need anything from me.

"I mean, maybe yes." He'd stopped jogging, his tone suddenly full of brevity. "It's a business proposition. Can you guys come over for dinner tonight? We can talk it all over. I'll cook."

This took me by surprise. When was the last time it was Finn's idea for us to hang out? Lately it'd been mostly me (and occasionally his wife) doing any planning. When I was feeling down, it seemed that my constant intervention was the only fuel kindling our entire friendship. Obviously, I'd have to agree to dinner. I'd just have to hope Dimitri was in a sociable and spontaneous mood tonight after a full work shift. I'd worry about that later.

"Tell me what's going on. You aren't funny," I muttered, my anger already melting away into curiosity. I whipped the car into the coffee shop parking lot, earning a blaring horn for forgetting to use my turn signal. I flipped the bird to the other driver in lieu of apology. Same thing, right? The shop was supposed to open in three minutes and there were already ancient people milling around the front door, peering in the windows, looking at their primitive watches. The hands would be displaying that I should have been there twelve minutes ago to start the coffee brewing, to put frozen pastries in the oven.

"Remember when we were kids?" Finn asked. His dreamy smile oozed through the speaker.

I laughed. "I mean, yes. Anything specifically? I need to get to work."

"Remember, we were going to move to the country, open a little hotel?"

I did remember. We were fifteen and in love, and he was going to be a famous photographer, and I was going to be a famous author, and we were going to open a cute little hotel to run, to live in, and to pay our bills. Even at fifteen, we knew that writers and photographers weren't going to do that last bit. We were very practical, we had it all figured out. I smiled in spite of myself.

"Well, I was thinking. Why don't we do it?"

I scoffed. "I think it's a little late for that, don't you?" Finn had been married for a while now, and not to me. We hadn't planned *everything* perfectly at fifteen, after all.

"Nah. Listen, we'll talk about it tonight. Seven?"

"I mean, I guess..."

"See you then." He hung up.

I sat, my seatbelt undone, but still settled across my lap. I stared at my phone. "What the fuck, man?" I asked Finn, but I knew he wasn't there.

I tried to pull on my apron as I power walked up to the back door. I had my keys in my mouth (gross) and both my hands fumbling behind me, trying to tie the straps in a little bow. I forgot my energy drink in the car. I snuck in through the back door into the kitchen, away from the prying customer eyes.

"Hazel, come on! I thought you were dead." My coworker leaned through the doorframe to glare at me, beyond pissed and well on her way to despondent acceptance. I didn't blame her. I sucked. "Just get on the register," She sighed. "I'm unlocking the door. Everything's done."

As I poured a half dozen black coffees and excitedly made one perfect cappuccino for a particularly daring gentleman, my mind wandered. Was Finn really considering opening a hotel? It really didn't seem like that plausible a dream, as an adult. Plus, he was married now and successful. He didn't need a hotel *or* me. We had our own separate lives now. Our own separate dreams. His just kept coming true and mine kept falling apart, but that wasn't his responsibility. Besides, maybe he deserved to have some things work out for him. And maybe I didn't.

"This cappuccino has too much foam in it." The daring gentleman slapped it down on the counter in front of me, sloshing milk over the side of the mug. He didn't know what a cappuccino was.

I smiled (or was it a grimace?), apologized, and made him a latte. I hated this place.

Dimitri worked later than me that day, so when I got off work, I drove down to his office building to pick him up. Like always, I felt a pang of guilt about the fact that he paid for the car, but he always seemed to be the one having to catch the bus to work. His schedule was always the same and there was a bus stop only a block from his building, so he insisted it was fine, that it made sense, but the guilt persisted. I didn't pull my weight. I was a drag on everyone around me. My friends had to offer to *pay* me to take the weekend off. The deficiency was so potent it manifested as nausea.

I'd been doom scrolling so efficiently that I swore I'd only been waiting a minute or two before Dimitri hopped into the passenger seat, but it must have been more like twenty. I looked at the time. Twenty-five.

"Sorry," he said, misreading my shocked glance at the clock. "Got held up on a call." He leaned over and kissed my cheek.

"Ew, don't, I'm all gross," I wailed, but he leaned again and licked my cheek. "Ugh! Disgusting." I giggled, even blushed a little, and put the car into drive. "How was work?"

"Sucked." He rubbed his eyes with the palms of his rough hands. "You?"

I knew he was tired, but I also knew that was a lie. He really did enjoy his work. It was never the *work* part of it, he was just content in any scenario. I'd known him through several jobs, and he never seemed to have the crippling dread I experienced at any of the jobs I'd had. He bussed tables, it was fine. He made friends and connections with diners and coworkers alike. He had a smile to spare every day. He became a line cook and I was so proud of him, asked if he had dreams of being a chef. He'd only shrug. Work was just work to him, a task to be completed daily before he got to come home and enjoy himself. He didn't feel the need for his work to define him, like I did. He was Dimitri and that was always enough. He enjoyed trashy space dramas and video games with epic storylines and pho, and if he happened to be an underwriter or a cook or a delivery guy five days a week, that part wasn't integral to his identity. I longed for that sense of self.

"Same," I replied. He did look exhausted. He'd probably like nothing more than to claim the comfiest spot on the couch and turn his brain off for the next few hours. *But...* "Lucy and Finn invited us for dinner tonight. Seven."

Why did I do that, I wonder? Why did I say Lucy's name first when I talk about them? I told myself it just had a better ring to it, rolls off the tongue easier. I never acknowledged that I was putting distance between myself and Finn for Dimitri's benefit. Making Finn sound less important to me.

Dimitri groaned. "Aw, I don't know, Nut. I'm pretty beat." Nut was by far, the worst pet name I could ever have possibly imagined for myself. How did that happen? Who let my parents do that to me?

"I already said we would," I said, trying to make myself sound annoyed, too. Like going out would be a chore. But I *did* want to go. I wanted to see Finn and Lucy (I mean, "Lucy and Finn," of course), and I didn't want to cook dinner. I wished Lucy would be cooking. Her dishes were always exciting, elegant, high-class nonsense I would never order on my own in a restaurant, but always enjoyed. Beggars can't be choosers, and even Finn was a better cook than me.

"Well, in that case, I guess it's settled," Dimitri said, the words more sigh than sound. He was annoyed, of course, but he was going to just drop it.

I felt shitty, but not bad enough to cancel the dinner. I was too curious about Finn's words. *A business proposition.* I reached over and patted Dimitri's leg. "Thanks, D." I made a little kissy noise that he didn't bother to reciprocate, his eyes already fluttering closed. The drive from his office to our apartment was only about fifteen minutes, but by the time I pulled into our parking lot, he was asleep. The pothole by our parking spot that never seemed to get fixed jerked him awake like an alarm.

"I've gotta shower," I said, hopping out of the car, leaving him staring around blearily while he reoriented himself after the dismal nap.

He picked up my mostly full, sticky, flat energy drink and dumped it onto the pavement before getting out. He gave me a resigned sigh that turned into a genuine yawn. "Yeah, yeah, get all gussied up. I know you have to show off for Lucy."

I laughed it off, but my cheeks burned. "Well, she's just too pretty. One of these days I'll steal her away."

I joked, but it was mostly true. I *had* to dress up for Lucy. She was beautiful, she was successful, she was smart, and always, *always* kind. All the things I wished I was. I wanted to impress her. I wanted her to be my best friend, too. Unfortunately, I felt like a slug around her. I was jealous of her. I'd spent all the time I'd known her letting that jealousy slide away into adoration. It wasn't her fault she was better than me and she'd never once insinuated that she even *knew* she was better than me. I couldn't hate such a nice person, no matter how hard I'd tried.

Finn said I was weird around her. "How's she going to get to know you if you never act like yourself?" he asked me once after my second or third time hanging out with them as a newly minted couple. "She thinks my best friend is a cardboard cutout. It's awkward. If she likes me, she's going to love you."

He didn't know that I'd forgotten to wear my social human costume around her those first few meetings because I was dead set on finding her flaws and exposing them. Deep in my soul, I had the desperate need for her to be a terrible person, so I tried my best to convince myself she was.

"I met a girl," Finn had said causally as I slid into the diner booth across from him. I wondered why he couldn't at least wait until I was sitting down and settled, but realized he might have been taking this opportunity to discuss it with me before Dimitri arrived. "Are you going to be weird about it?"

I took my time removing my coat and folding it next to me. "Why would I be weird about it?" I immediately hid my face behind a giant slightly syrupy laminated menu to disguise any reddening in my cheeks. I'd felt the heat creep up my neck, anger and shame spilling directly from my heart and out onto my skin.

Finn hadn't dated anyone since we'd split after high school. That maniac voice in my head told me that this was because he was still secretly in love with me and just waiting for the right opportunity to ask me back. I'd held a lot of hope over the fact he didn't date in those first few years. By the time he'd met someone, it shouldn't have bothered me at all. I was happy. I had Dimitri. Dimitri was, in every way, better for me than Finn had ever been. But it *did* bother me. I'd pulled the menu up close to my face and questioned why I already hated this "girl". I hated her and she wouldn't be good enough for my Finn. Obviously. Whoever she was. I hated her.

He hadn't answered, so I peered over the menu. He had an eyebrow raised and his arms crossed.

"What? You're allowed to date." I ducked back behind my sticky shield.

"She's really, really, great. We've been hanging out a lot."

I bit back how I should have guessed because he'd hardly been hanging out with me at all. Instead, I'd asked, "What's her name?" Like I cared. Like her name might make me not hate her.

"Lucy."

I hated Lucy.

I was getting better. I'd known her for three years and I was the "Best Man" at her wedding. But a slug is a slug, I guess. I agonized over what to wear. I redid my eyeliner twice. I cringed over the state of my hair, showing an inch of brown roots before the emerald green dye began, fading out and patchy. I put it up into a bun to hide it. I sucked in my stomach, let it out, then jiggled my upper arms around until I sufficiently hated everything about myself. Finally, Dimitri called from the hall.

"Hey, you said seven? We'd better go."

I did a little catwalk spin as I met him by the door, and he eyed me with mock criticism. "Well, not as pretty as Lucy, but I guess it'll have to do."

I punched his arm and let him pull me into a one-armed hug.

"You are stunning and only smell a little bit like coffee." He laughed. "Let's go."

Dimitri had only ever known me in my current form. I used to be dramatically gothic and took special care in my outfits, everything always had an intricate lace collar or a number of buttons or zippers that was *way* over the acceptable amount. I had long black talons and an hour of makeup and new hair dye every four weeks, on the dot. Clothes suitable for exercising were certainly not suitable for me, so I replaced food with coffee. I was *insufferable*.

Thankfully, college (or was it my split with Finn?) softened my obsession with my appearance. While it was mostly a terrible time, I also started dressing more comfortably, eating what tasted good, and generally not giving a fuck. In hindsight, it was definitely good for me. When I met Dimitri, I spent a long time trying to figure out what his "type" might be, because whatever it was, I was ready to morph right into it like an alien shapeshifter.

It turned out, he didn't have a type. He liked people when he liked them. I had to make myself an enjoyable person to be around to get his attention. It was hard work, I honestly just wished he'd had a thing for skaters or cowboys or whatever. It would have taken a lot less introspection, but the introspection turned out to be good for me, too.

So, here I was, the vestiges of my drama days still clinging on despite being almost thirty. I liked green hair and black eyeliner, what could I say? I didn't foresee myself skipping dinners and squeezing into lace outfits ever again though. Food was delicious, leggings existed, and I was goth enough for government work.

Finn had commented on my change in appearance a few times. Not necessarily nasty things, but things that hurt. Things I remembered, even though I forgot a coffee order seven seconds after it was placed. Things like, "I would have invited you on my hike, but I figured it wouldn't be fun for you." Things like, "Just a pajama kind of day, huh?" Like, "Let me guess, you're getting a milkshake again." It bothered me less and less as time went on, I just laughed it off, but Dimitri *hated* it.

He and Finn had developed the kind of friendship that two very dissimilar coworkers might. They'd be cordial and even chummy while they were together for the sanctity of the group setting, but they were never going to make plans together on purpose alone, and each was quick to criticize the other once the forced intimacy was over.

I realized as we were pulling into their driveway that I hadn't told Dimitri we were about to be "propositioned." I felt like it was too late to fill him in and hoped Finn would read the room and just act like he hadn't brought it up earlier. I nervously smoothed my dress while Dimitri rang the bell, like I hadn't spent a third of my life at this house.

Lucy answered the door, beaming at us with her million-watt smile. She wore a light green house dress, the cover model of some home decorating magazine. *Dazzle your guests with these five-minute tips!* She took my hand in both of hers. Her nails were a perfect, glossy white. "Hi strangers! Come in, come in!" She pulled me, stepping backward with light, dancer's steps.

I couldn't believe the changes she'd made to the place in the year she'd lived here. It was as gorgeous as her. Before she moved in, Finn had left everything pretty much as it had been when it had been his parents' house. Not in a weird or sad way, just in a "this is fine" kind of way. It had been all eighties' pastels, gaudy gold fixtures and thick carpets with walking treads run through the centers of them. Lucy changed everything. She'd had hardwood floors installed and painted the whole house in tasteful jewel tones and bright whites. All of the furniture had been replaced with modern comfortable pieces. The whole house seemed bigger, brighter, full of joy. She was the joy.

"Finn's out back at the grill. He's decided on hamburgers." She smiled, rolling her eyes playfully. She still had my hand, I hoped it wasn't sweaty. "I told him I'd cook, but he insisted it was his turn. I'm making salad and fries though."

I paused, letting her pressure on my wrist grow. This was one of those awkward things. She was implying that I should go to the kitchen with her while Dimitri should go stare at the grill or whatever men did. "She just wants to be friends with you." Finn would have told me, if he weren't a thousand miles away in the backyard. "She wants to spend time with you." Lucy was looking back at me expectantly. Dimitri gave me a little push forward.

"Let me help with the salad," I said, too late to not be awkward.

She beamed at me anyway.

"So..." She leaned across the kitchen island towards me.

I clumsily sliced mushrooms, displaying my ignorance of the simplest cooking tasks, praying she wasn't secretly judging me. I felt like I was on stage for a school play, and I didn't know my lines, or in one of those awful somehow-forgot-my-shirt dreams.

If she was judging, she was doing a great job keeping it a secret, she didn't even look down at the mushrooms as she spoke. She was an intense eye contact kind of talker, the kind that always seemed to be on the verge of spilling a secret, just for you. Nothing was more important to her than the face before her. It set my nerves on fire with self-consciousness, more worried on whether I had something in my teeth than whatever secrets she might tell. "Did Finn let you in on our plan yet? He swears he hasn't, but I know he tells *you* everything."

Perfect, I wasn't supposed to know anything either. I wondered if Finn had figured out that I hadn't told Dimitri. I glanced at the yard. There they were, their backs to the sliding glass doors, staring at the grill and laughing. "No, he said he'd talk about it at dinner. What's up? I'm dying here."

She grinned wickedly, which was, of course, adorable. "I'll let him tell you. He's *so* excited, Hazel. I am, too, actually. It was my idea, actually. He's bringing it to life."

If she was talking about a hotel, I should have told her it was *my* idea, but she might not have been. It was a strange, vague, conversation. I felt like I might say the wrong thing and somehow ruin everything. I concentrated on not cutting any fingers off instead of answering.

"I love this dress." She went on, abandoning the radish she was supposed to be quartering and feeling the material. "You're always dressed so *cool*. I wish I could be cool like that. I look like someone's grandma."

I looked down at my dress. It was black and boring. She must have been being nice? "You look beautiful, stop. You're the most beautiful grandma in the world." I added. That was something a friend would say, right?

She squealed and launched a radish quarter at me.

"Are you...throwing food in here? Do I have to separate you two?" Finn appeared at the back door, holding a plate of hamburgers, still sizzling. He set it down on the island between Lucy and I and headed to the cabinet for plates, squeezing Lucy on his way and making her bleat a feigned protest.

I looked around slightly desperately for Dimitri. I felt weird and ugly and unwanted being alone with the happy couple, even for a few moments. I needed to have my person, to display my own affection. I needed to remind myself that I, too, was loved, and did love. Dimitri had lingered outside to smoke, it seemed. I could tell by his slightly guilty smirk as he crept in and carefully shut the door behind him. He'd been trying to quit, and I was proud of him, though it didn't matter to me one way or the other, as long as he was happy. I hated the smell though. I didn't let him smoke in our car that he paid for.

I leaned out my jaw for him to kiss as he passed, but I didn't look up from the mushrooms. I was falling behind. The rest of the dinner was done and we were held up by my slow vegetable chopping. Dimitri washed his hands in the kitchen sink, then took the knife from my hands. His line cook days were just before he got his job in the insurance office, and he made quick work of the rest of the veggies while I grabbed silverware and help set the table.

I agonized over which side the forks and spoons go on, hoping that Lucy wasn't watching, but Finn noticed my struggle and honed in on my embarrassment like a shark smelling blood. He picked up a spoon I'd just placed. "They go on the same side, actually."

"God, Finn. Tell everyone I'm an idiot why don't you." I moaned, moving the spoons over.

"Well, I wasn't going to, but now I will. We're having burgers and salads, Hazel. What do we need spoons for?" he said with an evil grin. Well, maybe it wasn't *evil*, but it sure felt that way, his usually wide blue eyes slits of devious malice.

"Because we're having ice cream for dessert and I told her so." Lucy plucked the spoon out of his hand and tapped him lightly on the forehead with it before setting it back down. "Besides, she was right. Fork on the left, knife and spoon on the right."

"Fuck," he said and the smirk disappeared. "Alright, well, get your plates and eat or whatever." He grabbed one for himself and we all followed suit.

We ate in complete, tense silence. I forgot to put dressing on my salad, but was too embarrassed to go back to the counter and retrieve it, so I chomped on water flavored veggies one outrageously loud crunch at a time. I kept making eye contact with Finn, but he was resolutely not talking, completely focused on his burger.

Finally, Dimitri set down his own burger. "Is anyone going to tell me why everyone is being so weird right now? Is it my birthday or something and I forgot?"

Lucy set down her fork. She was grinning and it wasn't evil at all. "Well. Since you ask..." She looked expectantly at Finn.

Finn said, "Yes. Happy Birthday."

I rolled my eyes.

"Finn! Come on." Lucy looked like she might burst into a thousand rainbow bubbles any second.

"Alright, alright." Finn shoved the last three bites of his burger in his mouth at the same time and chewed forever as we watched. He was clearly enjoying himself. Finally, he said, "I'm thinking..." He stopped, looked at Lucy. "*We're* thinking of buying a bed and breakfast. Moving to the country. Getting out of this shit hole city." He looked at me specifically. "We were hoping you'd like to come with us."

I thought, if it wasn't for Lucy's bright and sincere face, I would have assumed he was messing with me. But Lucy wasn't joking. Lucy was so excited.

"What?" I managed.

"I'm serious. We're ready to get out of this house. I'm *so* ready to get out of this house. We've been talking about going up into the mountains since before we got married. The other day, Lucy was like, 'What's stopping us?'" Finn looked at his plate. He was suddenly embarrassed, but I couldn't figure out why.

Lucy answered my unspoken question. "It's you. He doesn't want to leave you guys and I don't either. I love you both." She said "I love you" so effortlessly, but with so much emotion, how did she do it? It took me over a year to tell Dimitri that I loved him. I'd never said it to Lucy. I might have loved her, I guess I'd never really thought about it. "Come with us."

I was a little shaken. I reached out and grabbed for Dimitri's hand next to me under the table. He'd been reaching out for mine.

"Well, hang on," Finn said. "This sounds weird and cult-y. Basically, we're going up this weekend to check out a potential place and wanted to know if you'd guys would like to come with us, help us scope out the area, see if it's somewhere you might be interested in. Nothing's set in stone. I just thought it would be a good excuse for us to take a little vacation and maybe think about it."

I looked at Dimitri. He tilted his head slowly, gazed away over my head. I wondered if he was imagining living in the mountains, imagining living anywhere besides our tatty little apartment we'd outgrown before we'd finished moving in. "I mean, obviously we'll have to talk about it," he said, each word a thousand pounds.

"But..." Finn prodded.

I squeezed Dimitri's hand in askance and after a moment that lasted a lifetime, he squeezed back. He was down to go. "But it could be fun!" I almost yelled in my excitement. "This weekend, I mean. I'll call off."

I studied Dimitri's face. Eventually, his brow unfurled, and he smiled. Not his polite smile, the one he gave acquaintances and salespeople, but a real, genuine, excited smile that showed off his dimple and turned his dark eyes into miniature firework displays. "Yeah. It sounds like fun."

Lucy actually clapped her hands. "Yay!"

Chapter 2

I was more than a little surprised that Dimitri didn't make a bigger deal out of me calling out from work for the weekend. He wouldn't have brought it up at dinner, not in front of our friends, he'd never embarrass me the way Finn loved to. But, after we'd retreated to the sanctity of the car and relaxed, I was sure it was going to come up. It never did, though we speculated on every other aspect of the weekend, reveling in the excitement of the prospect of our first trip together in a long time. Heck, our first time having the same three days *off work* together in a long time.

We were waiting for Finn and Lucy to pick us up and I couldn't help but ask. "So...you're not mad about me taking the weekend off?"

He was on our garbage picked couch, scrolling through his phone mindlessly. He wanted to look bored, but his leg jiggled like a thousand volts were running through it. He didn't glance up. "Nah, I mean, do you think they'll fire you?"

I cringed. "Maybe? I'm not really a star employee, anyway." I flopped down next to him. "They're probably looking for an excuse."

He put his phone down and deliberately caught my eyes with his own. "Well, maybe it won't matter. If we're maybe serious about this."

It was the first we'd talked about the possibility of this maybe being more than just a weekend. I was sure we'd both been thinking about it (obsessing in my case), but I knew we each wanted to take the trip first to see if it was even a remote possibility before getting our hopes up. There was no doubt that we'd be willing to go just about anywhere to get out of our perpetual poverty, but if Finn would need anything from either of us financially for the purchase *or* the move, we had nothing. We were basically just warm bodies.

I'd talked to Finn a little about it since our dinner, but he'd been frustratingly vague. I didn't think it was intentional, he just didn't have enough information yet.

"It wouldn't be like you buying in or anything, don't worry." Was all he could offer me through his choppy, healthy, jogging breaths. "I'd be selling the house and I've got some money saved up. Lucy does, too. It would be like, offering both of you live in jobs, basically."

"Live in jobs, doing what?" I'd asked.

"Well, we'll need someone to handle bookings, run the website, do advertising, whatever. We'll need a chef. We'll need housekeeping, bookkeeping, landscaping. It's like a whole thing. I feel like, between the four of us, we could probably play to our strengths, you know? Team effort."

It sounded plausible when Finn said it. It sounded *fun*, actually. But I didn't want to get my hopes up. I didn't go into details with Dimitri. I just said, "Yeah, maybe. Besides, *someone* is always hiring, I guess. I'm a terrible barista."

We sat in silence, letting that statement soak into the stained couch fabric. I gazed around our apartment. My mother wouldn't even come visit us there. She made pleasant enough excuses ("There's so much room in our kitchen, bring Dimitri here!", or "I actually have some errands to run, why don't you come with me instead?", and my personal favorite, "I just don't want to take up an extra parking space for your building."), but the truth of the matter was the neighborhood scared her. When we were moving in, she saw a rat by the dumpster, and someone asked her for change in the parking lot and she'd never once been back since. Finn and Lucy had come over a few times for dinner or a game night, but it was so embarrassing that I almost never invited them anymore.

"You think maybe it's time to try to move, even if this ends up not working out?" I asked quietly, staring out into the parking lot, our view from the couch.

Dimitri looked up at me. "I mean, that's always the goal, isn't it? I just don't know how we'll manage. They're not really allowing overtime at the office right now...I'll probably get in trouble for the yesterday—"

I cut him off with a kiss. "Forget it," I said. "I was just thinking out loud."

"Hey." He turned my face back towards his. "When we get back, we'll do some budgeting and look around. Maybe we could commute a little further and find something nicer. I'm sorry we've stayed here so long."

I didn't want him to be sorry. I felt terrible for bringing it up. He made twice as much as I did and held down a job. I should have been the one apologizing. I didn't though. I just nodded and smiled.

My phone buzzed a few minutes of silence later. It was Finn, *That pothole is a death trap. We're here.*

"Alright," Finn said from the passenger seat, slapping his hands to his thighs. "It's a two-hour drive. Did you pee, Hazel? Because we're not stopping, I don't want to get there in the dead of night."

"I peed," I said sullenly. "I'm an adult. I'll be fine." I buckled my seatbelt. "Hey, Lucy."

Lucy grinned at me in the rearview mirror. "Hey, babe." She got car sick, so she always drove. She had huge round sunglasses on that hid half of her freckled face, and her hair was pulled up into the most perfect messy bun. "You excited?"

"I think so?" I leaned forward, rested my hands on the back of her chair. "I don't know, tell me everything. Have the sellers been running the place as a B&B, or has it been sitting empty? How big is it? How many guest rooms? Is it in good shape?"

Finn counted off on his fingers. "Eleven rooms. So, we'd be fully booked with nine reservations. These old people have been running the place for like fifty years or something. It's got a good reputation, they stay busy, they just can't keep up anymore. They're ready to retire. I haven't seen it yet obviously, but the pictures look like it's in fine shape. It was built in 1890, though, so we'll see."

"1890?" Dimitri interjected. "Jesus. Probably haunted as fuck."

Finn shrugged. "It's supposed to be. That's why most people book it, I guess. Hey, an attraction is an attraction, people love that spooky shit." He gave me a knowing look. I used to write short horror stories back when I had time to write anything and he always thought it was a morbid hobby. "It's called 'Lovers' Leap'."

"That's the name of the B&B?" I asked through cackling.

Finn nodded. "Yeah, yeah. Apparently, some star-crossed lovers Romeo and Juli-yeeted themselves off the mountain around there at some point. The B&B was like a tavern back in the day that just named itself what the locals called the area and the name stuck." He looked around at us. "We'd be stuck with the name, too, it's pretty well known. It would be stupid to change it."

I shrugged. "I don't really care if it's called Hell, as long as it's not in Charleston."

Lucy giggled.

Dimitri took the opportunity to ask all of the questions I'd already asked and not shared with him, and I took the opportunity to stare out the window, enjoying the idea of never going back to my crappy job, my crappy apartment, my consistently late utility bills. I watched the city slowly recede like a bad dream. I already had to pee.

Thinking about leaving had me thinking about money again. I was embarrassed that Finn and Lucy had "money saved up." I was embarrassed that their car was so clean and big and nice. Finn and I'd started in the same place, with the same opportunities. Our houses were basically next door to each other. I was the one who went to college, I was the one who still had my parents' support, how had we ended up on such completely different levels? What had I been doing wrong?

He had a big, beautiful wedding with Lucy after they dated a year. Dimitri and I had been together twice as long, and he'd literally never even brought up the idea of getting married. My college friends were starting families, opening businesses, getting promoted. I was about to get fired from another minimum wage job.

College hadn't been easy for me, especially at first. I almost flunked out of several classes my first semester, reeling over the abrupt changes. Reeling over not having Finn around. He and I didn't even talk at first. I was afraid to call him. I wouldn't know what to say. Was I supposed to lie and tell him I was having a great time? Making new friends? That it was everything we ever imagined it would be? I wouldn't want to tell him that, to make him feel awful for missing out. But the truth was so much more embarrassing, I was sleeping through my alarms, living on cold ramen noodles that I always forgot about until one of my dorm mates needed the microwave and would give an annoyingly exaggerated sigh before setting the cup on some more obvious kitchen surface. The dorm mates whose names I didn't bother to remember, who made plans together in front of me while never inviting me. I had no academic drive, no social drive. I was depressed. Could I tell him that? After what happened to him and what he was going through, I was going to whine about having a normal college life? So, I didn't call.

He didn't call either and I bounced back and forth between being worried about him and being furious at him. It was embarrassing to admit, looking back, how much of my time I wasted thinking about Finn. And "wasted" not because of anything he had done, but because I was absolutely obsessing over him. Over the idea of the future that we had lost. I was sick.

Luckily for me, one of my professors noticed. Well, he didn't notice I was not handling life well, he noticed I'd missed almost enough classes to fail and was gracious enough to recommend I visit a guidance counselor on campus before I lost the ability to use any of the campus services.

"I'm just having trouble...adjusting." I mumbled at the floor in a humid third floor office. Flies bounced repeatedly against a windowpane, only inches above the open sill that would have released them back into the early autumn air. How could they be so stupid? "I've never been away from home before."

The counselor's baby pink suit jacket was draped over the back of her office chair, and she fanned her glistening neck with a hand as she spoke. "A lot of new students get homesick the first semester. I bet you have better air conditioning at home, right?"

I managed a tiny smirk. "I do."

"Well, it's only two weeks till our first long weekend. Try to at least make it to every class between then and now and you can reward yourself with a visit home. Sound like a plan?"

I nodded without really taking in what I was agreeing to. A stack of pamphlets were pressed into my hands.

"This is an assortment of study groups and student clubs I think you might find helpful or interesting, based on your major." She patted the top of my hand before leaning away across her desk again. "At least look through them and see if anything sounds fun. There's no better way to meet new people!"

I left the office trying to decide how I'd admit to my parents that I had screwed up so royally, and if Finn would consider taking me back if I moved back home. I held the stack of pamphlets over a trash can at the bottom of the stairs outside of the administrative building, planning to look through them right here and discard any that didn't look interesting. I expected to discard all of them.

However, a few actually *did* seem like they might be fun. There was a book club, an open mic, a short story group. I hovered over the trash can, arms outstretched, for quite a few minutes before taking the whole stack back with me to my dorm.

The short story club was meeting that evening and I decided to make myself go. Going anywhere on campus was a bad dream, a spotlight shone directly over my loneliness, my awkwardness, my guilt. Everyone was surely staring at me and judging me. Like they *knew*. Like they whispered about me behind hands. I was so full of myself. I'm sure no one on that campus spared me a single thought. I'm sure that even the counselor I'd spoken to had already forgotten my name by the time I teetered by the trash can at the bottom of the stairs. But back then, I was paranoid. Terrified. So, so alone.

I changed in the dorm, selecting clothes that might make me appear aloof, intelligent, interesting but uninterested. I stared at the ground, counted my steps. I thought I could hear whispers all around me. Every laugh directed at me. I wanted to go home. I wanted Finn to be here with me.

"You're new," said a man as I hovered near the doorway. The meeting was being held in a study room of the library, an assortment of single desks shoved to one side and a rough circle of chairs taking up most of the room. A few people lounged, laughed and talked in that easy way that felt so foreign to me.

"Yeah." I looked back at my feet. "It's my first semester."

"Cool, cool. Basically every month we meet, read our stories if we feel like it, get feedback if we want it, then we all choose a prompt for next month's story." He didn't rise from his chair or anything, or even ask my name. "If you're not feeling the prompt, don't write. If you don't want to share, that's cool. We're just here for fun, you know?"

I nodded.

I listened to four short stories that day with the loose theme of "Ice." By the third story's feedback, I offered critique and praise. By the fourth, I was laughing along with jokes being made.

I made friends that day and one of the friends happened to be in a few of my classes. I had a *person*. We were never close outside of the club and class, but that was the nudge I needed. I started going to classes. I started looking forward to club meetings, and I agonized over my own stories at first, hoping to dazzle. Maybe I didn't dazzle, but I at least fit in. My obsession with Finn (and what happened) took a comfortable back seat in my mind. It was still there, ready to lean forward and tap me on the shoulder and whisper in my ear, but there were whole hours of my day when I forgot. My academic and social life got better and I thought I was turning my life around.

But I couldn't find a job in my field after graduation. My manuscripts didn't get picked up. I didn't have the experience required for most of the "entry level" positions I applied for. I had to start waiting tables to make ends meet while I searched. The descent was insidious. I spent more hours working and less hours applying and finally no hours writing. One day, I woke up and realized that I wasn't a writer, I was a waitress. I wasn't even a good waitress. It was an insult to food service people everywhere to even call myself that.

I stared out the car window at the gloomy, blustery afternoon. It wanted to storm, but the sky couldn't muster up the effort. I related. I hoped it didn't pour, or Lucy would drive up the mountain roads going twenty miles an hour with her hazard lights on the whole way. It'd be midnight before we got there, and I'd still have to pee.

"That would be pretty cool. What do you think, Nut?"

"Mmm?" I turned back toward the interior of the car. I'd missed the entire conversation.

Finn was turned mostly around in his seat, both he and Dimitri were looking at me expectantly. Finn gave an annoyed little head shake at my inattentiveness. "Why don't you do some research on the creepy factor and do an article or something? Maybe we could get it on some travel destination sites or something."

"Why don't *you* do it?" I replied automatically before I even considered. "Isn't that kind of your job?" I tried to keep the acid out of my voice. I failed.

Finn sighed and turned back to the front, arms crossing. Dimitri clicked his tongue once and sat back in his seat, too, bowing out of the conversation. It was awkwardly silent. Lucy put the turn signal on to change lanes and the clicks were like explosions. I'd have to say something.

"That was...unfair," I said cautiously. "I'm—"

"A bitch sometimes," Finn said. He didn't turn around and he wasn't joking. It was fine. I guess I was.

Finn's fall from his dream job was a lot shorter than mine, in my opinion anyway. Finn wanted to be a photographer, but his photos weren't really what caught magazines' eye. His captions were quirky, funny, and smart. He got hired to write small blurbs for other people's work, and he became a fairly well-known commentary voice in the photography community. Now, he had a permanent spot with a major travel magazine and website, writing articles every month. Isn't that just hilarious. He didn't even *like* it, it was just a job to him. I knew it wasn't his fault, but I was obviously more bitter about it than I'd realized.

I picked at my nail polish, peeled off a few flakes. I didn't want to throw them on the floor of their car, so I stuffed them into my pocket. "You could take the photos?" I asked timidly.

He was watching the highway rush towards the windshield. Enough time passed that I decided he wasn't going to answer, and then he did. "It could be cool."

It broke the tension, each of us seeming to gasp the cool, clean air we'd been denied. Lucy put on music. We spent three songs complaining about her choice of boy bands, then another five songs singing along. We all knew every word, of course.

"We're going to have to stop," I finally said. "I'm sorry!"

Lucy immediately got into the right lane. "Oh, my God, I'm *so* glad you have to go," she said. "I've had to since we turned out of your parking lot."

"Me, too, but it was a matter of principal," I said, glaring at Finn.

He groaned with obvious sarcasm. "Forty minutes. You two can't wait forty more minutes?"

"Absolutely not," Lucy said primly. She already had her signal on for the upcoming exit. "This is our turn off anyway, no better place to stop."

"We should probably get some dinner, actually," Dimitri said. "This place isn't a functioning bed and breakfast right now, right? I don't want to make some old lady cook for us."

"They aren't going to be there," Finn said. "They left a key under the mat. I guess it's the kind of place where you can just leave a key under the mat." He rolled his eyes. "We're welcome to use the kitchen though, it looks pretty functional in pictures. We've got groceries in the trunk. We're going to check the place out and then meet with them tomorrow for lunch to talk business. If we decide we want to, that is."

There was quiet in the car while each of us pondered if we'd want to "talk business" come tomorrow. Lucy pulled into a well-lit gas station. We clambered out, each stretching sore necks and letting our joints crackle like popping oil. I couldn't believe how different it felt there, only a little more than an hour from home. The elevation change was a whole other planet. I breathed in, deep. It smelled like a gas station parking lot, but I don't know why I thought it would smell like anything else. Some things are always the same.

"Ooh, look!" Lucy pointed up at the awning covering the pumps. Dozens of shapes were fluttering around the lights, each as big as my hand and all a milky, alien green. "Luna moths! It's rare to see a bunch of them together like this. Maybe the bright lights are confusing them."

I watched them flit this way and that. They looked more like butterflies than moths and when they floated further away from the lights, I swore they brought a little luminescence out into the dark with them. They seemed magical, but also sad there at the gas station, like a unicorn in a zoo. There was only one other car there and the driver was paying at the pump. They ignored the moths.

"I thought you two had to pee?" Dimitri asked.

Lucy jumped like he just broke a spell she was under. "Right. Come with me, Hazel?"

Lucy was afraid of strangers. They talked to her, men hit on her. She got flustered, uncomfortable, and was too nice to tell people to fuck off. I was not. In fact, my powers of meanness were exponential when I was using them on someone else's behalf. It was a small superpower, but a useful one. "Sure," I said, and we headed in, matching our strides.

No one was visible when we walked inside. There was no music. I could hear the whine of the fluorescents, and one in the back corner flickered ominously. Lucy scanned the store, searching for the weird little hallway where bathrooms usually hide. "Hmm." She shifted from foot to foot, uncomfortable.

"Hello?" I called as I walked up to the cluttered counter.

A man popped out from behind a squeaking swinging door. "Hi there! Sorry, my door chime is busted. What can I do for you ladies?"

"Where's the bathroom?"

He produced a wooden yard stick from behind the counter, a key dangling on the end with fraying, dirty yarn. "Walk outside, turn right. Follow the building. Make sure to hang this," he shook the stick, "from the hook on the back of the door. I don't want it sitting on the floor in there."

"Is the floor gross?" I couldn't help but ask, eyeing the bacteria-ridden stick and key warily.

He shrugged.

I took the ridiculously huge key and handed it to Lucy. "You can go first. I'm going to shop." I didn't need anything, but I wanted to keep the attendant busy while she was out there, who knew where his little swinging door lead? I was paranoid. It was better than being naive.

I perused the shelves aimlessly, picking up random probably expired chips and reading the backs like I cared about nutrition.

The buzz of the lights made my skin crawl and my footsteps were too loud.

"So, where're you girls heading?"

I wanted to sigh, but managed to hold it in. I put down the flaming hot cheese puffs I'd been examining. "Just a little bed and breakfast for the weekend."

"Oh, Lovers' Leap?"

My heart skipped. I didn't mean to tell a random guy where we were going. I'd assumed there were plenty of B&B's that we might have been heading to in this part of the county so well-known for its scenic sweeping smoky mountains and rich history.

He continued before I managed to answer. "I've brought my wife there a couple times on years we couldn't afford to go far. It's a nice little place, she just loved it. She swears she saw a ghost in our bathroom one night." His laugh bounced around the cinder block walls, like he was everywhere and nowhere. "Wouldn't you know, she's been dying to go back and try to see it again. Women are so strange. It's too bad it wasn't open this summer."

I ambled towards the refrigerated drinks. The hum was even louder back there, with a random stutter as the bad light flickered. "Well," I called and plucked a few energy drinks and bottled waters out of the case. "Maybe it'll open back up next year, and you can take her again." I headed back toward the counter, and actually looked at him for the first time. He was an older guy, sixties, probably. He had a little driver's cap on that was both absurdly adorable and a little ridiculous.

He grinned. "Not next year. Next year, we're going to *Italy*. She doesn't know yet, I'll surprise her on her birthday. Been saving and planning for a long time."

I smiled back and plopped the drinks on the counter. "Well, that's wonderful."

Lucy danced back in, twirling the yardstick like a baton. "The boys say we're going to ruin the whole weekend if we're not back on the road in five minutes. Here, let me get those."

She handed me the yardstick key and had her credit card chip in the reader before I could protest. I pursed my lips, but managed mumbled thanks as we headed out the door.

"Take care now," the man behind the counter called.

"*Four minutes*," Finn yelled across the empty parking lot.

Dimitri was standing by the road to smoke. He probably needed to stop as badly as I did, that traitor.

I flipped them off and followed the building around its side. Another fluorescent light buzzed angrily above the door. There weren't any Luna moths there, just the regular little ugly ones. I opened the door with some trepidation, but was pleasantly surprised to be hit by the smell of lavender. It looked like I'd just walked into my own grandma's guest bathroom, there were decorative soaps, pale yellow walls, brilliantly clean floors. Across from the toilet, in a carved golden frame, a photo of the Leaning Tower. I smiled.

Chapter 3

"Look," Lucy said. "They've left the lights on for us."

The house was gigantic. A mansion. Ridiculous. I didn't know why I didn't expect it to be so imposing with eleven bedrooms, but I was absolutely caught off guard. While Lucy pulled the car around a circular drive and parked in one of the marked-out spaces along the side, I gaped at it, putting my face right up against the window like a kid at the zoo, leaving behind a greasy smear.

The wrought iron gates didn't look like they ever closed—the soil had crept and settled around the bottom, as though the metal had sprung from the earth—and the house was framed perfectly between them. Moonlight bleached the whole structure. I couldn't tell what color it might be in the morning, it was like a blank page. The clouds had all slunk away in the night, leaving a dark purple backdrop of sky and stars. The view from the rear of the building looking out over the valley would be incredible in the morning. But at night, it sat on the edge of a bottomless black pit.

It was...Victorian, maybe? I didn't know architecture or time periods. Were things even Victorian if they were in the United

States, let alone West Virginia? Dozens of arched narrow windows and little separate turrets of roof stabbed into the night sky. A candle flickered in every window. I assumed they were those LEDS meant to look like flickering flame and not the real thing, but the effect was nice. Warm light glowed from two sconces at the front door and bled out from beyond the ground floor's curtained windows. I hoped those window candles weren't real, the effect wouldn't be worth the fire hazard.

The quartz rocks that made up the drive sparkled in the moonlight and shaped topiaries loomed around the yard. I was honestly a little creeped out, but I kept telling myself how cute it will all be in the morning. Plus, it all looked to be in immaculate shape.

I realized that we'd all been sitting there, staring at the place in silence for more than a minute. I cleared my throat. "Um. Should we go in?"

Everyone else stirred as though from sleep, gathering phones and drinks and jackets.

"Should we grab our luggage or just make sure the key is there first...?" Dimitri trailed off, gaze returning to the monstrous structure.

"Uh." Finn looked up again also. He might have been counting the windows, eyes darting to and fro.

We all seemed very small. Could we really take care of a place like that? How did an old couple take care of it? They must have hired out all those jobs Finn had mentioned we could manage. They *must* have made decent money.

"Let's just go make sure we can get in first. I don't want to lug everything up there if there's been a misunderstanding or something," Finn finally answered.

None of us moved towards the gate.

The front door swung open with a creak that echoed across the valley sleeping below us. The yellow light of the foyer flooded out and blended with the moonlight, made the shimmering gravel path catch fire. Lucy squeaked with fright and sidestepped close to Finn's side.

"Mr. And Mrs. Murphy?" A voice called from the doorway.

Finn muttered, *"Jesus,"* and put a hand to his chest. Then called back in a loud, calm voice. "That's us!"

"You can bring your car through to the porch if you'd like," the voice returned. It was a man's voice, low and smooth. "We'll meet you inside. Follow the hall to the sitting room on the left."

The door closed, leaving us to the night once again.

We studied each other's faces, taking comfort in one another's disquiet.

"What the fuck?" Finn said. "I was told no one would be here tonight. Gave me a fucking heart attack."

"Well, you said they play up the creep factor, right?" I shrugged. "I mean, the guy at the gas station says his wife saw a ghost here and everything."

"You're just mentioning that now?" Dimitri said with a nervous laugh.

"I forgot!"

"Alright," Lucy said. "Let me go ahead and pull the car through. You guys can go on in."

"I'll ride up with you and take the bags and stuff in," Dimitri said quickly. He wanted to smoke again before we were trapped within the building for the night, I was sure. He wouldn't have wanted to come out into the night alone later on.

I rolled my eyes and grabbed Finn by the arm. "Let's go. It's probably way past the owners' bedtime. Hopefully, they'll leave after they make sure we got in okay."

I marched him decisively up the path, finally breaking the spell while Lucy and Dimitri climbed back into the car.

I didn't let go of Finn's arm the whole way up the walk. I didn't want to admit it, but I was definitely creeped out. The hedges were throwing strange shadows, and I couldn't believe how much larger the house kept getting as we moved closer. It was going to swallow us whole.

We paused at the door. "Should we knock?" Finn asked uncertainly.

"They know we're here." I pushed down the fancy doorknob latch and shoved the door open, dragging us across the threshold into the light of the foyer before I lost my nerve.

As we crossed, dizziness crashed down on me. My vision narrowed, turned to static. I stopped and put the hand that wasn't wrapped around Finn's arm to my knee to hold myself up. I felt him stumble beside me. My heart began to race. Something was very wrong. I was going to faint.

"Shit," Finn said. It was barely a whisper.

I started to tell him that I was sick or something and needed to sit, but as quickly as the vertigo had hit me, it was gone. I blinked a few times, searching for lingering waves of dizziness. There was nothing. "That was weird," I said.

"Did you get dizzy?" He spun in a circle, breaking out of my grasp. "I thought I was about to hit the floor for a second." He narrowed his eyes, sniffed the air cautiously. "Gas leak or something?"

I shook my head. "I don't smell gas. It's probably just the altitude change. Got us both at the same time?"

I gazed around the foyer. It was cute, decorated with plenty of floral patterns and doilies and plush furniture. It was nowhere near as imposing as the outside had me imagining. A gorgeous carved mahogany staircase lead up to our right and a little writing desk staged with an old typewriter snuggled in front of it.

"Should we wait for them or head through?" I asked.

Finn shifted from one foot to another in indecision. "Well, I don't want to keep these folks up waiting for us too long...let's just go. D and Lu'll find us."

I nodded and we headed down the hall. There were glass sconces flickering along the wall and I inspected one LED. The light splashing into the hall from the doorway in front of us was definitely coming from a real fireplace though, the shadows dancing along the floor were too wild to be an algorithm.

"Mr. Frey?" Finn called into the room before we entered. "I'm sorry we've arrived so late."

"Don't worry, my boy. Come in, come in. We have coffee." The man had the slightest accent. Was it German, maybe? I was terrible with accents, just add it to the list of things I was ignorant about. His voice was nice though. I thought so even when I heard it across the yard. He sounded a little like my grandfather.

We entered the sitting room, on the left, as promised. There was a cheery fire burning in a heavily carved mahogany fireplace. The room was all floor to ceiling windows on one side, the view nothing but blackness. There were two wing backed leather chairs on each side of the fireplace and on the side further from us, a man and woman sat side by side, smiling up at us. A coffee table situated near the door, in the center of another grouping of cozy furniture, had a glass carafe filled with coffee, two delicate porcelain mugs turned upside down on their saucers, a platter of assorted cookies. Sugar and cream rested in the center in painted bowls with little ladles.

"Mr. and Mrs. Murphy, welcome!" The man gestured towards the coffee table. "Please, help yourselves, and come and sit with us! I'm so sorry about the change of plans."

"Oh, I'm not..." I began, but the woman began to speak at the same time, so I fell silent.

"You are later than we expected to wait," she said.

I turned to study her, instantly annoyed. Like, yes. We were late, but they weren't even supposed to be there, so whose problem was it, really?

I forgot to be annoyed as soon as I took her in. She had to be in her seventies at least, and she was absolutely the most glamorous woman I'd ever seen, like someone from another time, a distant land. She might have been an elven queen. She sat rail straight, ankles crossed, her cup of coffee balanced expertly in her palm. She wore a satin green gown with a shawl. Gems on the shawl, her waist, her throat, her wrists, all glittered in the dancing firelight. She twinkled like the sky outside. Her thick, glistening silver hair must have been very long to accommodate the complicated braids swept up into a high bun, pinned in place with more shimmering stones. Her cheeks were pink and there were long lines from the corners of her eyes. Her eyes were deep, dark caverns, but I was sure it was only the dimness of the room and the twinkle of the accessories that made them seem so cold, so empty. She wasn't exactly *frowning,* but I felt as though I'd somehow disappointed her all the same.

"I'm so sorry," I managed to stammer.

Finn took a step towards them, but then Lucy's slightly quavering voice bounced down the hall. "Hello?"

"Oh," Finn said instead. "I'll grab her. Excuse me." He stepped quickly out of the room, leaving me enormously uncomfortable. I couldn't stop staring at the woman.

"Grab...who?" She arched a beautiful dark eyebrow. She had a slight accent, too, I thought. Or maybe I was just used to my own dumb sounding voice.

"His wife, Lucy. I'm not Mrs. Murphy. Sorry about the misunderstanding. I'm Hazel Andrews and we have my friend Dimitri Kriska here as well." I stepped forward to potentially take one of their hands in a way of greeting and as I did so, they turned and looked at each other for the briefest of moments. I didn't know exactly what those looks were saying, but I felt like they had an immense amount of meaning.

The man seemed very flustered, but stood to take my hand. I tore my eyes away from her to look at him. He was also extremely formally dressed, I realized. I felt like I was in my pajamas at a wedding. He had dress pants, a pin striped long-sleeved button-down shirt, a waistcoat with golden buttons. A giant green stone brooch was poking from his buttonhole. He had a hat on. It was weird.

He grasped my hand in both of his and they were warm and dry. A nice handshake. I looked into his face and my throat tightened unexpectedly with emotion. He *looked* a little like my grandfather, too. Pale blue eyes behind thick glasses and a large nose, a white mustache and big sideburns. He showed his age more than his wife, but still buzzed with energy. "A pleasure to meet you, Ms. Andrews. I'm so sorry, we didn't realize the Murphys wouldn't be traveling alone. Please excuse me, I must alter our arrangements. Please, sit, sit!"

He bustled out of the room, leaving me with his angry wife. "Uh," I said, rocking onto the balls of my feet anxiously. "I'll just. I'll just get some coffee."

I turned and realized the old man had taken the tray out of the room with him. Could it be any more awkward? I turned to instead sit in one of the chairs across from her, but as soon as I did, attempting to look as meek and posh as possible, the woman rose.

"I will go and assist my husband." She swept from the room, leaving me alone.

"What the fuck," I mouthed to myself.

"Where'd they go?"

I leapt off the chair and twirled around to see Finn and Lucy standing in the doorway. "Dude, I don't know," I aggressively whispered. "They're mad I'm here...I think. They took the coffee and left."

"What?" Finn pushed Lucy forward and gestured her to the chair next to mine. "Why would they be mad?"

"I don't know. Why are they here? I thought tomorrow—"

"If you'll be so kind, Mr. Murphy," Old man was back with a new tray of four cups and saucers. Why didn't he just bring extra cups? He set the tray down. "Help me relocate this settee by the fire to accommodate all of us?"

Finn hustled over to help. They guided a carved loveseat with yellow velvet cushions across the room and set it in front of the fireplace.

"There, now!" said the man and clapped his hands once. "You all, and your friend when he is done with the luggage, please sit and drink and eat. I will go and assist Opal in the kitchen with dinner arrangements. We will return to you soon." He smiled widely at us all and I felt crazy for thinking they weren't pleased to have me.

"Mr.," I began and then realized I don't know his name. What had Finn called him? Fern? Fay?

"Alexander Frey at your service, my girl. But please, call me Alex. We are all friends here! What can I do for you?"

I forced a smile. I would absolutely not be calling him Alex, (forever associated with one of my college exes). "I was wondering if you could show me the nearest restroom?"

"Of course, of course. It's on the way to the kitchen, no trouble at all. Come."

I followed him out into the hall, leaving Lucy and Finn re-arranging themselves, probably to sit next to each other. They were staring intently and raising their eyebrows back and forth. It was going to be a night of furiously silent conversations, I could tell. I saw Dimitri sauntering down the hall as I passed into an adjoining one. I waved and pointed back to the sitting room. Mr. Frey didn't notice, he was obviously on a mission to get back to his wife.

"Here you are Miss," Mr. Frey said, stopping and gesturing to a door to our right. "Will you find your way back to the parlor all right?"

"Yes, thank you," I said and without another word he marched further and turned left into a brightly lit room I assumed must have been the kitchen.

I put my hand on the knob, but paused. Opal (now that was a gorgeous name with no strings attached. I'd never known an Opal and if anybody was Opal it was that glorious, terrifying woman.) was apparently the *queen* of aggressive whispering and she was letting her husband have it in the kitchen. I couldn't help but strain my ears to try and find out what the huge issue with me and Dimitri being there was. It was no use though, I understood the tone perfectly, but the words weren't in English, so I was out of luck. I dove into the bathroom before anyone noticed I'd been attempting to eavesdrop.

I tried to go quickly, dying to get back and confer with the others before the Freys emerged from the kitchen. The real reason I came in was to check my face and hair, I felt doubly self-conscious in front of Opal.

The room was decadently decorated, painted a deep teal color and with all gilded accessories and fixtures. A bouquet of flowers took up most of the counter space beside the sink. I reached up and plucked a petal. They were real. A huge oval painting of Victorian ladies with huge skirts and parasols hung front of me, dominating the wall. I stood, admiring it for a moment, until I realized it was in lieu of a mirror.

"What the..." I gazed around. On the wall next to me, I discovered a golden shaving mirror on an accordion hinge. I pulled it towards me, its hinges soundless, and I squinted down into it to quickly check my face before departing.

I opened the door to the sound of clattering baking sheets in the kitchen. I cringed. I know all about angrily cooking and there was definitely some angry cooking going on in there. I bobbed back and forth. I wanted to go back to the sitting room, but I really felt like I should at least offer to help with dinner, since my presence was the one throwing off everyone's plans. I gritted my teeth and headed for the kitchen.

Opal was alone in there, Mr. Frey must have gone back to the parlor to keep everyone entertained. It wasn't a huge kitchen, but the appliances were all commercial sized and the marble counters stretched into spotless corners. I slid a tall baking rack (exactly like the one at the coffee shop I worked at) slightly away from the doorway to announce my presence. Opal stood at the center island, slicing red peppers. It was outrageous to see a woman dressed so poshly slicing peppers. She looked up quickly and her eyes narrowed at the sight of me.

I suddenly felt stupid for going in there. I wished I could just turn around and leave without speaking, but too late for that now. "Hi." I grimaced at my own dumb voice. "I just wanted to, uh, apologize. For the lack of communication, I mean. I'm sure you had dinner all planned for four. I just wanted to know if there was anything I could do to help?" My face must've been beet red.

She took a deep, steadying breath and let her face relax into a death mask of hospitality. "I'd like to apologize as well," She offered a tiny smile, and I found myself dying to get more smiles from her. I wanted her to like me. "I am a woman of routine and even the silliest little change of plan can feel catastrophic, sometimes. But, of course, I've overreacted. I'm sorry if you feel like you've upset me."

She looked down to resume slicing and my eyes followed hers. I gasped. Blood spotted the counter's pale marble, marinated the peppers, and poured down her thin fingers. She must have cut herself when I entered. "Oh, here, let me help." I rushed across the room.

She lifted her hand and examined it calmly. "It's alright, it's just a little thing." She turned to the sink and flipped up the faucet with no urgency. "I didn't even feel it. I'm sure it'll turn out to be no worse than a paper cut."

I stood at her side by the time she got her hand under the water. I snatched a wad of paper towels off the roll from next to the sink, ready to be of service. I was never the best in the kitchen, but clumsy enough to be a minor first aid expert.

"There now," she said and held up her finger for my inspection. True to her word, I could barely see the slice, just a little white line of separated skin, tinged pink at the edges. "There are bandages in a first aid kit in the pantry." She pointed to the door I'd slid the baking rack in front of. "Top shelf. Be a dear?"

I sprinted, eager to be useful. I slid the baking rack further along where it blocked a set of swinging doors. It seemed like way too many doors to have in a kitchen, but what did I know? Plenty of ways to escape, I supposed grimly. The first aid box was metal and looked like it had been in there for a hundred years, but I barely had time to wonder what condition the supplies would be in as I opened it and found it fully stocked with brand new items. I hovered over the box of bandages. The cut didn't seem bad enough to need anything more serious, but these had unicorns and Pegasus on them, and I could hardly bring myself to dare giving one to such a serious lady. I cringed and grabbed one.

"Thank you." Opal slapped a pink sparkly Pegasus over her finger without a second glance, and I exhaled.

"Now, please," she said, waving her hand as though I were a fly irritating her. "I truly appreciate you coming in here to help, but I work best alone in the kitchen. I obviously can't be trusted with distraction." I won another small smile from her. "Go, be with your friends! Relax, enjoy some coffee and biscuits. I'll be in soon enough."

"Alright, if you're sure..." I turned to leave, but stopped short. The kitchen island was an absolute horror show. *So* much blood. How on earth did she lose so much blood from such a tiny cut? Was it due to her age, was her blood like, loose in there, or something?

There was a gentle tap on my shoulder, breath on my neck. "I'll clean up, don't worry. Go on, now."

Her voice was very near my ear and very low, and for some reason it made my skin prickle. I imagined old, gnarled fingers digging into my shoulder. A no longer beautiful but terribly, incomprehensibly old and hideous face, inches from my own. The mouth opening wide and long teeth dripping. My body wanted to literally sprint out of that kitchen. I compromised by nodding without turning around and walking out just a little bit more quickly than my usual stride.

I'd only made it a few feet down the hall before Dimitri appeared in front of me. "Hey, I was getting worried. Do you not feel good?" He linked his arm through mine and spun back to walk with me.

"I'm fine, I went to the kitchen to see if our hostess needed any help." I didn't mention the blood, or that stupid little moment of fear that seemed so childish now.

"Is she pissed? Finn said she seemed pissed."

"She's just unprepared." I sighed. "She's in there trying to slap together two extra dinners. I'd be pissed, too."

"Well, to be fair, they didn't tell us they were going to be here, so..."

We walked into the sitting room.

Lucy and Finn were sitting on the newly moved loveseat, alone.

"Hey," I said, "where's the guy?"

Finn shrugged. "No clue. Hey." He leaned toward us like he wanted to whisper, but we were still halfway across the room.

We quickly crossed the floor and took two chairs, leaned our heads in.

"Sorry about this," Finn continued once we were close enough to hear his words, barely more than breath. "I just checked our emails again to make sure I didn't miss anything, and they *definitely* didn't say they were going to be here. Sorry it's weird. I hope they don't stay the whole time. I'd like to really look the place over and—"

He broke off and looked up over my head, eyes widening a fraction. My skin crawled.

I turned, but it was just Mr. Frey and he still looked like my grandfather. He was beaming. "Sorry to leave you on your own! I just went up and got a second guest room all ready for our second couple. Now, everything will be perfect." He sat in the wingback chair across from me. "Opal and I have business to attend to out of town this weekend. We didn't know until this afternoon that we wouldn't be able to make our scheduled lunch tomorrow! So, we decided the best thing to do would be to meet you here for dinner tonight instead. I hope this is not too big an inconvenience for you?" His question was directed at Finn.

"No, sir, not at all," Finn answered. He had his grown-up voice on, the one he used to get out of speeding tickets and schedule doctor's appointments.

There was a pause that lasted just a moment too long before Lucy rescued us. She ran her hand along the settee. "You have so much gorgeous furniture in here! You must have been collecting for a long time. And I simply *love* how you've decorated." She beamed around the room. She was as completely in her element as I was in a foreign land.

"Everything stays, it's all included in the purchase price." Mr. Frey patted the arm of his own chair. "Opal and I want a fresh start, a clean slate, and a lot less to dust. Can you imagine us," he grinned conspiratorially, "in a sleek, modern apartment that looks down on the beach? We are moving south. All the cleaning and maintenance done by someone else, nothing for us to do but relax, enjoys the view…" He faded off dreamily. "We are ready."

Finn looked around, scratched his head. "I don't want to look a gift horse in the mouth or anything, but have you gotten any of this stuff appraised? There are a lot of antiques here."

Mr. Frey waved his hand dismissively. "We don't want to trouble with it. Opal is ready to pack a day bag and never look back. We've been here far too long. We need to start enjoying ourselves before it's too late."

We all were quiet again, uncomfortable. What were we supposed to say to that?

It was Opal's arrival that saved us this time. She floated into the room and sat neatly beside her husband. He reached over and brought her hand to his face, planted a small kiss there before releasing her. I smiled, thinking of the man at the gas station and his wife's trip to Italy. Opal placed her hands delicately in her lap. "Dinner will be ready to serve in ten minutes. Now," she directed her gaze to each of the four of us in turn, "tell me, to what purpose do we find ourselves with two extra guests tonight?"

Mr. Frey shifted uncomfortably.

Finn stammered for a moment, but Lucy was not cowed. She responded pleasantly, evenly, "Hazel and Dimitri are our best friends. We were planning on all starting this new venture together, running the bed and breakfast together, starting new lives in the mountains together. It would be so lonely for Finn and me to come up here alone where we don't know anyone, and it would be such an adventure for all of us to be here." She smiled brightly.

"It's unnecessary," Opal said simply.

We stared at her until she expounded. "There simply isn't enough to do for four people here. The inn basically runs itself. Besides, you'll be a guest bedroom short."

"Now, my dear." Mr. Frey took her hand again, kept it this time. "We've been running this place a long time, everything *feels* easy for us because we are so used to it. Remember how difficult it was, at first?"

"No," Opal said. She was ice.

Finn was getting pissed, I could tell. "I don't really know why it's any concern of yours how we choose to staff this place, *if* we decide to buy it."

"*If* we decide to sell it to you," Opal retorted. "This house has been my home much longer than you've been alive, I won't see it mismanaged."

This was a nightmare. I stared down at my feet. Dimitri's leg jiggled nervously beside me. The fireplace crackled loudly, adding its own venom to the tension.

Finn stood up. "I don't know that this arrangement is quite what we're looking for."

Dimitri and I caught each other's eye. Should we stand, too? Were we leaving? I felt like I was staying at a friend's house when their parent was in a bad mood, a burden and source of contention with no way to redeem myself.

"Now, now, let's not be hasty." Mr. Frey stood as well. "You haven't even seen the house yet! Let's have dinner and then we'll take a quick tour. Opal and I will get out of your hair and you all can take the weekend to relax and talk it over amongst yourselves. We can discuss it again on Monday." His voice had a slight edge to it, an urgency. "Let's move on through to the dining room. We'll all feel better after some delicious food."

My stomach rumbled, but I couldn't stop seeing all the blood on the kitchen island. She was back with us pretty quickly, how well could she have possibly cleaned up the mess? Would I be eating pasta a la blood? I wished I'd had an opportunity to tell the others about it.

The three of us looked to Finn. We'd all do whatever he decided, and he knew it. He looked down at Lucy. She was unconsciously still running her hand along the smooth fabric of the settee, her gaze dreamy, and that seemed to make up his mind. He wanted this house for her. He nodded. "Alright."

It was a signal for us, and we followed him and Mr. Frey back into the hall without comment.

Chapter 4

The dining room was opulent. A glittering chandelier hovered above the largest table I'd ever seen in person and the walls were dotted with mirror backed sconces that made the place stretch into infinity, a dark forest full of fairy lights. The damask wallpaper glistened with silvery velvet. Lucy grabbed my arm as we entered and mouthed "Oh. My. Gawd." I was positive that was the pronunciation she was mouthing. She was completely entranced, eyes huge and reflecting the sconces' glow, and I knew there was no way that Finn would leave without making an offer.

I counted the intricately carved and richly upholstered dining room chairs. Ten on each long side of the massive table, two on each end. More people than would come to my funeral, but in a bed and breakfast with ten guest rooms, it was acceptable. Shimmering silver place settings for six waited the end of the table furthest from us and we wandered down the length of the room in a daze.

"Sit, sit!" Mr. Frey called, and he and Opal headed towards a set of swinging doors in the far corner of the room.

Dimitri sped up to join them. "Here, let me help serve."

"Nonsense, you are guests." Mr. Frey waved his hand. "Sit, my boy."

Dimitri shrugged and pulled out a chair on one side of the table and looked at me.

"Oh," I said. "Are we these kinds of people now?" I sat in the chair and laughed as he struggled to push me toward the table without dumping me to the ground.

"I mean, in a room like this, I feel like it's required." He gave up, left me siting a foot from the table, and took the place next to me.

I scooted forward on my own, the chair legs screeching on the wood.

Finn made a show of gesturing Lucy to the chair he'd pulled out for her, and as she sat, he slid the chair forward under her. He bowed and Lucy pinched her thumb and forefinger together on both hands at her sides, mocking a curtesy. She stage whispered, "I taught him that," and winked at Dimitri.

I plucked the plate in front of me from the tablecloth. "Holy shit, is this, like, *real* silver? Is silver even safe to eat off of?" I held it up to catch the light of the chandelier and squinted down at it. It had an embossed flourish pattern along the outer rim, and I traced my fingers across it. The white blob of my face reflected in it was distorting the delicate pattern in the dim light and I turned the plate slightly to move my reflection. Mine disappeared, but another reflection took its place. Another face, only inches from my own.

The plate fell from my hand and clattered onto the table, knocking my fork to the floor.

"Watch it there, butterfingers, I don't own this place yet," Finn said, but I barely heard him.

My heart was racing, and I stared at the wall behind me. The sconces twinkled innocently.

"Hey." Dimitri put a hand on my leg, and I jumped again, turning away from the empty space that held a reflection. "You alright?" He reached down and grabbed my fork, switched it with his own, and put my plate in its place in front of me.

"I'm okay, yeah. I..." I turned again, stared at the wall suspiciously. "I think I must be getting tired."

"It's this room. It's so dark, I bet people fall asleep in their dessert every night in here," he answered with a yawn and a stretch. Just seeing his casual, familiar body language helped slow my racing heart.

"There aren't any windows," Lucy said. "Can you believe, a room this size with no external walls? This place must be gigantic. I can't wait to see it in the daytime."

"Hot plates, coming through!" Mr. Frey sang as he backed through the swinging doors.

Serving plates rested on each arm and he set them in the middle of the table with practiced ease. One had some kind of delicious-smelling baked chicken and one was mashed potatoes. Opal came through behind him carrying bowls of salad and bread slices.

Before any of us could do more than exclaim with delight, Mr. Frey left again and returned with a huge pitcher of ice water, a bottle of wine, and one of those fancy glass bottles that I assumed held some kind of oil for the salad. He deposited each with a small clunk. "Well, tuck in."

We did. The weird reflection and even Opal's injury were shoved forcefully to the back of my mind by the best mashed potatoes I'd ever had in my life. I snuck a glance at Opal at the head of the table, on her husband's right. She hadn't started eating yet, she had instead been cutting her chicken into the smallest bites I'd ever seen for a grown person. She had removed her Pegasus bandage, and I couldn't for the life of me remember which finger she'd cut. She finally took a tiny chunk, while I watched her chew a full ten times before swallowing, and then wait another ten seconds before selecting another bite. I looked down at my mostly empty plate and decided to slow down a bit.

"This is really excellent." Lucy set down her fork and knife politely. "I can't thank you enough for making dinner for us, it's so kind!"

Opal set down her own cutlery in response. "Alexander, my love. We have such an early start tomorrow. Should we perhaps leave them to explore the house on their own? I'm sure they will manage." She'd taken three bites. I watched.

"Are you not staying here until morning, at least?" Lucy asked. "The road back down is so narrow."

Mr. Frey laughed. "Oh, I know that road as well as the insides of my own shoes. We'll be fine. We have a hotel waiting in the city, our flight is very early. Will you all be comfortable for the night? I'll show you where your rooms are."

He immediately stood, his own dinner half eaten. When Opal said jump, he didn't even bother to ask how high, he was already in the air.

Finn set down his water glass. "Uh sure." He pushed back from the table. "You guys go ahead and eat, I'll just show you later." He looked suddenly nervous, patting his clothes and running a hand through his hair.

"We'll take care of cleaning up, Mrs. Frey," Lucy offered. "Don't worry about a thing."

Opal rose gracefully. "Thank you, child, that's very kind. Hazel, was it?" She turned her gaze upon me as she said my name, and I suppressed a shiver.

"Yes, Ma'am?"

"You'll find plastic wrap and refrigerator containers in the pantry I showed you earlier. For the leftovers. I'm sure they'll make an excellent lunch." With that farewell, she glided from the room, her dress glimmering in the fake candlelight.

Dimitri dropped his fork onto his plate as soon as the Freys and Finn were out of the room. "Are we just going to pretend that this isn't, like, super bizarre? I feel like I'm in a weird fever dream."

Lucy leaned back and exhaled, let her stomach expand into a normal position. "Oh, my God, I thought it was just me. Food is good though."

"I'm sure it'll be less weird in the morning," I offered.

Lucy smiled. "I'm sure it's going to be amazing! And besides..." She leaned forward, rested her arms on the table. Her long hair trailed dangerously close to her dinner, and she dropped her voice to a whisper. "It's not like they come with the house. They're weird, but they're moving to the beach, right? This could be so cool, right? I mean," She sat up and spreads her arms wide like she was hugging the whole room. "*Look* at this place!"

I grinned. Her enthusiasm was infectious.

Dimitri smiled, too, but it was a sad little thing, barely quirking up one side of his mouth. "The house is wild. It's as big as our whole apartment building, probably. I just don't want us to get our hopes up."

"D, don't be a downer," I murmured. Lucy's face had already fallen slightly.

"I'm not, I'm just being serious. I'm getting a weird vibe. Like maybe there's some kind of catch that they'll spring on Monday. Let us all fall in love with the place and then let us know that... I don't know. It's no longer zoned to operate as a B&B, or that there's an incurable mold situation, or whatever." He shrugged. "Just, don't get your heart set, okay? There will be other places we can consider."

I noticed he spoke directly to Lucy and that didn't bother me. Lucy always had things go her way, she might not have understood disappointment or even compromise. I don't think it was really her fault, she'd just been lucky. She got into her dream college, got hired into her dream career, found that career satisfying and enriching. She met a man, fell in love, he loved her back, and married her. Everything came up Lucy.

Dimitri didn't bother telling me what could go wrong because I already assumed it would. He'd be preaching to the choir. I really didn't have any inkling of hope that Finn might actually end up buying this place and hiring us on, I just wanted a fun weekend off work.

Lucy's lower lip trembled and slightly poked out. "You really think it won't happen?"

Dimitri held up his hands. "I didn't say that. Let's just let it be a nice surprise if it does, that's all."

Lucy nodded, but didn't pull her lip back in. She looked down at her plate, still half full of food. "I just think it would be so perfect..." she said quietly.

"Say, Lu," I said, trying to change the subject a little. "So, you're fine leaving your job and all to come up into the mountains?"

"Well..." She was still staring hard at her potatoes. "I am. I'm getting a little too...attached, I think. Bringing some stress home. It's hard, sometimes."

I nodded, but I knew she didn't see me. Lucy taught remedial English and math at a high school in the city. She used to teach French in a fancy prep school and made great money, but the kids were difficult, and the parents were worse. Maybe she struggled for a bit, doubting her own abilities as a teacher, and decided to get some practice in different settings by offering free tutoring in public high schools. She found her true calling then, helping kids out who really needed her instead of kids just filling up a credit.

When one of the city schools had a teaching position open up, she jumped on it, took a huge pay cut, and never looked back. She continued her after school and even before school tutoring and ran a bunch of different work and extracurricular programs to help underprivileged kids land on their feet after graduation. I didn't know how she did it, but she didn't know how she could *not* do it.

When Finn first started dating her, he confided in me that his number one fear was the fact that she adored kids so much. "I don't want to be a dad, Hazel," It was as close as he ever got to discussing the trauma of losing his parents so young. "I know it's going to be a deal breaker when I finally tell her."

It ended up not being a deal breaker at all. Lucy never wanted children of her own, she only wanted to help the ones that were already around. She wanted to be five hundred kids' fairy godmother. Recently, though, she'd brought up the idea of fostering a few times. To *me*, anyway, I didn't know if she's gotten up the nerve to talk to Finn about it. "I want to foster kids before they age out. I want them to become an adult knowing they've got someone they can ask advice from, get help from. Remember how hard it is being eighteen? How much you needed your parents?"

I remembered. I was still eighteen some days. I thought the reason she hadn't brought it up with Finn yet was because he didn't have his parents during those years, when he really needed them. She tried not to remind him. She stepped around it like glittering shards of glass that surrounded his past, his family, his memories.

I wanted to tell her that the more we visited those memories and ground their sharp points into sparkling snow, the easier it would be for Finn to walk across them to meet us and to carry on with his life. But I didn't know how to say it and I already knew what her response would be, "But I wasn't there. I didn't know his parents." She wouldn't mean it to sound like jealous, but it would. A lot of things might never be spoken between us.

I was seventeen and Finn was eighteen on the day of the accident. We had graduated high school four days prior. We had big plans, the two of us. We had it all worked out. When I remembered that day, I remembered it this way. It might not have been *exactly* the truth, but everyone assumed it was.

Finn had just turned eighteen the day before. We were going to his favorite steakhouse to celebrate. Just him, his mother, father, and me. It was a big deal that I was invited. Finn's father was either a private man, or he just hated me specifically. Even though Finn and I had dated through most of middle school and all of high school, he didn't consider me family. I was Finn's "friend." Friends weren't included in family events like holidays or vacations. I wonder if he just didn't want my face marring family photos when Finn and I inevitably split, as he seemed sure we would.

But I'd forgotten about the birthday dinner. I had picked up a babysitting gig to help fund our post-graduation cross country trip and would be spending the evening watching princess movies with a very demanding three-year-old.

"I'm so sorry!" I genuinely was. "I can't believe I forgot. Are you pissed?"

Finn had shaken his head. "No, but I'm upset. Not about my birthday, I couldn't give a shit about this dinner. But this was a chance to show him that we're serious, you know? That you're going to be around."

I'd hung my head and let tears slip down my cheeks. I didn't have a whole lot to cry about in those days, so any little reason was good enough for them to escape. "*Him*" was Finn's dad, Frank. "It'll be okay. Maybe I can bring by a cake before I go to the Connors, we can have it for dessert after dinner. I should be done babysitting by then. He likes cake, right?"

Finn rolled his eyes. "Everybody likes cake, Hazel. But I'm still going to have to spend this whole awkward dinner without you."

He did not have to do that.

I'd received the call halfway through the eighteenth performance of "Let It Go" sung by a child who only knew those three words of the song. The call was from my mother. "Hazel? Sweetie. Where are you?"

The words had stopped me dead. There was nothing strange about them individually, but my mother hadn't called me sweetie in ten years, and she'd *known* where I was. At least, if she had not been a complete wreck, she would have known. She might not have remembered her own address in that moment. "I'm...I'm watching Amelia, remember? The Connors' kid?"

"Your dad is coming to get you. He'll bring Amelia to me."

"What?"

"There's...there's been an accident, sweetie."

Amelia was tugging on my sleeve. "Play the let it go song! Play the let it go song!"

"What? Is everyone okay? What happened?"

"Finn and his parents. They got in an accident."

"*Let it go song!*"

"Oh, my God." My vision had tunneled. I'd stood from the couch when my mother called me 'sweetie', but sank back down again, oblivious to the toddler tugging on me. "Is he okay, Mom?"

"He's okay. Your dad is going to bring you to the hospital." She paused.

"Mom?"

"Frank and Matilda didn't make it."

"What?" I whispered, forcing the words passed the absence of air in my lungs. But I'd heard her. *What had I done?*

They'd gotten sideswiped by an eighteen-wheeler that hadn't seen them on the onramp of the highway, less than two miles from their house. The truck driver had panicked and jerked the truck to the shoulder, and inadvertently crushed the car between his cab and the cement barrier. Finn's parents were both dead on the scene. Finn had been sitting in the middle of the backseat, seatbelt off, attempting to reach the steering wheel. He had only received bruises and never lost consciousness. It took almost an hour for the EMTs to extract him from the wreck. Almost an hour in the confines of that crushed vehicle with the bodies of his parents. An eternity. Hell on earth.

Finn had told the police that his father had been suffering some kind of medical emergency right before the accident. He had lost consciousness. Finn told the sobbing truck driver it wasn't his fault. He'd said it with dead eyes and a monotone voice as they loaded him into an ambulance. He was in shock, obviously, but he'd repeated it all later, with a clearer head. It wasn't the truck driver's fault, his father had been sick, unable to control the car.

The truck driver had refused to leave the scene until Finn was safely loaded in, just yelling, "I'm so sorry, I'm so sorry!" through snotty tears.

It all might have happened whether I'd been there or not, whether I'd done what I had done or not. I told myself this over and over. Survivor's guilt, I guess it's called. But I never talked to anyone besides Lucy about those feelings, because whatever Finn was going through was undoubtedly worse. I didn't want to make it about me. I needed to support Finn. Besides, I couldn't ever tell anyone, not even Lucy, that I had more guilt than the average survivor.

This all had been brought to light between Lucy and I during our forced alone time together over the last two years. I hoped it made her feel closer to me and hoped it made her understand her husband a little bit more on those days he might seem unreachable. I hoped it made it feel like we could be there for each other, like sisters, sharing heartaches.

So, it had been me she'd confided in about her students. How they struggled at home. How they might not have internet, or didn't always get dinner, or how their parents were addicts or worked three jobs to make ends meet. She wanted to take them all home with her and keep them safe. Every day was becoming heartache. I wonder now, if that was the main appeal of a bed and breakfast. I wonder if she imagined that one day, when we were too old (and hopefully too rich) to want guests anymore, that she could fill all the bedrooms with wayward teenagers and give them a year or two of the good life before letting them fly from the nest like so many baby birds.

"It'll be good to take some time away," I said. It sounded lame, but she looked up and smiled at me, as though she knew all the things I'd been thinking. Maybe she did.

"Alright." Finn reappeared, shoving open both swinging doors dramatically. "The weird old people are officially gone. I've just waved them all the way down the driveway."

"Shh, Finn!" Lucy giggled. "What if they've got cameras or something? Be nice!"

Finn scoffed at her. "Look around you, Lu. Where the hell would they be hiding cameras, in this eighteenth century wallpaper? Let's get this food put away so I can show you the bedrooms, they're *wild*."

We all started haphazardly grabbing plates. Dimitri and I did most of the work, condensing and stacking the way only people who have worked forever in food service could do. Lucy grabbed the dishes of leftovers and Finn handled the drinks.

The hallway between the dining room and kitchen was a long corridor of cabinets and counter space. All the appliances that were missing from the kitchen were there, a huge coffee pot, eight slice toaster, mixing stand, blender, even a tabletop bread maker.

Lucy was in love, of course, and said, "I can't wait to see the kitchen! Wonder what it's like."

Covered in blood, I thought, but said nothing. I was apprehensive. The cloud of bad feeling should have lifted with the caretakers' departure, but instead, it was denser, heavier. It was as though the Freys had kept the house in check for us and now it could be as weird as it pleased. I knew Finn has just walked through the kitchen, and he definitely would have said something if it were still gruesome, but unease tickled my spine all the same.

Finn backed through the swinging doors at the end of the corridor, and the kitchen stood before us. If it hadn't still smelled like chicken, I'd have thought no one had ever used it before. Dazzlingly clean, not a pot or pan or bloodstain in sight.

"Wow," I said. "That Opal can *move,* I guess."

"She was definitely in a hurry to leave." Finn caught the refrigerator door with his foot and yanked it open to deposit the drinks. "She was basically dragging ol' Alex by the ear. Wonder what their appointment is."

I set my stack of dirty dishes by the sink. There was no dishwasher. I guessed antique silver probably shouldn't be put in the dishwasher, but it seemed like an easily avoidable inconvenience. Dimitri set his stack down, too. "We can do these later," he said, reading my mind as usual. Half our conversations (especially disagreements) were completely silent, his intuition leaping beyond my irritations and focusing on solutions like I was dating Sherlock Holmes. "It'll take no time at all."

I nodded, but was only partially listening. I stared out the window over the sink. It was *so* dark out there, I felt like I was looking at a glossy black wall, or maybe a hole where I could tip forward, fall straight in, and just careen down and down forever.

A face loomed up next to mine in the glass, floating from the abyss. My chest tightened with the threat of a scream. Was I *that* tired?

Cold fingers swatted my hair from my neck and a squeak actually escaped my throat before Finn said, "Hurry up," and the face in the window's mouth moved. It was only Finn's reflection, his hand cold from the ice water pitcher. I was apparently *that* tired.

I turned the rest of my scream into a slow exhale, blowing the air out like I was cooling down a mug of tea. "Alright, alright, lead the way."

Lucy yawned and stretched like a cat. "I'm exhausted. Do the beds look comfortable? Clean?"

"Yeah, yeah." Finn waved a hand over his shoulder dismissively as he marched us down the hall. He swung around the banister and ran up the stairs, his feet thudding on the carpet runner.

Dimitri took off after him with a boyish grin, leaving Lucy and I standing at the bottom of the stairs, rolling our eyes at each other.

"Do we have to run?" she asked, her voice a little whiny. She was allowed, she'd been driving all day.

"I won't if you won't," I answered.

She grinned. "I won't if you won't."

We climbed the stairs languidly, studying the wallpaper, the carved rail, the paintings hung along the wall.

"I wonder if this is the view." I gestured to a painting of a rough estimation of mountains and valleys, all in thickly applied burnt oranges and soft lilacs.

Lucy smiled and touched the frame tenderly. "I hope so. I feel like this night will never end. It feels so heavy!" She pulled her hand back, shivered a little. "Like a big black blanket over the whole house. I want to see the view!"

"Well, go to sleep and when you wake up,"

"Santa will have brought us all gifts, right?" She laughed. "I might not be able to sleep, it *is* like Christmas Eve! I can't wait to see this place tomorrow."

Sleep probably wouldn't come easily for me either, but not for longing of sweeping Appalachian views. I couldn't shake the weird creeping sensations that niggled me, raising my arm hairs, making me repeatedly turn and look back down the stairs behind us, as though someone would be there, following. I hoped Lucy didn't notice.

We finally arrived on the landing of the second floor. There were no lights on, just horrendous emptiness pressing on our cozy life-filled square of wooden flooring. The second floor may as well have been an abandoned barn on a moonless night, or a desolate airplane hangar. Instead of commenting or fumbling for a light switch, we leaned in unison to peer up the stairs to the third floor. Warm light bounced down the walls in flickering waves. Dimitri's head appeared over the rail high above, staring directly down at us, and his eyes caught the light and glimmered for a moment. Lucy yelped in surprise.

"You coming or what?" he called down, and his head disappeared again.

Suddenly, the second floor seemed much too quiet, and much, *much* too dark. Lucy and I shared another glance. It was clear she thought so as well, so we nodded to each other and pelted up the stairs as fast as our legs can carry us, laughing and out of breath.

A sitting area at the top of the stairs welcomed us, presumably positioned so one had a place to rest after running up like the hounds of hell were following. We collapsed into fainting couches, still laughing. A chandelier with Edison bulbs in glass votive holders bathed us in warm, cozy firelight. There were tiny tables placed near the couches and chairs, and I realized they were actually ash trays, though it didn't look like any had ever been used. Then again, the kitchen didn't look like it had ever been used either. I breathed in deep to see if I could catch a hint of smoke.

"Pretty neat, huh?" Dimitri lifted up my legs so he could sit on the chaise next to me. "I feel like we could have a seance here. Creepy."

He pointed down and I followed his gaze. There was an intricate circular rug underneath the furniture grouping. I rolled my eyes. "Those are just the zodiacs." I pointed to the woven ram by his feet. "That's you."

He glanced down. "Stunning resemblance. Alright, are you two done fainting? I'm *so* ready to go to sleep."

Lucy bounced up from her chaise. "Where's Finn?"

"Unpacking, I think."

I rolled from under Dimitri. "Alright, let's see these 'wild' rooms. Are we near each other?"

Dimitri heaved himself up. "Yeah, we have a connecting bathroom." He headed down a dark hallway, no sconces burning. Two doors stood open along the left side of the hall spilling light. There were two closed doors on the right and a huge bay window with dozens of throw pillows in a window seat at the end of the hall. The black night pressed in.

Finn appeared at the nearer of the two doors. "Did you get lost?" He handed Lucy a small cloth bag that I assumed held toiletries. "Dug this out for you. Alright, should we plan on like, ten tomorrow?"

We agreed and Dimitri and I headed to our own door, Lucy calling dibs on the bathroom first. I knew there were a lot of bathrooms in the place, but I would absolutely be waiting my turn to use that one, I wasn't about to sneak around the place in my pajamas in the dark. Not tonight, anyway. I wondered if we would move in and I'd get used to the decadent halls and shadowy corners, and wander around with my toothbrush in my mouth like I would in our tiny apartment. I couldn't imagine it. I could certainly imagine Lucy sweeping through the halls in one of her ridiculous long lacy nightgowns, clutching a candelabra dramatically, straight out of a gothic romance. Somehow, the scene just didn't work with the bike shorts and huge t-shirts I usually wore to bed.

"Well, here it is." Dimitri stood at the other door spilling light and swept a hand in front of him. "After you."

My jaw dropped. We were under the eaves of the house and the ceiling had high vaults and steep corners. Narrow windows were deep set in the walls with benches and pillows built in like the one in the hall. A huge four poster bed sprawled in the dead center of the room, the part with the highest ceiling, draped in gauzy gold cloth, with heavy black velvet drapes tied back at the corners. There must have been twenty pillows on the bed, all in various shades of gold and with every texture I could have imagined. A fireplace was set into one wall and the fire had been kindled. It glowed comfortingly. Next to the fireplace was, outrageously, a claw foot bathtub.

"Are you serious right now?" I stammered and laughed as I rushed to the tub. The slate tiles of the fireplace stretched out in a wide semicircle and encompassed it and a little stand holding a tiny shaving mirror, basin, water pitcher, and a rack of huge fluffy towels. "What's in the actual bathroom?"

"An actual shower and toilet for actual people," Dimitri said. "Do you feel like, very out of your depth here? I feel like I'm a kid sitting at the grown-up table."

I picked up the shaving mirror, running my grubby little hands over its delicate details, smudging the glass, soiling it with my inadequacies. "This probably cost more than our groceries this month. What's the catch, D?"

He shrugged. "Maybe there isn't one. Maybe it'll all work out and you'll start wearing tiaras to dinner."

"Hmm." I squinted at my tiny reflection. "I could rock a tiara. I think. I don't know, I can't even see my hair in this thing. I hope the bathroom has a bigger mirror." I set it back down carefully.

"You're not going to like this, but it doesn't. It's got a big painting of angels instead."

My cup curled up in annoyance. It was certainly bizarre. I was honestly surprised there wasn't a dressing mirror there by the tub.

Dimitri vaulted across the room, jumped on the bed with a flop. "The guests here are probably all old rich people. They don't want to see their whole reflection while they're trying to enjoy themselves. Too many skin folds," he said, or at least, I thought that was what he said. Half of it was a yawn.

"Get your shoes *off* of that bed," I commanded.

"Oh!" He jumped up. "I forgot to show you something neat."

He grabbed my arm and dragged me towards one of the windows. It didn't have a bench set in like the others. He flipped the catch on the windows and pushed them both open and revealed a small balcony set into the roof. A low wrought iron fence surrounded it, just high enough to keep one from toppling to their tragic hillside demise, if one was careful, and the same slate tiles from the fireplace and bathtub had spread out there into the night like eager moss. Two intricate iron chairs were placed to look out over the view, which was endless nothing. In true West Virginia fashion, the clouds must have reappeared in the last hour and soft rain pattered onto the slate. At the sound and smell of it I was instantly the most exhausted I'd ever been.

"Neat," I repeated dully. "I've gotta sleep."

He nodded, shielded his lighter from the gentle rain and mumbled around the cigarette that had appeared between his lips. "Sure thing, Nut. I'll be in in a minute."

I closed the door (window?) on him and saw the flare of his lighter through the glass. A dark reflection stood beside my own on the windowpane and I gave a small start, a twitch of the neck and heart, before I recognized it, just Dimitri's hunched shoulders and lean frame out in the dark. I turned away without another glance to pick through our messily packed bags and Lucy called, "I'm all done in here, goodnight!" from behind the closed bathroom door.

Chapter 5

I slept like the dead.

No new environmental noises kept me tossing and turning, no visions of blood or strange reflections. My head hit the pillow and suddenly, it was morning, and Dimitri was tapping my shoulder. I groaned and pulled the quilt up to my face. "Ten minutes?"

"I gave you ten minutes ten minutes ago." He gave the blanket a yank that my sleepy, half dead arms couldn't hope to overcome. I opened my eyes a smidge. He sat on the edge of the bed, already shaved, and showered, his hair still wet. Droplets of water soaked his collar.

I took a moment to appreciate that he was a beautiful, beautiful man, but the moment was cut short by a yawn I couldn't contain that made my jaw pop. "What time is it?"

There was a rap on the door. Dimitri leaned his head to the side, raised an eyebrow. "Who...who is it?" He sounded uncertain.

"Lucy! May I come in?" She was practically singing.

Dimitri deferred to me, since I was obviously not prepared for company, but I shrugged and answered, "Come on in."

The door swung open, and Lucy appeared, carrying a tray on one shoulder like a waitress. Like a *good* waitress, not like me. It had a small carafe of coffee and two mugs on it. "Good morning, sleepy head!" She set the tray down on the nightstand by my head. "Hazel, I'm *dying* to explore the house, we're all waiting for you! I brought you coffee."

I rubbed my cheeks, yawned again. "Alright, I'm awake. What—"

"It's nine thirty," Dimitri answered before I could repeat my question.

"Sorry." Lucy giggled. "I just couldn't stand waiting anymore! I've been up for two hours."

She was dressed like Samantha in Bewitched, a high necked, sleeveless pink dress and a wide yellow belt. She had chunky yellow square plastic earrings in to match, her fiery hair in a braid with perfect little flyaways at her temples she had to have pulled down on purpose. She sat down on the other side of the bed, and I suddenly felt like a hospital patient with both her and Dimitri's curious gazes resting on me.

I pushed myself up to sit against the pillows, leaned over and flipped a mug to the upright position. Their eyes on me made my doubly self-conscious as I tried to pour from the carafe. "So..." I said in the dead air. "You haven't looked around at all yet?"

Lucy gave a mocking gasp, clutched invisible pearls. "We wouldn't dare! We're going to explore as a group. Finn is *finally* in the shower. Don't let him give you a hard time, he's a hundred times more grumpy than you are in the morning, you know."

"What have you been up to, then?" I sipped the coffee. It was delicious and cool enough I wouldn't burn my tongue. I took a bigger gulp.

"Well..." She leaned over conspiratorially. "I *did* check out our balcony. Oh, Hazel, you are going to just *die* when you see the view. It's so beautiful!"

I bobbed forward to peer out the nearest window, and she put a hand out to block my view. "Wait, get dressed first and we'll go out!"

Dimitri reached back and grabbed the other mug. "Thanks for the coffee, Lucy. You found your way down to the kitchen alright alone?"

"Definitely not." She shivered. "There's a little coffee bar and the teensiest little fridge on the landing by those couches we were on last night, how cute is that?"

Dimitri smiled. "Adorable."

"Thank you, thank you." The bathroom door swung open again and Finn stepped into our room, bowing slightly in the steam that chased him out of the bathroom. "You're pretty cute yourself, D. Too bad Hazel still looks like trash."

I chucked a tasseled gold pillow at him, but the room was too wide, and it fell about five feet short of reaching him. The motion also sloshed coffee out of my mug and onto my t-shirt. "I'm getting up now," I moaned, dabbing at the wet spot with a different part of my shirt. "Everybody get out. I'll transform."

Lucy jumped up. "I'll show you guys the coffee bar! Meet you on the landing, Hazel?"

"Don't forget to draw your eyebrows on," Finn called back to me as he ushered Lucy toward the hall.

Dimitri leaned over and planted a kiss in my hair before he stood. "I'll push him out a window, just say the word. You should draw angry eyebrows on today."

A smile crept across my face. "Not necessary...yet." I shooed him off the bed. "I'll be ready in ten, maybe twenty tops."

He followed the others out and the door shut with a soft clunk, like the first shovel of dirt on a grave. It wasn't like that at all, of course, but the finality of it, the silence that dropped into my lap with the realization of my solitude, made it the same. The hairs on my arms stood in a wave, my discomfort in the house hadn't dissipated with the night. It had to be only the sheer size and strangeness of the place that had me on edge, but it was embarrassing. I didn't want the others to know. Despite the sunlight shimmering off of every surface in the room, I was afraid and slurped my coffee to create noise. I needed to get out of the warm bed and make my way to my suitcase, to the bathroom, but the distance across the floorboards seemed insurmountable. This bed had become, in moments, my coffin.

"All right," I said decisively to the empty room and let the mug clunk down onto the tray. "Time to quit with the bull-shit."

"No," the empty room replied.

My ears rang, my muscles all stiffened without my consent. I leapt out of the bed, the sheets tangling around my ankles, attempting to drag me back. "What? Who..." I stumbled towards the door to the hall, pulling the sheet with me most of the way. "Who's in here?" My heart was absolutely hammering against my ribs. I *knew* someone had just spoken. It had been clear as day, clear as the blue sky outside I tried to avoid peeking at.

I crouched down, looked under the bed. There was a foot of clear space under there and I could see the other side of the room. When I stood, I knew as I crouched there, someone would be standing right next to me. I'd seen scary movies. But there was no alternative, so I rose, both my knees popping from being used so early in the morning. There was no one.

"Hello?" I called, louder than I wanted to.

No one answered me. My fingers drummed against my sweatpants, trying to hammer a coherent thought into my head. After very little thinking, I bolted for the door and out into the hall, sans eyebrows.

"Dimitri?" I slammed the door shut behind me. I could hear them talking in the siting area, the hallway wasn't terribly long. Their voices all hushed at once.

"Is that you, Nut?" Dimitri called back.

"Of course, it's me. Can you…" Suddenly I felt very childish. I was certain I'd imagined a voice. I didn't want to tell them about it. I didn't want them to think I'd lost my nerve. I also definitely couldn't go back into the bedroom alone to get ready. "Can you come here for a second?" It was lame, but I was actually shaking with fright. I was proud my voice was working at all and didn't sound hysterical.

He didn't answer, but he appeared in just a couple of seconds, cruising down the hall at a jog. "What's wrong?"

Maybe I sounded a little hysterical.

I hooked his elbow and started walking him down to the window at the end of the hall. I sat us down on the window seat. "I don't want to freak anyone out, but I think someone might be in our room."

Dimitri eyed me carefully. "That seems like a good reason to freak out, actually. Did you see someone in there?"

"I heard a voice."

"Not our voices?"

"I don't think so." I looked at the closed bedroom door. "But maybe I imagined it, I don't know. I'm a little frazzled."

He stood. "You're very frazzled. You look like you're going to puke. Should we leave? Call the cops?"

I grabbed his hand. "Can you just come in with me while I get ready?"

"That's not what I'd recommend in the case of an intruder." He tilted his head a little, studied me again. "You think it's something else?"

I blushed. "Maybe? Don't tell them I got scared, okay? I've got a rep to uphold."

He rolled his eyes and pulled me up by the hand I still clutched him with. "You'll tell them yourself. The reason Lucy has been up since the crack of dawn is because she had a nightmare, thought someone was whispering. I felt like someone was in the bathroom with me while I was in the shower. Do you ever get like that, like in hotels or whatever?" He gave a dramatic shiver which was fairly convincing, even though I knew he was making it up to make me feel better. "Finn…"

He opened our door, but held me back from entering, scanning the room. There weren't any closets, just a tall dresser and armoire. I hadn't thought to look in the armoire. I looked at Dimitri instead, afraid to see someone or something in the room that shouldn't be there. "Finn, what?"

"Oh," Dimitri said distractedly, still scoping the corners. "He hasn't seen or heard a single thing. He thinks we're all jumpy in a strange place."

I narrowed my eyes. I assumed Finn was lying, but I didn't know why, because I was also sure he was right. "I didn't check the armoire." I pointed an accusatory finger at it.

He strolled over and pulled it open without preamble. Empty, except for some fancy wooden hangers. He glanced back to where I lingered still halfway in the hall. "I guess we should check both rooms. You stay there and watch this door and their door."

I nodded and my nerves jangled again as he disappeared into the bathroom, closing the door behind him, but he was only out of sight for a moment before he reappeared at the other bedroom door and stepped into the hall. "There's not a lot of places to hide, really," He admitted with a shrug, "There's no one here."

He guided me through the door and to the bench at the end of the bed. "I'll be right out on the balcony, just yell if you need me, okay?"

I nodded. I felt stupid.

I squinted around the room, sneaking the tiniest peek towards the balcony, but I didn't want to ruin the surprise of the view for myself, not really. Lucy would know if my reaction was faked, I was pretty terrible at feigning surprise. Dimitri lingered with his back to the door, his hand resting on the latch, ready to run right back in if I need him. That should have made me feel loved, but the blood rushed to my ears as they reddened in embarrassment. I didn't need to be babied. I could handle a few disembodied voices. I had green hair and drew on my eyebrows, this was supposed to be my thing.

I popped up and picked a random dress and tights from my bag. They all looked the same, it didn't matter which ones. I headed for the bathroom to change and fix my face, and felt my wrist pop as the knob I expected to turn in my hand resisted me. It was locked.

I knocked. "Hey, are one of you guys in there?"

There was no answer.

I sighed. Dimitri must have locked it behind him when he went through. I backtracked through the room and out into the hall. My slight annoyance had quickly taken center stage in my mind, and I could dimly hear Finn's voice down the hall. Not his words, just his cadence. The familiarity ticked my anxiety down one more notch. Pretty soon I wouldn't even be trembling.

I considered calling down the hall to let them know I was going in their bedroom, but the door was standing open, and I decided not to bother. Their room wasn't the mirror image of ours I'd for whatever reason imagined it would be. Instead, an entire wall of windows opened up onto a stone balcony. I couldn't help but finally take in the view. It was so panoramic in there that my vertigo from last night returned. Instead of tumbling through nothingness, I felt like I was tilting right down into the valley, like any moment the flaming array of autumn leaves would slice me apart with a million paper cuts as I tumbled through them. The valley was a dazzling orange and yellow bowl of foliage. Morning mists still clung on to the darkest shadows in the basin. The gray sky was full of circling birds and the occasional startling white puffy cloud. It was the most beautiful fall morning I had ever gazed upon.

I forced myself to turn my eyes back and check out their bedroom. Their room was even larger and fancier than ours somehow. The ceiling was high on the wall I clutched the door-frame on and swept down dramatically to the arched windows. Three huge chandeliers hung, dark for now. The room was all glittering gray velvet, black wood, pewter and artfully tarnished silver.

"Wow," I managed, but then I turned towards the bathroom, hugging my clothes tight. I had to pee. The door was closed, and I had a sinking sensation as I touched the handle. I was already letting out an exasperated groan before I'd even begun to turn it, because it was locked. Of course, it was locked.

I stomped back down the hall again and caught the sound of Lucy's laughter and suddenly their happiness grated on me. Two minor inconveniences in a row were enough to transform me into a raging bitch. I flung our door open, ready to start howling at Dimitri, but stopped, my mouth hung stupidly open. His back was still there, leaned against the patio door, hand on the handle. The bathroom door stood wide open.

I pressed my lips together and nodded. "Okay. Sure. Whatever," I said to the empty room, forgetting momentarily that I didn't want to speak to this empty room. I stomped to the bathroom and swung the door shut behind me, too annoyed to be nervous any longer.

There was a little vanity in the bathroom complete with a tufted stool and a tiny cosmetics mirror. I'd dumped my make-up bag on it unceremoniously the night before, and after brushing and washing, I plopped down on the stool and took my makeup bag up in my hands.

I didn't open it right away, I just stared down at it, running my thumbs over the fabric. I didn't know why it hit me so strongly in that moment that I'd bought the bag for my big high school graduation cross country trip. I turned it over a few times, my brushes and blushes clinking softly against each other within. I'd spent way too long crouched in the aisle at the store, searching for the perfect bag with all the right pockets and a fabric pattern I didn't hate. The bag in my mind didn't exist, so I'd decided to get the one I held now, blue and white striped with cartoon bananas all over it, but damned if it didn't have perfect makeup pockets.

I remembered smiling to myself as I'd checked out, thinking of how much of a kick Finn would get out of making fun of me for the bag. But in the end, he didn't go on that trip with me like we had planned. In fact, I didn't think he'd ever even seen this bag, unless he'd noticed it this morning. We had both changed into entirely different people in the few days between me buying that bag and me going on that trip.

"Then go," I heard him say, and it was like he stood right next to me, not ten years in the past when he uttered the words, not even right down the hall like he actually was. This impossible voice didn't freak me out though, I'd heard those two words echoing around in my head for a long time.

"I just think, maybe, it would be good for you. Be good for both of us. Let's get out of here for a while. This is all too much." I had tears streaming down my face as I spoke, each one like punctuation. I'd cried for two weeks straight after the accident. It really *was* way too much. Finn having to handle all of the end-of-life details for both of his parents, suddenly having the responsibilities of a house and utilities, meeting with countless lawyers, making appointments, endless phone calls. He was in a daze. Like a zombie. I didn't know how to reach him, but also, I was afraid to reach him. I was afraid to see the wall he'd hastily built himself while in the backseat of that crushed car come crumbling around him. He was only a child under there, I knew he was. He had to be hurting.

But he looked at me with the face of an old, tired man. "I can't, Hazel. This stuff can't wait. I..." He broke off, looked down at his hands. "I don't even think I'll be able to go to school in the fall. Maybe I'll just start a semester late, but—"

"Hang on, hang on, what? Finn." I'd waited to continue until he dragged those cold dead eyes back up from his hands. It took a long time. "You've got to go to school. They'd want you to go."

His jaw clenched. "I just don't think I can do it right now, okay?"

"Okay," I said. "But—"

"I'm not going on a dumb road trip right now either. Sorry your plans are all fucked up. It must be so difficult for you."

I stood there, my mouth stupidly hanging open.

"You want to go?" His voice was tepid water. He didn't care about this conversation, about me, at all. "Then go."

I closed my mouth. Nodded slowly. I walked out of his empty tomb of a house and onto the sidewalk. I walked home. He didn't follow me, and he didn't call out to me.

At the time, I thought that he should have. I thought he should have called me back and apologized for forgetting that I also had feelings. Apologized for shutting me out. I had the audacity to be angry with him for not being considerate of me and my plans.

Yep, I went on our road trip. I went alone and I cried all across the United States. I cried at Niagara Falls, I cried at the House on the Rock, I cried in the redwood forest, I cried in ghost towns in New Mexico. While I drove, I wrote myself a story in my head.

It was the most important story of my life, and I made sure to repeat it to myself every day. It wasn't true, but after enough repetition, it replaced a truth. A truth I told myself I would never think of again.

I didn't take any pictures. I only answered phone calls from my parents. Finn didn't call me at all during that trip, and I never called him.

There were times during the trip that I knew I shouldn't have gone, that I understood I was selfish and stubborn, but those times were brief. Most of the time was spent wallowing, upset that my plans had been fucked up, it was true.

I'd been back in town for a little over a week when he walked into my bedroom. I was sitting at my desk, working on a story I told myself I'd finish before fall classes began. A story that didn't really matter at all. The doorbell hadn't chimed, I didn't think, but he might have just walked in. He used to just walk in.

My bedroom door stood open so the cat could wander in and out as he pleased. That cat would lay in one spot for hours at a time, but he liked to know that he could leave, if the mood struck him. Finn's voice, after almost two weeks of not hearing it, nearly made me jump out of my skin.

"What are you working on?"

"Jesus Christ!" I'd shrieked.

"A ghost story, huh?"

I spun around, and he was taking a seat on the chest of drawers at the foot of my bed.

I recovered from the jump scare, but impending doom quickly took its place. He was here. We were going to have to talk. I wasn't ready.

He began, "I'm sorry about what I said before you left." His voice was plain. Honest. "It wasn't fair. You're sad, too, I know that."

I shrugged. "I'm not mad. You don't have to apologize." I took a breath, tried to compose my face into one that was indifference instead of gloating satisfaction. "I don't know how to help."

He nodded. "You could start by apologizing, too."

My pulse quickened and my face reddened. "I..."

Finn held up a hand. "You weren't planning on apologizing. Okay. Well. Think about it, okay? Really step outside of your shoes for a goddamn minute."

"I'm s-sorry," I stammered.

"I don't actually need to hear it," he said. "I just want you to think about it."

I'd thought about it every day since. I thought about it then, staring down at the stupid banana fabric.

There was a knock on the door, and I let out a little yelp. "Nut? You okay in there?" It was Dimitri.

I cleared my throat. "Fine. Be out in five."

I was out in ten. Maybe eleven. My eyebrows weren't even mad.

Chapter 6

Our tour of the property was slightly delayed by a combination of Lucy and I's need of more coffee to be fully awake and insisting on starting the tour downstairs to make a full pot. Lucy had already realized her adorable shoes were too uncomfortable to trot around the giant house in, and she detoured back to her bedroom "for just a second!", but we all knew it would probably be a full twenty minute outfit change.

The guys decided to go out to the patio off the parlor to wait for us to get our shit together. Dimitri beckoned for me to follow, but I shook him off. "I'm going to run back up and grab my mug from earlier to use," I said. "I'm already tired of doing dishes."

Dimitri pinched his newly lit cigarette and stuffed it unceremoniously in his pocket. "Want me to go grab it?" His face was eager, and I knew he was looking for an escape from the impending few minutes he'd have to spend alone with Finn.

"Nah. I'll be right back," If we were going to live together, Dimitri would have to attempt to have a more in-depth relationship with the guy, move beyond faux cheeriness of casual acquaintance. I knew, deep down, they'd get along great. Once

Dimitri understood Finn's sense of humor, he'd surely realize that Finn wasn't *actually* an asshole. "You guys relax."

When I returned, I cupped my mug in both hands like I was one of those happy women in a dietary supplement commercial and paused in the hall, gazing into the parlor. The glass doors to the balcony were all thrown wide, letting in the chilly autumn air. The view was just spectacular; I actually felt my breath catch at the sheer beauty. Mist curled and billowed in the valley and reached up toward the small, cold sun. I watched the tendrils lift and disperse as the warmer air consumed them.

"A guy could get used to this."

Finn and Dimitri were both relaxing in rocking chairs on the deck, their own mugs cooling between them on a little wooden table, the rising steam mimicking the mist. I took a few steps across the parlor to join them and leaned against the door frame behind them. Neither of them noticed my approach, their eyes filled with the valley before us, their minds apparently each turned inward.

Dimitri sat forward a little. "What do you think Hazel would think of a wedding up here? Maybe like, right here." He cleared his throat. "I mean, if you decide to take this place. I've been wanting to ask her, but... Well, you and Lucy had such a nice wedding, and you know we haven't really been in a position to afford anything crazy. I want her to have a nice day, you know?"

I tamped down a squeal escaping my lips like I was a tire deflating by simultaneously biting onto my hand and dumping a good slosh of my coffee down my front for the second time this morning. I was dying to hear what they said, of course, but I would have probably just disintegrated on the spot if I got caught eavesdropping. I tried to slowly and silently step backwards, praying they didn't notice me.

"She'd love it, D." Finn laughed loudly, bless him, he covered some of my noise. "You know, I've been wondering when you were going to ask her. She's been wondering, too."

"Has she? I wasn't sure if she even wanted to get married. I'm afraid I'll ask her, and she'll laugh in my face."

"She'll probably ugly cry, so maybe you shouldn't after all."

I made it back to the door of the parlor. I stood there, an idiot grin on my face, leaning back and forth trying to decide whether to walk back out there and join them for real, or dash upstairs and immediately tell Lucy what I'd just heard. I bounced from foot to foot for a moment longer and then set my mug on a small table and ran for the stairs.

I had a lot of casual boyfriends once I relaxed in school. I never really cared too much for a single one of them, always subconsciously telling myself that they were temporary, that I would go home and end up with Finn again one day and none of the interim people would matter.

One of those men were in my short story group. Actually, several of them were, including the man who had laid down the rules at our first meeting. The nice thing about never having any serious boyfriends was that there were never any serious feelings left once it was over. I could sit across the reading circle from Brad, or Jeff, or whoever and not feel awkward at all, and not care at all when they brought their new partners to meetings.

It was Jeff that brought Dimitri with him in my senior year. "Hazel, come sit with us!" Jeff called when I walked in.

It had been pouring that day, hard enough that I'd almost skipped our meeting, but I'd written a fun little rhyming poem and was dying for feedback on it. We had moved our get togethers to a little coffee shop off campus, which was nice not only because it sold coffee and the chairs were much more comfortable, but also, we could expand the group to include more people that didn't attend the school. I knew at first glance that

Jeff's friend must not attend, because I definitely would have noticed him. His hair was soaked, and little runners of water dripped from the curled-up ends and fell from his eyelashes. His collar was turned up on his peacoat, his hands jammed in the pockets. He looked like 60's era Dylan. I *loved* 60's era Dylan.

Suddenly a little more self-conscious, sweating under my damp, heavy coat, I smiled nervously and headed towards them.

"This is Dimitri," Jeff said, in the sing song voice someone uses when introducing a new partner, or a new puppy. "He's not much of a writer, but he enjoys a good story. Cook up anything good for him to listen to?"

I forgot. In that moment I didn't even know if I'd brought a story. "Maybe," I said coyly. "I'm Hazel." I stuck out my clammy hand and Dimitri took it and squeezed it briefly, didn't even shake it. That night, I didn't think about Finn even once.

I took the stairs two at a time, literally giggling to myself. Echoes of my heavy footsteps whispered back down to me through the empty space beside the stairs. I slowed as I hit the second story landing, out of breath and a little dizzy. The second floor was silent as the grave, just as it had been every time I'd moved past it.

I only paused to catch my breath for a moment before starting up to the third floor a little more slowly. A door opened and closed somewhere in the second-floor hall. I stopped, one foot hovering above a step. I leaned slowly toward the railing and peered out. I saw nothing. No one. I almost called out, but I knew before I opened my mouth that it wasn't Lucy. Lucy was just as uncomfortable as I was on this landing in the dark the night before, she wouldn't be down there wandering around without one of us with her. I continued up the stairs and tried to put the sound of the door out of my mind.

I didn't have to look for Lucy, she was stretched across one of the chaise lounges with her laptop balanced on her knees.

She jumped when she heard me on the stairs and then smiled when she saw me. "I thought you were Finn. Do *not* tell him I've been working up here. I promised no working this weekend. But—" she grinned "—the cell signal is surprisingly excellent. I was worried about that!"

I plopped down across from her and wiped a trickle of sweat from my temple. "Lucy."

She peered over her laptop at me and raised an eyebrow. "Hazel?"

"I just overheard D and Finn talking," My cheeks hurt from grinning so widely. "Dimitri is going to propose!"

She slammed her laptop shut and squealed. She tossed it on the cushion next to her, bounded across the zodiac rug and grabbed my hands. We squealed together. It was the happiest I'd been, maybe ever. Maybe we *were* friends. She felt like a friend.

"Oh. My. God!" She leaned in and whispered, like they might hear us two floors below, but somehow did not hear our shrieks a moment ago. "Does he know you heard? Did he say when?"

I shook my head twice. "I don't know, I don't know! But," I whispered back, "he was talking about having the wedding *here.*"

We squealed again, shaking our clasped hands back and forth.

"Be my maid of honor?" I asked, surprising myself.

"Really?" She gasped. "But I thought you'd want Finn to be maid of honor? Get him in a dress and everything?"

I laughed. "He's D's best friend, too. I bet anything he'll want him to be best man." I knew that wasn't true. Dimitri had probably twenty friends he liked better than Finn. Hell, he liked our drunk neighbor whose name I could never remember better than Finn, but I couldn't think of another person Dimitri might choose as a best man, and I was sure he'd be okay with it. For me.

Lucy turned serious for a moment. "It would really mean a lot to me. To be your maid of honor, I mean. I don't have a lot of other friends. I've always hoped we'd end up really close."

I surprised myself a second time by hugging her.

We spent over an hour just touring the property and "oohing" and "ahhing" over every detail. We all had sparkles in our eyes and even Dimitri started speaking as though we'd be living there in the future, offhandedly mentioning things we should change or update. Lucy was absolutely enchanted.

There was one locked door down the second-floor hallway, and we all unanimously agreed it must have been the bedroom the Freys had taken for their own and skipped it without venom. There was no need for us to snoop where their private items were stored. There was too much else to take in for any of us to have room for curiosity about what might have been in there.

"Oh. My. God." I whispered when Finn pulled open a huge set of heavy double doors on the second floor. I'd been surprised that the floor hadn't been particularly creepy. It was bigger than the third, with more areas besides the bedrooms and bathrooms. Not only was there a sitting area like the one on the third floor, complete with a coffee bar and ashtrays, but a wide open area beyond housing a pool table, poker table, and two beautiful chess sets.

This room was a library. A huge, ancient, straight out of a fairy tale library. The ceilings arched up past the third floor and rose into open beamed peaked roof. Books covered two stories of walls. There was one of those ladders on a track reaching halfway up the walls, and a grand staircase erupted from the center of the room, spreading out into a catwalk and narrow walkways that ran around the upper perimeter. Another sliding ladder rested along the upper portion of wall.

I dragged my gaze downward with considerable effort. The place was furnished with groups of comfortably worn leather armchairs and sofas, low tables, and several small desks with old lamps placed on each one. I wandered, dreamlike, up to the staircase to touch the banister. Behind it on the far wall was a huge, ancient fireplace. It was wide and tall enough for all four of us to stand inside. I didn't know why we'd ever want to do that, but we could.

"Thought you'd like it," Finn said with a dismissive shrug. "It was in the pictures of the place obviously, but I will say it's a lot more impressive in person."

Lucy had already skipped across the room and was doing her best "Belle" impression on the ladder. Before we left the room, I was sure each of us would do it, at least once. Right then I was more interested in the meat of the place, though. What kinds of books were stored there? How were they organized? As I floated towards the nearest wall, I told myself not to be disappointed. That I'd likely find mostly encyclopedias, or maybe even fake books. It was probably for ambiance.

My fingers ran along some spines. *Secrets of Trans-Allegheny, Blackwater: An Adventure, Beauty of Appalachia.* I noticed a small brass placard fixed to the shelf. It read, *Local Histories.* I squinted around the room and spied dozens of other brass placards. Smiling, I envisioned all the time I'd spend exploring each shelf when we lived there. *When we live here.* Despite my best efforts not to get excited, despite my *knowing* that nothing ever just "worked out", the tingles of possibility, of anticipation, buzzed in my chest.

"Somewhere, out there!" Dimitri called in a squeaky falsetto, sliding down the room on the ladder with one arm outstretched.

"Dimitri, you idiot. That's not even the right movie. A mouse sings that," Finn said distractedly.

I looked over at Finn, mouth open to admonish his attitude. He sat at the largest of the desks and was jiggling the single wide drawer on it. It popped open with a screech that matched Dimitri's song. Yellowing spiral notebooks and assorted pens filled every available inch of the drawer's interior.

Unimpressed, I turned to continue perusing book titles and was smacked with an enveloping wall of cool air. It felt like walking into an air-conditioned supermarket from a warm parking lot, a pressure change into another world. My hair fluttered for a moment. I looked down, assuming I was near a vent or something, but there were only solid, gleaming wood floors.

"Hey, come look at this stuff." Finn was talking to the whole room, still with that distracted air. Dimitri hopped down from the third rung of the ladder with a thump and Lucy pattered back down from the staircase she'd been slowly ascending.

I didn't move right away, still halfway turned towards the books. Should I say something about the gust of air? It brought a sickening wave of apprehension with it and placed someone else's fear directly into my own stomach, a little voice in my ear whispering caution, as though I were about to topple over the balcony outside our bedroom. I was suddenly trembly and a little nauseated. But surely a room that size would have some strange air currents, of course. It could have been just from Dimitri screwing around on the ladder across the room. What was it they say about a butterfly flapping its wings in China? I moved slowly towards the desk with cautious steps, where all three of them were thumbing through the notebooks.

I glanced over Finn's shoulder. The notebook he had open was full of mathematical equations, written longhand. There were some illegible notes in the margins, and each equation was crossed out with an X in red ink. "I guess somebody isn't good at algebra," I said. My joke fell flat, and nobody responded. Dimitri and Lucy each squinted down at their own notebooks, seemingly identically marked.

"I think the writing is maybe Polish?" Dimitri said after a minute of silence. "Maybe? My language skills aren't great. But..." He closed his notebook and replaced it in the drawer. "The equations are done correctly, I think. It's weird that they'd be crossed out when the sums are right." He shrugged.

Lucy closed her notebook as well and braved an excited smile. "I'm sure they've just been sitting forgotten in here forever. We should just leave them. A little mystery for guests!"

We all stood for an awkward few seconds while Finn continued to flip pages, oblivious to the rest of us. Lucy put a hand on his shoulder, and he jumped. "Whoa, sorry." He looked around at us. "Didn't realize everyone was waiting on me. Let the tour continue." He threw the notebook casually back into the drawer and pushed it shut again with some effort.

He took four long steps with us all at his heels and then instead of leaving the room, plopped down onto one of the sofas. "So. What are you all thinking?"

I sat, glad for the detour. The slight nausea hadn't left me. I felt like I'd recently thrown up. My rings clacked together on my fingers, and I folded my hands to keep them still. I didn't know what was wrong with me and I hadn't even had a chance to slide around on the ladder yet. "Could we manage it?" I glanced around. "I don't care what ol' Opal says, there's no way they've been keeping this place up on their own. This house needs a *staff*. It's...it's a lot."

"Come on Hazel," The groan of Finn's frustration was so familiar to me that I heard it in my own head when I was disappointed in myself. Was he ever *not* annoyed with me? He continued, "Don't be lazy. If we all *worked* during the day I'm sure we could keep it up just fine. Better than fine."

His words stung a little regardless of how often he said similar things to me, and Lucy slapped his shoulder as she perched on the arm of his sofa.

"She's not being lazy, she's being pragmatic," she said. "*Somebody* needs to be, because I'd just die for this house. Can we keep it, please?" She drew her "please" out like a child asking for a new toy.

Dimitri remained standing, picking at his fingernails. "What if it's, like…" He wasn't looking at us, eyes on the floor, or maybe his nails, I couldn't tell. "I mean. Why's it so cheap, you know? What if there's something wrong?"

Finn gestured around. "Like what? Everything seems to be in pretty good shape. Phenomenal, I'd say, for the age. Should we have it inspected, you mean?"

Dimitri shook his head. "No. I mean, yes, you should, obviously, but that's not what I—"

"What if it's haunted?" I said with a grin. I said it to sound silly and to diminish any weird little feelings I'd had into a joke. But. *But.* It felt haunted. I *felt* haunted. I wondered if they were feeling it, too. It was heavy in there.

Finn scoffed. "Ghosts aren't real." His voice was quiet. Sad. The tone ruined the light heartedness of the question. "It's just a big old house with a bunch of fancy furniture. That's synonymous with ghosts in the movies. It's how we're going to make our living, remember?"

"Do you think it could be?" Lucy asked. "Haunted, I mean?"

I looked up. I didn't know exactly why, but the question was directed at me.

I opened my mouth to reply, and that cool touch of breeze caressed me again. I watched as Lucy's artful flyaways were pushed back from her face. She shivered. I closed my mouth again. I didn't know.

Chapter 7

The day seemed to have flown by us. We scavenged the leftovers from the night before for lunch, having all skipped breakfast in our eagerness to explore. Lucy tried her best to get us to allow her to reheat everything in the oven, but once we discovered the microwave in the hallway between kitchen and dining rooms, her battle was lost. We were too hungry to wait, and the nuked food was good enough.

We ate our hasty lunches on the wide covered deck. The glorious view persisted, accompanied by a perfect crisp autumn day without the cold autumn wind. I left the doors into the parlor hanging wide open, inviting the valley inside.

"I feel silly using these dishes out here for leftovers." Lucy stared down at the silver plate in her lap. She was sitting cross legged on the wooden planks of the deck (she'd changed into yoga pants and gym shoes), the rest of us lounged on the oversized rocking chairs. "There has to be a more informal service packed away somewhere."

"We can bring ours from home," I piped up. "They're the most informal dishes I've ever seen in my life."

"Do you still have the jam jars with cartoon characters on them in lieu of drinking glasses?" Finn asked.

"Those are *collectibles*. So, of course."

The glass paneled doors suddenly both slammed shut. We all jumped, and I dumped my entire plate of (slightly dried out) mashed potatoes onto the deck.

Dimitri hopped to his feet. "That was weird. Must have been a good gust of wind." He pulled the doors back open, and Lucy caught my eye and held my gaze for the full five seconds it took him to do so. I couldn't quite read her face, but I would have hazarded a guess at panic. We both knew there was no wind.

She shook herself and scooped up my plate and the majority of the potatoes from my feet. "Want to help me with the dishes, Hazel?"

Subtlety wasn't her strong suit. Her tone basically proclaimed, "Would both of you men leave so I can speak to Hazel alone?"

Both Finn and Dimitri seemed to grasp that (or just didn't want to help clean up) and handed over their empty plates.

"I want to check out the basement," Finn said. "Make sure it looks dry or whatever. Want to come, D? Since I actually have no idea what I should be looking at?"

Dimitri grunted an agreement, still looking at the doorway. He knew there was no wind, too.

We headed inside and parted ways in the hallway. Lucy stopped and turned back to Finn. "Wait, show me where the basement is? In case we need anything?"

"There's stairs past the kitchen and also an elevator," he said.

"There's an *elevator*?" I gasped.

"Well, sure. You've gotta have one in a building with customers. Actually, we should take it down there," this last part was to Dimitri. "Make sure it's got an in-date inspection and all that."

The three of them headed down the hall to see the ridiculous elevator and once I recovered from gaping at the idea of one, I carried the dirty plates towards the kitchen, where I almost dropped them all over again.

The kitchen was drenched in blood. *Covered* in splatters of disgusting, almost black, dripping blood. More than when Mrs. Frey cut her hand. More than a kill scene in a slasher flick. The smell was horrendous. I staggered, leaned against the doorframe. A scream welled up in my throat. A slimy tendril of partially coagulated blood threatened to drip onto me from the door frame. Blood pooled at my feet, slowly inching toward the soles of my boots. The whine of hundreds of big, fat bloated flies filled my ears.

I sank toward the floor, toward the blood, sliding down the frame. I shut my eyes tight. *This isn't happening,* I thought. *This is too ridiculous.*

The buzzing stopped. I kept the stack of plates in a death grip, my link to normalcy. I could feel them scraping against each other as my fingers tightened, tightened...

"Hazel?"

I let out the breath I'd been holding to keep out that coppery smell. My eyes popped open involuntarily, showing me Lucy's knees. She sank down to a squat beside me.

"Let me take those." She whispered. She gently pulled the stack of plates from my clawed fists. She set them on the floor next to her and then shifted to kneel beside me. "Do you need anything?"

As she shifted, I received a full view of the kitchen once again. Of course, there was nothing. No blood, no smell, no flies. A perfectly clean kitchen. "I..." I began, fully intending to say I was fine, but my body knew something I didn't and made me say, "I actually would love a glass of water." The kitchen swam before me, retreating from me down a dark corridor.

Lucy said something, but I couldn't hear her. She took me by both shoulders and guided me towards the kitchen floor, so I was thankfully horizontal when I passed out.

When I opened my eyes again, Lucy's face hovered above me. "We're home!" she said in a high, sing-song voice. "Wake up and put your shoes on."

I smiled, then chased it with a groan. "How long was I out?"

"Oh..." She looked down at her watchless wrist. "Maybe fifteen seconds? I'm going to go get you that glass of water now, okay? Do *not* sit up until I come back."

I waited obediently on the floor, staring up at the plaster ceiling. I listened to the cabinets open and close and the sink run. I closed my eyes again.

"Okay."

I opened my eyes. Lucy was back, holding out a glass of water with ice cubes and even a straw in it.

"Now, sit slowly, lean against the wall here. Then sip this water, don't gulp it."

I did as I was told. I realized as I started moving that I was soaking wet. I'd sweat through my clothes. "Ugh." I managed.

"Sweaty?" Lucy asked cheerily. "Totally normal."

"Normal?" I asked. I was more than a little concerned, but Lucy was perfectly calm, acting like I'd fallen and skinned my knee.

"Sure. I knew you were going down before you did!" She laughed. "Vasovagal Syncope."

"Bless you."

She giggled again. "Kids in school will pass out pretty often. If they're standing in line too long, if they haven't had enough to eat that day, if they get too nervous for a presentation. And oh, my God, blood donation days. So many kids will just drop at the sight of blood or a needle, sometimes even at the *idea* of blood."

I bit my lip.

"Maybe you stood up too fast or had too much coffee or something," She continued. "It happens! But we should definitely slow down for the rest of the day. Have you been feeling alright?"

"Uh," I tried to think back, but my memory was all blood. Not necessarily my gruesome vision, or hallucination, or whatever the fuck it had been. It was Opal, bleeding all over the green peppers. "Well, I had a little dizzy spell in the library earlier."

"You should get your bloodwork done. Maybe you're low in iron or something. When's the last time you saw a doctor, anyway?"

I didn't answer right away. Was that two sentences in a row she's mentioned blood? Everything felt weird and fuzzy. Was this real? Was I being fucked with? "Um. I broke my finger a couple years back."

Lucy pursed her lips.

"What? I don't have insurance, you know."

"Well, we're going to have to fix that," Lucy said, and grinned.

I couldn't tell her about the blood right then, looking at that face. A face full of dreams and stars. I smiled back weakly instead. "Am I going to get a 401K?"

"Oh, yes. And stock options and whatever the hell else they say to snag people into office jobs. You're getting it *all*, mama."

I laughed and tried to wipe the sweat off my temples. "I need a shower. This is gross."

"Not so fast, I want to keep an eye on you for a bit. Plus, we have dishes! I'll pull up a chair for you. I wash, you dry."

Two minutes later and I had been guided across the kitchen like I was a little old lady crossing the street and settled into a chair. It was too low, I couldn't actually be useful from down there and when Lucy handed me a dishtowel, it was cool and damp. It was for my sweaty face, I knew. She had no intention of making me dry dishes.

For a few minutes, the only sound was the water filling up the sink. I got the feeling Lucy wanted to have a "talk" and she didn't want to shout over the running water. She absently scrubbed a dish before she finally spoke, and by the time she did, I was sweating again. This had been the silence of the time between a "call me" text, and actually making the phone call. Of a "see me after class" note. Of a looming performance review. I watched the side of her face with growing apprehension. What was so serious?

"Have you had anything weird happen to you here?" she finally asked. She meant it to sound casual, but it didn't. It sounded like the exhale of a breath she'd been holding since she turned on the sink. She was as anxious as I was.

Should I have told her? Over the course of the day, it didn't seem like it'd been weird, but now that I thought about it...there's been a lot of weird. I compromised. "You mean, besides collapsing in the hall just now? I mean..."

"Someone was talking to me this morning," she said abruptly. She abandoned the plate to the depths of the sink. "Someone was whispering to me. Finn says I must have been dreaming, and admittedly, I *was* asleep. At first, but..." Forgetting her hands were wet, she reached up and nervously played with one of her loose locks of hair. "I can't stop thinking about it."

"What were they saying?" I asked. I didn't really want to know, I didn't think. I only asked so she knew I was taking her seriously.

"He said, 'They'll keep you.' I'm sure that's what I heard. He might have said other things, but I wasn't quite awake, so I don't know..."

"He?"

"Yes. It was a man whispering, I'm almost positive. I thought, when I was still kind of asleep, I thought it was my dad. Like, him when I was little. I didn't tell Finn that because I'm sure that would confirm his whole dream theory. But I don't, like, randomly dream about my dad, you know? I can just call him if I need him." She blushed.

"Hey, you're allowed to have parents around Finn, it's okay." I said it like a joke, but she looked close to tears.

"I'm jealous of you," she said abruptly.

I gaped at her for a heartbeat, the towel pressed to one side of my face. This was an unexpected left turn in the conversation. Of *me?* How? Oh. "Because of Finn and I?"

"No," she said, too quickly. "Well, yes. That, too. Maybe that was the first thing, but it's grown a lot since I've gotten to know you. You're so smart and cool and unique."

I rolled my eyes. She wanted to talk about Finn, of course. She was just trying to butter me up. I decided to just let her continue. She'd get to whatever she really wanted to ask me eventually and I was a sucker for a compliment.

"And you're so funny, you always have something funny to say. I feel like a mouse when you're around. You and Finn can just talk for hours and hours, and" She paused, took a breath. "He and I will never have what you two have. It hurts."

I shrugged. "Well, of course, you won't."

She looked shocked, offended. I must have not explained myself adequately.

"Look," I continued. "He and I will never have what you and him have, either. Hell, he and I will never have what *you* and I have. I can't imagine having this conversation with him." I laughed and hoped that I wasn't imagining her shoulders losing a little of their tension. "Every relationship is special, and important. You can't have a good relationship if you pin all your needs on one person and expect them to lay all their needs on you. That gets lonely. You start to resent the other person." I paused before accidentally telling her that I knew this and so did Finn, because we were each other's entire worlds for too long, and it broke us both when we weren't enough for each other. When I couldn't support him. She didn't need to hear that.

Her face lit up. She glowed like the moon, how was she so beautiful? "You are *so* smart, Hazel. That makes me feel so much better."

"About the whispers?"

She laughed. "I mean, kind of, but it doesn't answer my question. Have you—"

"You two are the slowest dishwashers I've ever seen in my life. Hazel, what the fuck are you even doing down there, cheerleading?" Finn sidled up on Lucy's other side and gently scooted her to his left, so he had access the sink. He immediately began washing and drying with efficiency.

"Thanks, babe," Lucy said. "We got distracted."

She was looking at me. She didn't want to tell the guys I passed out without my permission. I was trying to decide whether I wanted them to know at all when Dimitri walked in, carrying a full-length dressing mirror on a stand.

"Look what we found down there!" Finn said while Dimitri thrusted the mirror forward like a trophy. "There's probably more, there's tons of furniture all covered in sheets."

"Not the least bit creepy." Dimitri muttered.

Dimitri was covered in dust and sweaty from carrying the mirror. He plunked it down by the kitchen island and stretched his back. "Scoot over, Nut. I need to sit for a sec," he said, but then looked up at me, really took me in. "Jesus, you look awful!"

"Thanks, darling," I said as offhandedly as I could muster.

He came toward me, one hand outstretched at my face. "Hey, are you sick or something? What's wrong?"

He was actually panicking a little. I must have looked like garbage left in the sun. I leaned around him slightly before answering to check my face in our new mirror.

A woman stood next to me in the reflection. Her jaw was unhinged in what should have been an earsplitting screech, though no sound reached me. Her thin arms waved above her head in rage or frustration. She should have been screaming right in my ear, mere inches from me. I didn't hear anything except Finn washing dishes, but that seemed dim and far away. I blinked and she was still there. My breath caught in my throat. Tears blurred my vision. I needed to turn and look beside me. I couldn't look away from her reflection.

She was desperate, wailing. She reached towards me to grab me by the shoulders, to make me look at her. I felt the pressure of fingers on my collarbone. I finally screamed and jerked away from the touch, fell from the chair to the floor. I broke eye contact with the mirror and saw that it was Dimitri grabbing my shoulder. He dropped to his knees beside me, calling my name, but I only watched it being formed on his lips. My heart thudded in my ears, and everything tunneled. I was going to pass out again. Before I did, I heard a very clear voice right next to my ear, screaming desperately as though I was about to step into traffic, and she was trying to stop me.

"They will *keep* you!"

Chapter 8

I came to again in the parlor, draped across the yellow velvet couch, my feet propped up by several expensive looking pillows. My cool cloth was slapped wetly across my forehead and three faces hovered above me. "You guys," I muttered. "I'm getting sweat all over this couch."

"Doesn't matter, stay put," Lucy said in her most teacherly voice.

"Hey, Nut," Dimitri whispered, as though I were dying. Maybe as though I were already dead. "Are you okay?"

"I'm okay. Just a little shaky. Sorry. Was I...was I out a long time?" I asked this because I *dreamed*. I dreamed about the woman I'd just seen in the mirror. I dreamed that I knew her. That we were friends. I dreamed that I was at lunch with her and Lucy, and we all laughed and talked together, but I was afraid. Not of *her*, she was my friend after all. And we had known each other for a long time in the dream. I was afraid because I had forgotten her name, and I was terrified she was going to realize.

I kept snatching glances of her out of the corner of my eye in my dream, trying to remember. She was thin and pretty and had very long dark hair loose around her shoulders. She wore high waisted black slacks with very wide legs and a form fitting turtleneck sweater. A simple silver cross on a fine chain peeked out from the fold at the neck of the sweater. She kept catching me staring at her and smiling. "What?" she'd asked with a laugh.

"Less than a minute, probably. Dimitri ran you in here like you were a football," Finn said. He looked worried, too. "Hey, should we go home, you think? You need an urgent care or something?"

"No, no." I began to sit up and Lucy reached forward and pushed my shoulder back.

"Stay," she said firmly. "You need some sugar. Orange juice?"

"Okay."

She whisked out of the room.

I watched until she was around the corner and then propped myself up on my elbows. "I don't need to go. I feel much better already. I woke up a little dizzy this morning and all the walking around and late breakfast just made it worse, but I'm sure I'm completely fine. I just need to be waited on hand and foot for the rest of the day, obviously." I dramatically reached for one of the pillows under my feet until Dimitri grabbed it and placed it under my head. I grinned, dried sweat cracking on my cheeks.

"Okay. Let's all take it easy for a bit." Finn agreed.

I furrowed my brows and glanced over at him. He looked shaken and I didn't think it was over my wellbeing. "So, how was the creepy basement?"

He and Dimitri shared a look, which was exactly what I was hoping to see.

"What happened down there?" I asked.

Neither of them had answered by the time Lucy floated back over to me with orange juice. Her hand trembled slightly as she handed it to me. I squinted at her and she averted her eyes.

"Alright, we need to talk," I said after taking a sip. "This place is haunted as shit."

They all turned to look at me, but nobody laughed.

"I'm seeing stuff. Hearing stuff. It's messing with me. I..." My eyes filled with tears, and I was furious about them. I should have been ecstatic, how many people could say they'd seen a literal apparition? But it wasn't like the movies. My mind simply couldn't process what I'd seen, outside of pumping water from my eyes and making my hands tremble. "I don't think I could live here. Not like this. It's been less than a day and I'm already literally swooning. I'm obviously...more delicate than I thought." It was hard to admit.

Still, nobody spoke. I knew that Finn would be upset, would tell me I was being ridiculous, tell me I'd get used to the house. I knew Dimitri would be supportive, but devastated to go back to our apartment after this glimpse of a future we could have had. I knew Lucy would cry. I tried to catch each of their eyes, but everyone was lost in their own heads.

Finally, Dimitri said, "I could have sworn was a man standing *on* the desk in the library this morning. Right when we walked in, for just a second. I saw him. It was the same desk Finn opened." Dimitri paused for a moment, eyes closed in the memory. "He was screaming. He was looking right at me and screaming. I couldn't hear him. I felt a little dizzy and brushed it off as...I don't know. Trick of the light, maybe?" He laughed, embarrassed. "Don't laugh at me, it's stupid."

I should have been terrified to hear the proclamation, but more than anything else, I felt relieved. It was so similar to what I'd just experienced, I could maybe cross "hallucinating" right off the list of things wrong with me.

"I saw a woman in the mirror in the kitchen, right before I passed out just now." I couldn't deny that I was pretty excited. "She was screaming, too, like yelling in my ear. I can't say for certain because I was definitely checking out, but I think she said the same thing you heard, Lucy."

Lucy went a little pale, moved from my side to a chair and sank into it.

"Alright, I think we all need to just relax for a second. Don't start scaring each other on purpose," Finn said.

"Have you seen anything, Finn?" I asked. "Heard anything?"

He didn't meet my eyes. "No. Ghosts aren't real, Hazel." He shifted a little, realizing we were all waiting for him to elaborate, to settle our nerves. He was the leader, after all. This was his expedition. "Listen. When we first walked in here last night, we got really dizzy, right, Hazel?"

I nodded slowly. My brain was sloshing around in there, I didn't want it to leak out.

"Well, I'm betting the altitude change or something like that is messing with us. I'd say a gas leak, but I haven't smelled anything like gas, have any of you?"

I let Dimitri and Lucy shake their heads for all of us.

"Plus, this place is spooky as shit and that's obviously on purpose. The Freys are creepy, and I bet that's an act, too. This place is *supposed* to be haunted. That's what gets it so many reservations. We *want* a haunted bed and breakfast, right? We want people to be a little freaked out and have a good story to go home with, otherwise our only guests are going to be boring old snotty people. So," He looked at each of us, slowly and seriously. "If you want to do this, let's try to be rational and take things with a little salt, yeah?"

I had to admit to myself that it was a pretty good pep talk. I felt kind of silly. It was interesting, how desperate a mind was to reject anything that was outside the normal experience.

I easily said, "Okay."

"You're right." Dimitri grinned at me. "What do you think, Nut? Still better than our neighbors in Charleston, right?"

I did my slow nod again, but I grinned, too. I looked at Lucy.

She chewed on her lower lip and gazed at Finn, as though he were a work of abstract art and she was trying her best to "get" it. Eventually, she felt our eyes on her and nodded. "Okay. I just don't want anybody to get hurt."

Finn reached out and put a hand on her. "Hey. No one's getting hurt. Okay?"

Our predicament at an uneasy truce, I relaxed enough to remember I felt gross and really wanted to shower, but Lucy forbade it for the time being.

"The last thing we want is for you to pass out and hurt yourself in that shower." She gave me a very motherly glare.

"Fine," I whined and flopped back against the pillow.

"Well, as I'm not currently dying," Dimitri said. "I'm going to go wash all this basement dirt off of me."

"Oh, rub it in." I snapped.

He shrugged. "Hey, maybe you shouldn't have paper skin and glass bones or whatever." He kissed me, grimaced dramatically, and left the room.

I groaned. "I'm fine!"

Lucy stood as well. "You *will* be. Just give it a few minutes, okay? I'm going to go clean up that mirror. It's going in our bathroom." This last sentence was obviously directed at Finn, who still sat on the couch by my feet.

"Alright. Tell me when you're ready for me to grab it." He sounded a little distant. I wondered if maybe his pep talk didn't work as well on him as it did on the rest of us.

I tilted my chin down a little so I could see him in my peripheral. It was quiet for a minute. "So..." I was trying to be casual. Not accusatory. "Have you *really* not seen anything?"

He rolled his eyes skyward. "Hazel. Stop."

"Hey, don't get defensive, just asking. Neither you or D looked great when you came back from the basement. I'll wheedle it out of him if you won't talk."

"Can you just back off?"

I clapped my mouth shut at his tone. He was mad, sure, but also scared. It frustrated me. Why couldn't he just talk about things that bothered him? We could have worked through things so much easier if he'd just admit a little weakness for once in his life. I opened my mouth again, a threat to say those thoughts out loud, memories burning me.

He wasn't having it. He abandoned me on the sofa and walked out of the room without a word. I thought back on all the times we'd stormed out on each other mid "discussion," stopping before they became arguments. I remembered it was usually *me* that would do the actual leaving. I took my time alone sifting back through time, trying to recall if it was him or me that was the problem. My brain got stuck on a particular argument and, of course, it was from *that time*, the time of all the arguments. When everything fell apart.

"I don't think it's a good idea for you to come tomorrow." Finn had blurted suddenly that day, breaking our comfortable silence as we'd studied.

I looked up from my very last paper of high school. It was after graduation, but my English teacher was accepting a few extra credits to help with my final GPA. The paper was mostly a blur of smeared pencil lead. I never understood why ballpoint pen wasn't allowed for our written assignments in high school. As a leftie, the side of my hand was always a shiny gray, and my papers looked like they'd been recently excavated from an ancient civilization. "What?"

"To dinner."

"I know where you're talking about, Finn." I couldn't help my smartass tone. "I mean, why do you think that? It's your birthday dinner!"

He didn't answer for a moment, just bobbed his head back and forth like he was weighing options. "I mean, my birthday is over, anyway. We already celebrated."

I set my paper aside. "What's going on? Just tell me."

I watched his face carefully. His eyes darted to me and back to his hands, which he was flexing, pushing on his knuckles like he wanted them to crack and relieve some pressure. The moment lengthened without a response. My heart began to race. Suddenly the sunny late afternoon air of my bedroom seemed heavy, full of bad news threatening to pour down over me.

"My dad doesn't want you there, okay? He says it's a 'family dinner'." A red flush of embarrassment was creeping up his neck.

I wasn't necessarily shocked. Hurt, yes. But this thing was fairly normal coming from Finn's dad. He used to like me just fine, but as the years went on, little comments had been growing in both severity and frequency. He'd mention that Finn should "get out there" more. That he should focus more on his studies. That he should better manage his time and his youth. I assumed there were more comments that never made their way to my ears. The man thought Finn was wasting his time with me.

It was my turn to weigh my response. I'm sure my own skin was heating up now, turning patchy and red, allergic to humiliation and anger. I was mostly angry. I shouldn't have to respond at all. This conversation should never have made its way to me. Finn should have stuck up for me to his father. He should have said there would be no birthday dinner without my presence. He should have been in my corner. I felt the anger overtaking the hurt until there was almost no hurt left. "Fine." ended up being my eloquent response. I felt it lacked something, so I added, "Fine." as I scooped up my paper and book and stood.

"Hazel," Finn began, starting to stand as well.

I wanted him to follow me, to take my hand and apologize. I expected him to, but he sank back down to his chair and just watched me storm out.

I was down the stairs before I realized we were in *my* house, I'd stormed out of my own room and had nowhere to go. The embarrassment sent me straight into the guest bathroom by the front door, homework and all. I shut and locked the door and sat on the floor and cried until I heard him open and shut the front door a few minutes later.

I stared at the fancy parlor ceiling and sighed. *That* was a memory I needed to forget. A memory that *didn't happen.* Forcing it back out of my mind, I couldn't help but focus on my disgusting clamminess. My clothes and hair were sticking to me. I carefully sat up, testing my balance. I felt pretty stable. I cocked an ear towards the kitchen, listening for the sounds of Lucy. The house had too much furniture dampening the acoustics, I couldn't hear a damn thing. Oh well, Lucy wasn't my mom, what would she do if I disobeyed her? I *needed* a shower, and I also wanted to talk to Dimitri on his own. He wasn't too self-conscious to tell me what happened in the basement.

I rose slowly, like I was on the moon and unsure of the gravitational pull. I bounced on the balls of my feet a few times and deemed myself cured.

I crept into the hall and skittered along the wall, listening hard for Lucy. I guess I was a *little* afraid of her finding me being a deliberately bad patient. The muffling of the carpet runners on the stairs was a blessing and I dashed up the first flight as fast as I could manage in my slightly shaky state. I felt a little safer from being heard once I hit the second-floor landing.

A door opened and closed somewhere down the second-floor hall.

I sighed.

I had to go take a look this time, I decided. We were maybe going to *live* there, after all. I wasn't about to go around being frightened of an entire level of the house, especially not the one with the library on it. With some mental effort, I stepped off the landing and into the reception seating area.

"Hello?" I called, but not loudly. I didn't want anybody to answer. I wanted to find a door with loose hinges and a window accidentally left open to the sneakily forceful breeze around mountain.

I made my way down the hallway of bedrooms, and all of the doors were shut. Of course, they were. The culprit could have been any of the doors, or all of them. I walked purposefully to the first one on the left, and pushed on it without turning the knob. It didn't budge. Properly latched.

I made my way down the hall, repeating my very scientific process. The last door on the right swung forward at my touch. I smiled in victory and peeked inside.

The rooms on this floor were just as decadent as the ones above, though without the wild ceiling slopes and peaks. This particular room's theme was orange. Crushed velvet orange draperies and smooth carved wood finishes. It was beautiful, but I was momentarily distracted by the view from the generous smattering of narrow windows. The fiery valley fell away to one side and rose up into deep, dark woods that weren't visible from my room. They felt close and threatening, full of tall, moody pines that mocked the changing, frivolous leaves down in the valley. Wise and eternal, and maybe a little menacing. It might have just been that the sun was setting and the shadows of the pines were long and deep.

A creak in the room brought me back to myself. I jumped. How could I have forgotten that I was in there investigating a strange noise? I realized with some regret that I was definitely not final girl material. I turned back to the room and continued my investigation. The windows, of course, were all closed. The door gaped open, as I left it when I entered. I put my fingertips along the edge of the old, dark wood and gave it a gentle shove.

It swung easily and returned to its frame. There was a small click as the latch caught. I stared at it, waiting for it to reopen on its own. It didn't move. I tugged at the handle without turning it, just to see how much force it needed to open. It didn't move. I turned the knob. It didn't turn.

"Oh, geez," I said out loud and the room devoured the words, leaving me in abrupt silence. The realization that this door was the one locked tight on our earlier investigation crashed down on me, too late. "The Freys don't have any stuff in here...where's their stuff?" I put bravery into my voice that didn't belong to me. Who was I pretending for? I was the only one around and I knew I was a little bitch.

I jiggled the handle more forcefully, yanked on the door, begging it to pop back out of its frame. It remained firmly in place. It was getting dark so quickly. My breathing surrounded me, bounced back into me, too many breaths, too close together. The light switch was right next to me and I flipped it. Two chandeliers of orange light blazed to life above my head and reflected off of all of the orange velvet. The whole room flickered.

I tried the door again, like maybe the light switch was also a secret lock. It wasn't and so the door ignored me. "Fuck."

I considered knocking, but if I were anywhere else in the house and heard desperate knocking, I might have had a heart attack and I didn't want to put any of the others through that. My phone was in my back pocket though. I plucked it out and without considering, dialed Finn.

"Yes?" He answered on the second ring.

"Hey. So...I kind of accidentally locked myself in a bedroom. Can you come get me out?" I tried to keep the rising panic out of my voice.

He was laughing. "Which room are you in, yours? How did you manage—"

"I'm on the second floor. End of the hall on the right."

"Why the hell are you in there?"

"Just...Just come get me, please? I thought I heard something down here."

He was still laughing as he hung up.

My hands shook as I tried to replace my phone in its pocket. I told myself I was just still shaky from earlier and definitely not terrified. I considered sitting in the window seat until Finn arrived, but the deepening shadows in those ancient pines made me increasingly uncomfortable. I felt like I was being watched from the trees, even though they were definitely too far away for anyone to be able to see me from out there. Maybe I felt like I was being watched *by* the trees.

I remained standing by the door, my hand hovering over the doorknob. I didn't even know if Finn would be able to get me out easily. There was a deadbolt on my side of the door, and it wasn't shot. The door shouldn't have had a lock on the outside, should it? It must just have been stuck. I wished this room had an in suite bathroom, but it didn't, just its weird clawfoot bathtub by the fireplace.

There weren't any other doors in this room at all. I jiggled the handle one more time just to quadruple check that it was really stuck and I heard Finn faintly from the other side.

"Chill out, I'm on my way."

I exhaled.

A knock sounded on the other side of the door, vibrating through my hand on the knob. It seemed so loud in the silent pyre of the orange room. "This the one?" Finn asked. His voice was overloud to ensure I could hear it through the door.

"Yeah, I'm in here." I called back. "It wasn't latching properly, and I kept hearing it swing open—"

I was cut off by the door swinging smoothly inward. Finn stood there, his hand outstretched. He raised an eyebrow at me. "Very funny."

"Seriously?" I groan, all my panic melting into exasperation. I actually glared at the door as I spoke, like it could hear me. "I've been tugging on it for like ten minutes!"

"I didn't even turn the knob," he said. "It wasn't even shut all the way."

"It was, too. It was shut and stuck."

It was Finn's turn to look at the door. "You really want to argue this? I mean, it's obviously not stuck now."

I huffed past him, storming toward the stairs. I didn't realize Finn was following me at a distance until I heard his tread on the stairs below me. I turned back. "Not going back down?" I waited for him to catch up to me.

"Nah," he said. He had that same preoccupied air from earlier. "I'm going to go over some paperwork. I'm going to make coffee, you want some?"

"Sure. I'll be back in a few."

I must have missed Dimitri during my second-floor adventure, because the only evidence left of him was a wet towel on the bathroom floor. I was overly upset about him not being there, tears threatened to fall as I glowered down at the towel. I really wanted to just have a few minutes alone to talk to him and make sure we're on the same page. I *also* really wanted to know what happened in the basement.

As the shower water heated up, I stared at my face in the tiny circle of shaving mirror. I looked absolutely disgusting. The sweat had dried into crusty patches under my eyes and my bangs were plastered down to my forehead, stiff as undercooked noodles. My eyebrows had been reduced to transparent black smudges, one trailed all the way down my temple.

I couldn't believe I let Lucy see me like this. I actually considered just locking the doors, curling up on the floor, and dying of embarrassment. I flipped the mirror up, so it faced the ceiling. Maybe the tiny mirrors weren't such a bad thing.

I scrubbed myself pink in the shower, using somebody's tiny travel three-in-one soap they'd left in the corner, as I had forgotten my own in the bedroom and couldn't be bothered to make the ten step walk back to my bag. I told myself I'd use the shower time to think about the future, to prepare myself for the now very real possibility of never walking into that shitty coffee shop again, to maybe finally be able to have a little time to write. I didn't, though. I focused my attention on scrubbing, exfoliating. My mind was steam.

Chapter 9

It felt late (I had no idea what time it actually was, that day had been a lifetime long), so I put on pajamas and didn't bother reapplying makeup. My bare face was less embarrassing than what everybody in the house had already seen me like that day. I considered replacing the mirror to its original position, but remembered the reflection in my dinner plate and in the kitchen, and Dimitri's library ghost (*he was standing* on *the desk),* and I left it like it was, trained on the innocuous ceiling.

I was surprised to find Finn still in the sitting area by the stairs, still alone. The paperwork he was looking at must have been on his phone or he'd abandoned it and was mindlessly doom scrolling, because his eyes were glued to the little screen. "Don't forget to turn the warmer off after you get a cup," he said, but didn't look up.

"How'd you know it was me and not a *ghost*?" I ran my voice through several spooky octaves on the last word. I'd forgotten about coffee, but I was more than happy to have some to warm me up. My wet hair was making me shiver.

"Because you stomp like a Clydesdale."

"You are *so* kind to me." I poured the rest of the coffee into a new mug (I'd finally lost track of mine from the morning) and dutifully turned off the warming plate. "Where is everyone?"

"Not sure." He was distracted.

I sat and slurped obnoxiously until he looked up. "Can I help you?"

"You got games on your phone?" I asked.

"No." He sighed and rubbed his eyes with his knuckles. "Just contracts. I'm still wondering what the catch is, you know? I've read over this stuff like five times, and it all seems legit."

"Maybe the ghost situation lowers the price."

He locked his phone screen. "There's no ghosts, Hazel. And stop freaking out Lucy. She's not going to get any sleep tonight if you keep this ghost shit up."

"Me?" I cried. "It's not just me, Finn."

I was gearing up to argue, but he stood.

"I'm going to go find them. We should probably be eating. I think it's late."

My stomach growled, right on cue. I supposed my leftover mashed potatoes were quite a while ago. I stood, too. "Don't leave me up here with the—"

"Don't say it," he said sternly, but I caught a little grin. Grimace. Something like that.

We spent the trip back down the stairs trying to freak each other out. He tapped my shoulder when I wasn't looking, and I about had a heart attack, so I let him walk ahead of me and ran my hand over the top of his head, barely moving his hair. He stopped and started slapping his hair and shaking, sure there's a spider in it, until he noticed that I'd just about keeled over from silently laughing.

He leaned back to whisper, "We should scare them. Come on."

"What about Lucy not sleeping?" I asked, but I tiptoed behind him, grinning. "Do you know where they are?"

"D came up looking for you, but got tired of waiting and said he was going to help Lucy make some dinner. Since no one bothered to bring food to me while I was lounging, they'd better still be in the kitchen."

"Charming."

He held a hand up as we crept through the front hall, making me pause. He then performed several complicated hand motions like a baseball catcher or something and I snorted laughter, trying to desperately to stay quiet and making twice as much noise for the effort. He crouched down and did a somersault across the doorway to the empty parlor, and I sauntered casually behind him. We were right outside the kitchen doorway communicating our intricate scare plans though hand motions and excited whispers, ready to pounce from either side of the frame on our unsuspecting victims.

"What are y'all up to?"

I jumped out of my skin and landed against the doorframe and Finn let out the squeak of a frightened guinea pig. Dimitri was standing in the hall behind us, hands on hips.

"Dang it, D!" I gasped, running up to him and giggling. "We were going to scare you!"

Dimitri didn't smile. He cleared his throat and said quietly, "Not a good time. Lucy's upset."

"What's wrong?" All the silliness dropped from Finn immediately. "Where is she?"

Dimitri turned. "Come on, in the dining room. Dinner's ready."

We found Lucy sitting alone at the table. There was macaroni and cheese in a big bowl, a plate of apple slices and crackers beside it. She looked up at us and gave us a watery smile. "I thought kid food sounded good. Comforting." She started to cry.

"Hey, hey..." Finn dashed across the room and squatted next to her chair. "What's going on, babe?"

While she sniffled and ran her fingers under her eyes, trying to save her mascara, Dimitri put an arm around me and guided me to the table. I realized I'd been just standing in the doorway in shock, gawping. Lucy had spent all morning being in charge and taking care of me, what could have broken her so quickly?

"It's nothing, nothing. I just—" Another sob cut her off, and she gave up on fixing her face, threw herself into Finn's shoulder and cried into his shirt.

He wrapped her into an awkward hug, him half crouched and her still mostly in her chair. He made eye contact with Dimitri over her shoulder and mouthed, "What the fuck?"

Dimitri cleared his throat again. He seemed supremely uncomfortable. "Do you want me to talk to them about what's bothering you, Lucy?"

Her braid bobbed up and down in the glimmer of the sconce light, but she apparently didn't trust herself to speak yet. She leaned back from Finn and gestured to the seat next to her. He took it gratefully and reached out to take her hand. She resumed wiping mascara all over her face. I imagined her picking up a plate to use as a mirror and wanted to somehow warn her to definitely *not* do that, but didn't know how. Instead, I kept an eye on her, like I could somehow protect her. I hoped she didn't think I was just staring.

"Well," Dimitri began slowly next to me. "We were finishing dinner, and I stepped out for a couple minutes. When I came back in, Lucy—"

"It was nothing," Lucy said quickly. She carefully picked up her napkin and unfolded it onto her lap. "I'm sorry, Dimitri. I just got a little freaked out being on my own. I shouldn't have bothered you with my nonsense."

Dimitri's mouth hung ajar for a moment before he recovered and held up both hands. "Alright, no big deal. Let's eat?"

I stared at the empty bowl in front of me. I wasn't even a little hungry anymore. I vaguely tried to convince myself I was sick, but I knew it wasn't true. I was anxious. Scared. I wanted to know what happened to Lucy, or maybe I wanted to pack us all in the car and get away from there and never think about it again. Something was definitely going on.

Dimitri ladled the macaroni into everyone's bowls. I put my hand up when he turned to me. He raised an eyebrow.

"I think I should maybe just stick to crackers," I muttered. "Not feeling so hot still."

"You want to go home?" he asked.

That was my moment. I could have said yes. I could have brought us all away from that place. I looked up from the empty bowl. Finn was staring intently at me, and Lucy was gazing down into her lap. She was deep in her own head, I didn't even think she realized that the question had been asked.

"Nut?"

My eyes found Finn's. His narrowed just a tiny bit. *Don't you dare ruin this for us,* they said. "Uh...no. No. I'm okay. Just not a hundred percent, you know?" I was a coward. "Probably just tired."

Dimitri wasn't convinced, but he dropped it and pushed the tray of crackers towards me. I took one and held it stupidly.

The silence that followed was monumental. None of us ate. Finn bravely pushed macaroni around his bowl and the scrape of his spoon echoed down the length of the hall.

"You sure you don't want to talk to us, Lucy?" I finally asked. I couldn't stop myself.

"Drop it, Hazel." Finn's voice was a command, and it pissed me off.

I set down my cracker to cross my arms and glare at him.

"It was really nothing," Lucy whispered to her plate. "I'm being silly."

"Are you just saying that because this dining room is so beautiful?" I snapped. My venom at Finn had turned on her, and I was too heated up to care. "You willing to doom us all to getting haunted for some nice antiques?"

She looked like I just slapped her, and I felt like I did and that she deserved it. She scooted her chair back to stand, but Finn put a hand on her arm. "No, I think Hazel should go. She's not even hungry." He turned to me. "Are you?"

I didn't bother responding, I just threw my own chair screeching back across the hardwood and stomped out of the room.

I power walked down the dark hallway, but only made it a few yards before Dimitri caught my arm. "Hey, hey. You want to talk?"

I shrugged out of his grip. "No. I want to seethe privately. Go eat."

He shifted around for a second. "Alright. I'll make notes of any mention of you and report to you later?"

That was enough to get a tiny smile from me, and I nodded.

He began walking back, but paused to say, "Just call me if you need me, okay?"

I didn't really know where I wanted to go. I had planned on just going up to bed, but now that I was on the stairs, by myself, I didn't know if I really wanted to go just hang out up there alone. I hadn't forgotten about the voice this morning, and after all the other weird shit that day, I didn't really know if I could handle any more. I thought maybe the landing seemed like a cozy place, with its chaises and soft rug. Maybe I'd just hang out there until Dimitri came up from dinner.

But what would I do there? I didn't bring my laptop like the others. I didn't even have a book...I paused on the second-floor landing. I should get a book from the library.

The thought shifted from a vague idea to an imperative. I *needed* to be able to get myself a book from the library. I steeled myself and gazed into the darkness of the second floor. I could do it. I wasn't a child.

I ran my hand along the wall by the stairs. The wallpaper was textured and I traced fuzzy damask shapes. It wasn't comforting, it was gross. I wondered how many other hands had trailed along there, searching desperately for the light. I found it and the Edison bulbs flared to life above the sitting area. It was the same as the one above, but the rug was different. This one had numbers circling in incomprehensible patterns of navy and silver. Maybe a calendar? A phantom whiff of cigar smoke filled my nose.

I didn't linger, headed straight across the expansive space toward the tall double doors of the library. They were closed, and I hovered in front of them for far too long, losing my nerve. There had been a man standing on the writing desk. I was terrified to open those doors and see nothing but blackness and to scramble in the dark for the light switch. I didn't know where the switch was in the library.

My phone buzzed in my back pocket, and it startled me so badly I chomped down on my tongue, tasted blood. I fumbled the phone out, welcoming the delay. It was a text from Dimitri. *"You okay?"*

I sent back a quick thumbs up and was about to put the phone back before I realized I was holding a flashlight. I opened the app and pressed down the lever of the door handle, phone held up before me like a shield.

I was surprised to find that it wasn't actually as dark as I assumed it would be. Deep purple light still oozed in from the highest windows, casting the whole room into murky shadows. The windows seemed impossibly high without the rest of the room being fully visible, and as I looked up at them, terror seized. Dragging my eyes downward to face the murky room was impossible. What might have been lurking in the glow of my flashlight, silent and waiting for me to discover it? I was paralyzed. My hand still clutched the door handle, and I considered just stepping backward and dragging the door shut before me without ever looking down.

You're here for a book. I scolded myself. *Can't you even get a book on your own?*

My breath released in a slow, even exhale, trying to blow away my nerves. I forced my chin downward. I couldn't see anything besides the odd glimmer of reflection off random shiny surfaces. The room was too wide, and my little phone flashlight didn't even fully illuminate the nearest piece of furniture.

I needed to find the lights, which meant I needed to cast *my* light onto the wall behind me and turn my back on the abyss. I could do it. I stepped inside and turned to my right. The door swung gently closed behind me, and I immediately told myself that was a totally fine and normal thing to happen. Doors swing shut, right?

The switch was there, right where it should have been. I rushed toward it, giving my fear the tiniest outlet in my mad dash. I hit the wall with force and flipped all four switches up. The room illuminated behind me, and I let out a shuddery little laugh.

I took my time turning off my flashlight app, and texted Dimitri to tell him where I was before I turned around. I was acting casual, but really, I had to give whatever creepy crawlies that might have been going bump in the night in there a chance to get out of my sight.

I jammed the phone back in my pocket and turned. The library greeted me, just as beautiful as it was earlier in the day. Inviting, comfortable, glamorous. No ghosts standing on furniture, no whispers of breath or gusts of wind. Just hundreds upon hundreds of books.

I stepped onto the ladder, gave myself a little push, and glided halfway down the wall. I couldn't manage to sing, though.

My fingers ran absently down the book spines, but I wasn't really looking at them. Now that the room was bright and warm and my breaths were coming slowly and evenly, I finally wondered what the fuck I was doing up there in the first place.

Not the library specifically, but the house, the whole trip. Forget the potential ghosts. Could I really have been happy there? Could I really have accepted being *employed* by Finn? Being around him all the time? It was easy to forget, now that we were older and only chatted on the phone, saw each other once or twice a week, but he really got on my goddamned nerves sometimes. How long would we be there in house before he started bringing up the fact that he owned everything, and I was just around out of pity? Could I handle that?

And poor Dimitri and Lucy. They'd be sitting sideline to our constant bickering, balancing between keeping the peace and having our backs. It sounded exhausting. If I were either of them, I surely wouldn't put up with an arrangement like that.

It had only been twenty-four hours, and I was already hiding out in another part of the house pouting, Lucy in tears at the dinner table. What would we be doing in two months? In two years?

A rattling sound sent me careening off the ladder with a cry. I spun around and looked at the doors, thinking someone was jiggling the handle.

It happened again. I froze. It wasn't the doors. It was coming from somewhere in the room.

I crept towards the center of the room, head cocked to the side, waiting for it to happen again so I could pinpoint it. It didn't. I looked around for anything out of place. Maybe there were mice? I scanned the floor. The hardwood gleamed.

It sounded like a doorknob turning, I decided. I glanced at the doors again and they stood silent and closed. A shriek of wood scraping wood brought forth an almost identical sound from my throat and I turned so fast toward the noise my spine crackled.

A desk drawer stood open. Not just a desk drawer, *the* desk drawer. The one we riffled through earlier in the day. The one where Dimitri saw his ghost. Was it open when I came in? Did Finn close it earlier?

I glanced around the empty room again, shrugged to myself, and took the seat in front of the desk.

The notebooks were presumably how we'd left them earlier in the day, but I had to admit to myself I hadn't been very interested in them at the time, so wasn't really paying attention. I started pulling them out, one by one, looking for something different, something meaningful.

The notebooks seemed to be getting older as I reached further and further back into the long shallow drawer. The last one, crammed toward the back, was just yellowing paper held together with a binder clip. There was writing on the front, but I couldn't read it. "Hmm...."

I pulled out my trusty flashlight, since it was also a computer. I started typing the letters one by one into a search bar, followed by *translation*.

I squinted at the results. It's Czech, so Dimitri was pretty close with his language guess earlier. *The Trouble with Souls* was written at the top of the page. I frowned. I flipped through the pages, wondering if that one was different than the others, maybe musings or even a short story. Nope. It was more equations, all so similar that to my untrained eye they looked pretty much identical, all crossed out. I flipped back to the front and typed in the next line of letters to the best of my ability.

An Alchemical Pursuit. What the fuck did that even mean?

My phone buzzed in my hand. Lucy. She was apologizing for earlier and asking if I'd like to come down and have some tea with her before bed. I declined and told her I'll see her in the morning. I didn't apologize in return, even though I knew I should have.

I gazed up at the walls, realized I hadn't even been to the second floor of the room yet, but instead of selecting a book, I took the bound pages from the drawer.

Chapter 10

I knew in my bones that my second night in the house would not be as restful as the first.

"What are you thinking, D?" I asked. He was closing the patio door, and I was already snuggled up in the giant bed.

I watched him. He seemed to be running through several conversations in his mind; eyes flashing left to right as though a book was open in front of him. "I don't think we should stay," He finally read aloud from the imaginary pages, then sank down to the edge of the bed, shoulders slumped. "I don't think it's a healthy arrangement for us."

Healthy. It seemed like a strange word choice, but hadn't that been exactly what I was thinking in the library? I tried to decide whether or not I was upset by his decision. I couldn't tell. It felt good to have some kind of input, but the crushing idea of going back, of forgetting what things might have been like, of losing Finn and Lucy to this place, it hurt. I sighed and reached for his hands. "You're probably right."

He obviously felt better about continuing after being assured that I wasn't mad. "You're not happy around Finn, you know? And honestly, I don't know how you put up with the way he talks to you. I've always got my mouth halfway open to tell him off for the shit he says to you, but by the time I've worked up the nerve, you've already brushed it off like it's no big deal. A little distance might be good. We can do our own thing."

"Wait, what are you talking about?" I asked, genuinely confused.

He raised an eyebrow so high it was completely hidden in hair. "He's a complete dick to you. Like, all the time."

I laughed. "What? No...that's just. We're friends. That's just how friends talk to each other, right?" Right?

He shrugged, backed off. Maybe he felt like he'd overstepped himself. "I mean. I guess?"

"What happened to Lucy?" I asked suddenly. I'd actually just remembered something had happened. Something to make her cry. Something I hadn't been sensitive about at all when I'd snapped at her.

He rubbed the back of his neck, a nervous habit, but a hot one. "I don't want to say anything she told me in confidence..." he said slowly, delicately. I hated that he felt he had to tip toe around me right now, like I was a landmine. *Not healthy.*

I didn't want to be a landmine. "That's fine. She'll tell me if she wants to."

He spun around and flopped onto his stomach, legs kicking up behind him like a gossipy teenager. "It wasn't about the house, at least not really. She was just..." He trailed off, then brightened. "You want to hear about the basement though? That's *my* story to tell."

I grinned. "Duh. Spill it."

Dimitri told me about the basement, and I tried to picture it in my mind's eye as he spoke. Unfortunately, he was pretty shit at storytelling, bless his heart. "So, we go down there, right? Well. First, we get in the elevator and Lucy leaves and it's just us, okay? Just me and Finn. And we hear, like. Well, the elevator is like one of those old ones, right? Like with wire cage door?"

Apparently, after Lucy had returned to the kitchen to discover me on my way to the ground, the guys spent a few minutes trying to figure out how to work the elevator. The accordion door wouldn't close, and they were afraid they were going to break it. Finally, Dimitri realized that the accordion had been hooked together by a simple latch to keep the door open. When he flipped it, the door closed smoothly, and the floor buttons lit up.

Finn pressed the button marked "B" and at this point, Dimitri heard a voice that did not belong to either himself or Finn.

"She said, 'Don't'." Dimitri told me and he was whispering. I leaned in close to catch every word. "A woman's voice said, 'Don't'. Clear as day. And me and Finn like stared at each other, right? But we didn't say anything about it because the elevator started moving and it kind of caught us off guard. He denies he heard anything, but he looked at me right after and he was scared as shit, Nut. He heard it."

They arrived at the basement level without further incident and the elevator was in great working order with a current inspection. The basement was "full of stuff, like clocks and couches and chairs or whatever", but it all seemed to be fairly well organized. Unfortunately, everything was also shrouded in dust covers and they never did find a light switch.

"I wanted to go straight back up," Dimitri admitted. "I was so scared down there. I don't even like a regular dark basement. But Finn wanted to walk the whole perimeter and make sure everything looked solid."

They did. Apparently, the elevator shaft was pretty central to the house, so they crept out into the dark, glancing back to keep the lit elevator in view. "You'd better believe I hooked the door back open so it couldn't go anywhere," Dimitri laughed. "That was a genius addition."

The basement didn't extend the full footprint of the house and only had a few small, enclosed rooms at the edges of the open space. They didn't check those rooms, as Finn said he knew what was in each from the listing. "He said one had all the Internet equipment in it, and another had like the lower level furnace or something." Dimitri shrugged.

It was the mirror, the same mirror that ended up in the very bathroom we were now sitting adjacent to, that chilled Dimitri to his core.

"We heard whispering. It was coming from all over the place. Too quiet to make out words...it might have just been the sheets moving around on the furniture. Finn said that's what he thought it was anyway, the heat kicking on and moving stuff around a little. I don't know if it had been happening the whole time we were down there, and I just didn't notice it right away. Finn said that it had been."

I frowned. Finn seemed to be going to awfully great lengths to ignore the fact that the place wasn't right. Why would he want it so badly when it was obviously so creepy? He didn't even like my scary stories. I let Dimitri continue without interruption, because he was on a roll.

Dimitri wanted to get out of the basement as quickly as possible, so he walked the perimeter of the large room with his phone flashlight trained where the cement floor met the stone walls, trying not to focus on anything else. Finn lingered in certain areas, got distracted by certain bits of furniture, wandered back and forth across the space. When Dimitri had made a complete circuit, he called to Finn from near the elevator and Finn didn't respond.

Dimitri teetered between trying to keep his cool and completely losing it, and thought the whispers were getting louder.

It took him a few seconds to find Finn in the dark. Finn had apparently been pulling sheets off random pieces of furniture and looking them over, and Dimitri followed a trail of shiny wood desks and decorative knickknacks until he found Finn squatting down, staring into the dressing mirror. Finn's own phone flashlight dangled in a loose grip in his right hand, pointing uselessly at the floor.

Dimitri shined his light on Finn and the mirror, and Finn didn't immediately turn. He seemed too interested in his reflection. Dimitri looked into the glass as well.

"*There were people.*" He whispered to me. "There were so many people standing there and they were all looking at Finn."

Dimitri did what any sane man would do, screamed as loud as he could (surprisingly not very loud, he mused. He could barely get a squeak out of his frozen throat.) and ran back towards the elevator.

Finn called for him to come back and Dimitri initially refused, telling Finn to get his ass to the elevator or he would leave Finn down there. "He came towards me, so slow. He was carrying the mirror, and he was still stopping to pull sheets off shit, not a care in the world. He asked me what my problem was. He acted like he didn't see them. He *saw* them, Hazel. He saw them. But he just said you girls were wanting a mirror and that we should bring it up for you. And he was so chill about it! I finally decided I must have just scared myself. Imagined things in the dark, you know? But...I'm not so sure, honestly. I've never imagined anything like that before."

Heat crept up my face as Dimitri finished his tale, a good compliment to the sheen of sweat spreading across his freckled nose. I was mad. I was *so* mad. Not at Dimitri and I took care to make sure he didn't think I was. It was Finn gaslighting everyone. *Why?* I could deal with Finn being an ass, but I couldn't deal with him being an ass to Dimitri. Dimitri shouldn't have been second guessing himself, thinking he wasn't brave enough, whatever. I crawled back up to my spot at the head of the bed and pat the pillow beside me.

"I believe you," I said. "I don't think we should move up here."

Dimitri scooted up and got under the covers, wrapped me in a warm, slightly sweaty hug. "Thank God," he whispered.

I laid on my back with the covers pulled up to my chin, gazing at the intricate ceiling. A warm glow was cast under the bathroom door, where we unanimously decided to leave the light on.

Dimitri was fast asleep beside me, his breathing deep and easy. He was turned away from me, just a darker, denser shadow. I turned onto my side as well, away from him. I couldn't bear the thought of my back being exposed to the empty room. I'd decided that I hated how the bed was set in the center of the room. I felt like we were adrift in a sea of night. Untethered.

I let my eyes slide to the crack of light under the bathroom door. A warm, yellow light, just like the rest of the ones in the house. It made me feel a little cozier just gazing at it and I let my eyelids start to flutter close. I pretended that I wanted to stay awake, widening my eyes again whenever they rested fully closed. It was an old trick from when I was a kid, a little child's version of reverse psychology. *Oh no, I mustn't sleep. I should stay awake.* Nothing helped me fall asleep faster, in usual circumstances.

As I widened my eyes though, I started to imagine what it would be like if there were suddenly the twin shadows of feet breaking through the slit of light. If they started to creep back and forth behind the closed door. If the doorknob suddenly started to twist. I heard the phantom sound of the drawer in the library being jiggled. Was that little shadow at the edge of the doorframe always there? I squinted hard at it. Did it move?

My lashes began to obscure my vision again and I stretched my eyes back to full awareness. But my vision didn't return. Instead, a curtain of darkness descended, and the glow of the door was gone. There was a fraction of a second of confusion and I thought the light had been turned off. Then, I saw it.

The long, dark sheet of hair that was blocking my view of the bathroom door was only inches from my face. The faintest glimmers of light shone through it as it slid down through the air. The hair puddled onto the pillow beside me. A few strands tickled my cheek.

The head the hair belonged to sank down into my field of vision, almost upside down. She stood beside the bed, bent double to peer at me. Her face was so close to mine our noses might have accidentally touched. How long had she been standing here?

I could barely see her, backlit in the low light, but a faint glimmer caught in the wet of her eyes. I tried to scream, and the tiniest asthmatic wheeze managed to escape. Dimitri wasn't wrong about that. I was completely useless with fear. I couldn't even turn my head, couldn't even avert my gaze from the terrible, glistening eyes. My chest was caving in on itself. I thought I might actually just die, for lack of another way of ending the terror suffocating me.

"Jesus *Christ*!"

The mattress shook as Dimitri flopped around on his side of the bed. I felt him scramble partially over the top of me. There was a loud *whump*, fabric on fabric. The scream I'd been trying to scream finally made an exit from my throat. The mattress rose as Dimitri jumped off the bed. I was still screaming. He was both screaming and running, I heard his bare feet across the floor, his voice being thrown around the room with mine. The chandelier popped to life and dazzled me.

There was nothing on the floor beside my side of the bed except a heavy brocade pillow.

"Who the fuck was that?" Dimitri yelled. The words came out in a rush, all one long word. He tried again. "Who. The *fuck*. Was that."

I turned to face him, finally breaking my paralysis and propping myself up. He was standing by the light switch, both arms raised and grabbing the hair on the back of his head, staring at the floor in front of him. My chest finally began rising and falling properly, my screams dying down into long, slow breaths. I couldn't talk yet.

The bathroom door flew open, and Finn appeared in tatty joggers and a t-shirt. "What happened? Are you guys alright? Hazel? Hazel. Are you okay?"

"No, she's not fucking okay! There was someone in here! Someone standing over the bed. What the *fuck*!" Dimitri was pacing, throwing his arms around. It was wild to see him so worked up, he was usually such a passive guy.

"Hey, D," I said, almost a whisper. I reached for him.

He came toward me. "Come on, get up. We've got to leave. All of us." He glanced back at Finn, still standing in the doorway, looking completely baffled.

"D," I said again. "Did you...did you throw a pillow at her?"

"I...Yeah! I guess!" He couldn't lower his voice. Everything was a scream.

I snorted. I tried to cover it with a cough, but it dissolved into insane giggles. "You," The word barely squeaked out, I was almost in tears. "You threw a pillow at a ghost."

He was rubbing his eyes and lets out a tiny huff of a laugh as well. "Well, what was I supposed to do?"

"There are no ghosts," Finn said, almost whining. "Come on you two, stop messing with me."

"Is it safe to come in?" Lucy appeared behind Finn. "What happened?"

"D threw a pillow at a ghost." I wailed and then started absolutely crying with maniac laughter. I thought I might pass out all over again. I realized that the reaction was possibly my body attempting to keep me sane but I was suddenly incapable of taking anything seriously. As long as I didn't think about that face, so close to my own. The glimmer of her eyes appearing and disappearing as she blinked...

"We've got to leave." Dimitri repeated firmly. "I never want to experience anything like that ever again. You," he pointed an accusatory finger at me, "might have gotten hurt. And I still might have a heart attack. Might be having one. I don't know. Never again. I want out."

It hurt to hear it out loud like that, even though Dimitri and I were already in agreement before we turned the light out. I felt bad for Finn and Lucy. I knew they wanted it. I maybe wanted it, too. But Dimitri was right. It was too much. I couldn't even imagine sleeping the rest of the night there, let alone living there. The idea of going back to Charleston made me sick to my stomach, but there would probably be other opportunities. Maybe.

Trying desperately to compose myself, I swung my legs over the edge of the bed. "Okay. Yeah. We should go."

"What? Come on, you guys. What happened?" Finn demanded.

Lucy came the rest of the way into the room and linked her arm through Finn's. "We have to leave?" She bit her lip.

I studied Dimitri's face. He was pale, chest heaving, and sweat ran down his temples. Terrified. "Yes," I said. "We need to pack up and go."

A deep chime reverberated through the house. The doorbell was ringing.

Chapter 11

"Is that the goddamned door?" Dimitri asked no one in particular. "I hate this place."

I was still weirdly giggly. Was I in shock? Was this shock? Maybe I was just stupid.

"I'm not answering the door at fucking midnight," Finn said. "They can stand out there all night."

Lucy scratched her face sleepily. "What if it's the Freys'?"

"I don't—"

Finn's answer was cut off by the door chiming again.

"Alright," he continued. "Alright. Let's go down together. Just let me get some shoes on."

We all kind of shrugged. I climbed over Dimitri's side of the bed to get up. I didn't want to stand where *she* was standing.

"Maybe I'll stay and pack up our stuff," Dimitri said as I reached him. He was grabbing his shoes as well. "We are *not* staying." This last bit was directed at me, like I might get my mind changed in his absence.

"No," I grabbed his arm. I was freezing in my pajamas. "Just come with us, okay?"

He glared at the bed before acquiescing.

The doorbell rang three more time as we descended the stairs like the worst Scooby doo cast. None of us were dressed to be out wandering the halls, all of us were jumpy, snatching quick glances into dark corners and stopping short every time the bell tolled again. There were a few times when I felt sure there were five or six of us walking together, in the darkest parts of the staircase, but when I turned to check, I only saw the three familiar faces. I kept thinking that one of them was whispering, but I couldn't seem to catch anyone in the act of doing so. Each time the bell rang, we all jumped and gasped and momentarily clung to each other.

"It had better be the cops, to be this insistent," Finn muttered. "Should we even answer it? What's the etiquette for this situation? It's not our house."

None of us answered him before we reached the door and Finn pulled it open without hesitation, despite his previous comments. Mr. and Mrs. Frey stood on the other side. I wished the door had a peephole or something so we could have at least exchanged looks about them arriving in the middle of the night. I was supremely uncomfortable.

"I must say," Alexander Frey said, and passed a huge plastic dome into my hands. "It is very strange to knock on one's own door. But, what's the etiquette for that situation?" Finn and I spun and shared a look after all, etiquette be damned. Maybe we were too quick to dismiss cameras in there.

I looked down at the dome in my hands and was hit with a wave of nausea.

"We brought cake!" Mr. Frey said brightly, answering the least of all the questions I would have liked to ask.

"Great." I smiled woodenly. "I love cake. I'll just...I'll just get this in the kitchen."

"I'll accompany you," Opal said. She looked me up and down.

My cheeks flamed. I knew I looked terrible. I hadn't recovered from the shock of the whatever it was upstairs, or really from the whole day. My hair was a nest, my t-shirt read, *The Mothman helped me commit tax fraud, Point Pleasant '05!* Her eyes narrowed slightly and then she swept past me, leading the way.

I followed her dreamily. I felt a little strange, couldn't seem to shake the feeling of unreality, like I was under water, and everything was deadened, distant. Maybe I *did* have a fever. Opal's long hair was pulled back into a single braid that fell to the end of her spine, even with the lump of the hood of her coat making it bulge out a bit. "Coat', but it was actually a long black cloak, with slits in the sides that her delicate arms protruded from. I could see the shimmery amethyst material of whatever she might have been wearing underneath clinging to her spindly arms and also a few heavy silver bangles at her wrists. She might have been dressed down from the last time I'd seen her, but she could have still been on her way to attend an opera or something. It was weird to imagine her sitting in the passenger seat of a car, I could only picture her in a horse drawn carriage, like she was Cinderella. Her hair glimmered in the sconce light and I followed its dance dreamily, a lost traveler focused on a willow-the-wisp.

"Have you had an eventful stay so far?" she asked, without turning.

Eventful? What a strange word to use. Accurate, but strange. "Yes, actually," I managed to answer. "Much more eventful than I would have expected."

She paused then, and turned to look at me. She revealed small white teeth in a predator's knowing smile.

They set us up.

In that moment, I was positive that it was all some elaborate game they'd been playing, though I hadn't decided what the goal of it would be. I tried to smile back at her, but I couldn't quite manage it. Speaking slowly, making sure my voice was steady I said, "How was your meeting? We didn't expect to see you again so soon."

She seemed about to answer me or maybe to let me in on some great secret. Her dark eyes sparkled malevolently, excitedly. I remembered the breath on my neck last night, the impression of her being unimaginably ancient and cruel.

But her eyes left mine and instead locked on something behind me, and in the shift in focus, a normal woman once again stood before me, her face passive. "Ah, Ms. Murphy."

"Anything I can help with?" Lucy asked cheerily, stepping beside me.

"They've brought cake," I said stupidly.

"Yes, what a lovely thing to do... Let's serve it up!" Lucy turned to the wall of cabinets and opened one, amazingly the right one, and pulled down a stack of small plates. "How was your trip, Mrs. Frey?"

"I'll put coffee on," I murmured, sliding the cake onto the blood island and heading for the small hall.

"Short and to the point," Opal answered. "Just how I prefer things."

Lucy didn't bother to reply, it was obvious that Opal wasn't willing to make small talk.

I considered running down the appliance hallway and through the dining room to talk to Finn and Dimitri, but I was sure Mr. Frey was with them. I wished I had my phone, but it was plugged in on our bathroom counter, right next to everyone else's. We were going to have to have our private conversations the old-fashioned way, all raised eyebrows and nudges under the table.

"We won't be staying long and again I apologize for the out-rageous interruption," Mr. Frey said as we all sat in the parlor with coffee and cake. "I realized I'd forgotten some important documents in the study and am really only here to retrieve them. However, I am curious, have you come to a decision about the purchase of the property? Any questions I can answer or worries I can relieve?"

Those last questions were directed at Finn, and he fidgeted with his t-shirt collar for a moment before answering. "We love the property and are leaning towards moving forward with the purchase. I'll just need to speak to my agent and attorney and schedule a few inspections before we finalize."

I almost dropped my cake. Dimitri cleared his throat, but didn't say anything. Instead, he gave me a long stare, and I returned it with wide eyes.

Mr. Frey clapped his hands together once, loudly. "Excellent, my boy. That's excellent. Well, we'll be out of your way again shortly, and you four can continue to enjoy the rest of your weekend here. Opal and I will now be staying in town, so we are nearby if you need us for any little thing."

I'd been awkwardly picking at my cake throughout the ex-change, just to do something with my hands. I was frankly shocked by Finn's decisive answer. I assumed he and Lucy must have done some more talking after I stormed out from dinner, but they definitely hadn't talked since the ghost in the bedroom incident. Finn obviously wasn't taking me (or even Dimitri) seriously. I wondered again what might have happened to Lucy earlier that day and I wondered if she had shared it with Finn. Was he even taking *her* feelings into consideration? I leaned my head onto Dimitri's shoulder for just a moment, the hug of a person who had one hand full of cake and one full of coffee.

"Guess it's happening," he whispered into my hair. "But we aren't going to be here for it. Is that okay with you?"

Lucy and Mr. Frey were talking, so I assumed that Dimitri's words wouldn't be heard by anyone but me, but Opal turned her head slowly to us and smiled that same maddeningly knowing grin again. I shivered.

Some painful small talk continued while everyone pushed cake around their plates. A grandfather clock chimed way too many times. I let my exhausted mind relax, let everyone's meaningless words wash over me, and dreamt of sleeping on our too small, horribly uncomfortable mattress in Charleston.

"What I am really trying to wrap my head around," Finn was saying. "Is how on earth the two of you keep up with a house this size, especially with guests." He waved an arm around the room. "I mean, you *must* at least staff a maid or two during busy season?"

Mr. Frey laughed. "Oh, no. The real secret is we just don't sleep!"

He and Opal both thought this was very funny for some reason and had a little giggle together. Then Opal leaned forward slightly, all business, and said, "I keep the cleaning and maintenance of the house on a very strict daily, weekly, and monthly schedule. I would be happy to share my maintenance calendar with you. It really does make the work quite manageable, as long as you stay on top of the tasks. Don't put things off." This last sentence was a command.

"Yes, Ma'am," Finn said respectfully. "That would be wonderful."

Suddenly my plate was being tugged out of my hand. I jumped to full consciousness. Lucy leaned in front of me. "Are you done with this?" She whispered, because Mr. Frey and Finn were talking again.

I nodded, but didn't relinquish my plate and instead started to get up. "I can help wash up."

Lucy shook her head and gave my plate a slightly more forceful tug. I allowed it with a sigh.

Opal stood as well and collected the dishes from Finn and Mr. Frey. She hovered for a moment in front of Mr. Frey, and they shared a brief and silent conversation of their own before she removed his plate. Poor Lucy was going to be stuck in the kitchen with that terrifying woman again.

"Actually, Dimitri here pointed out a few spots in the foundation on the west side that I wanted to mention," Finn said, oblivious to everything except his chatter.

"Ah! A jack of all trades, are you, young man?" Frey turned his attention to Dimitri.

Dimitri shrugged. "I dabble."

"Well, no time like the present...why don't you show me?" Mr. Frey popped out of his seat like a jack in the box.

Dimitri and Finn both moved to stand, but Mr. Frey waved Finn back. "Not to worry, not to worry. We'll only be a moment."

Finn shrugged and settled back. I shook my head forcefully, gripping Dimitri's arm in both of my hands. He pried me away gently. "It's okay. I'll be right back." He followed Alex Frey out into the hall and all the sleepiness and silliness that had been keeping me anchored fell away. I was terrified, confused, and I just wanted to leave.

"Do you think this is a good idea?" Finn asked, literally the moment he knew everyone else was out of hearing range. Unless they had cameras installed, that is.

I considered for a minute. I wanted to know where his head was at. I needed him to be my friend and confide in me. I was also dying to lay back down on the couch, my head was swimming, but I would probably *actually* die at the look on Opal's face if she walked back in here and saw me sprawled out on the sofa like some bratty teenager. "Well..." I said cautiously.

"Like Lucy said before, it's not like they come with the house. As long as they're really moving far away and won't be popping up every few hours..."

He nodded. "Right. Let's say we don't have to worry about them ever showing up again. Let's say it's just the four of us and this house. Do you think it'll be okay?"

"I don't know, Finn. I am really having some seriously bad feelings and worse experiences," I answered vaguely.

"Let's pretend, for the sake of argument, that you probably just have a fever or something and there's no such thing as ghosts."

I frowned. "Hey, it's not just me, okay? Why are you being such an asshole about this?"

He gave a little condescending laugh that I loathed. "It's not just you *now*, but you've got your little hooks into D and Lucy. You're feeding them scary stories, getting them all spooked. I get it, it's what you do. But don't you want this to work? When are you going to stop? Save it for the brochure."

I wished that I could have just stood up and walked out and been done with the conversation, like usual. Why did Dimitri agree to go with Mr. Frey? We should have been on our way home. A creepy ghost lady had been watching us sleep not even an hour ago, where was my head at? "We're not staying, Finn," I said firmly. "Me and Dimitri aren't staying even if you buy the place."

"Are you serious?" He sat forward in his chair. "Are you that scared of the dark? Come on! This is a once in a lifetime opportunity I'm giving you."

I'm giving you. That sealed it. Not healthy. "It's not that. It's you. I can't live in the same house as you. You're a dick." The last sentence was said with a shrug.

He sagged back into his seat, ran his hands through his sleep tousled hair. I liked seeing him wrong-footed like this, messy, not in control, no smart little comeback.

"Look," he began.

I waited.

"I'm sorry. I'm stressed. Things with Lu have been..."

I perked up. I was expecting some kind of excuse for his behavior, but I wasn't expecting *Lucy* to be it.

"She's having a hard time," he continued earnestly, looking down into his lap, searching for words there. "And you're right. I'm a dick. She doesn't have a lot of friends besides me and I know I'm not exactly the greatest friend a lot of the time. I thought that maybe it would be good for her to have another friend around, you know?"

Shit. He had me cornered. I couldn't abandon Lucy if she needed me.

I pursed my lips, decided to change the subject. "Alright, if it's honesty hour, tell me what happened in the basement."

He shook his head, shook the cobwebs of weakness from his shoulders. "It was creepy and dark down there, a field day for the imagination. We didn't *actually* see anything down there."

I gazed around the parlor. The dark wood and antique furniture and flickering candles (*fake candles*, I reminded myself) really did make my brain whisper snippets from Hill House, or Dracula. A house meant for so many, but only holding a few didn't just feel empty, it felt hungry. *Could* Dimitri have imagined what he thought he saw down there? Could we have imagined our bedroom peeper? No, I didn't think we could have. I could see her clear as day in my mind, feel the tickle of her long dark hair brush my cheek.

"So," Finn began again casually. He drew out the space after the word until I turned back to face him. "How are things going with D? Good?"

I smiled my first real smile in hours. I had to tread very lightly. I couldn't let him know that I'd overheard the wedding talk and it didn't take much for Finn to notice that I was hiding something. "We're good. Great, actually. I think," I leaned forward conspiratorially, "he *was* actually really excited. I think he thinks you're going to pull this thing off. He's just pretty shaken up right now."

He laughed. "I'm guessing *you* aren't as optimistic?"

"You got me. I don't know. I have a weird feeling." My voice was barely above a whisper. "It's not the ghosts I'm worried about, dude. It's the Freys. They're up to something, I swear."

Finn held a hand up, silently asking me to stop talking. He glanced around the room warily. "Let me just get through the sale and be rid of them, then we can figure out the rest." His voice was below a whisper. I was basically reading his lips.

The traitorous nod I gave hit me with an immediate pang of guilt, but I never could say no to Finn.

We were both quiet then, listening for the Freys and our partners return, but there was nothing but the ticking of a mantel clock somewhere. Had it been a while? I felt like it had been a while. I caught Finn's eye without breaking the silence, and was considering mentioning that we should maybe go see what everyone was up to, when Lucy and Opal materialized in the doorway.

They weren't speaking, but in the silence Finn and I had left, their arrival was like a marching band. Lucy came forward casually and took a seat on a chair across from Finn. She smiled a cherubic smile at us. "All washed up."

I barely registered Lucy as my gaze lingered on Opal. She stood ramrod straight in the doorway looking...lost. Her glassy eyes lingered somewhere over our heads, and the cavern of her darkened mouth was exposed, her jaw jointless and gummy. Her arms dangled at her sides, palms slightly forward. I was about to ask her if she was feeling alright, when Lucy spoke again.

"We'll tell Mr. Frey that you'll meet him at the car."

I frowned at Lucy. Did she just kick Opal out of the house?

Opal's face didn't change in the slightest, but she abruptly turned and marched down the hall. The expression—or lack of one—sent goosebumps spreading over my skin like wildfire. A breath of cold air fluttered across my face for just a moment, and with it came an overwhelming sense of sadness and loss. Just like in the library, the feelings were *in* me, but not exactly mine.

I closed my eyes and thought I heard the faintest crying, the tiniest whisper, "*No. No, no.*" I thought I heard it, but maybe it was just the heat register kicking on. Just sheets fluttering in the breeze.

"Jesus, does the weirdness ever end?" Finn whined. He flopped back against the sofa.

I turned my attention to Lucy. Smiling prettily, hands clasped in her lap and ankles crossed. "It's almost over. Just some paperwork to sign?"

I could count so many of her perfect teeth in that smile.

"Did you run into D and the other Frey at all?" I asked.

"No, but I'm sure they'll turn up soon. Mr. Frey won't leave Mrs. Frey waiting. Maybe Dimitri is seeing them out."

I nodded and peeked at the doorway. Suddenly I wanted Dimitri with me immediately. I felt panicky, like I didn't know where he was or like he hadn't returned phone calls. Like he was missing. I stood up quickly, sending a burst of static across my vision. "I'm gonna go see what's taking so long."

I expected Lucy to stop me, but it was Finn that said, "Hey, aren't you like, delicate, or something? They've only been gone a couple minutes. I'll go down there if they aren't back soon."

I bobbed between sitting back down and going to the basement, and then I realized I didn't know where the elevator even *was*, exactly. I couldn't sit back down though. "I'm just going to go start packing up." It seemed like the smart thing to do, Dimitri would surely be ready to go as soon as possible.

I could tell that Finn and Lucy were waiting for me to leave before they started talking and I grimaced. Had I been that insufferable? I padded slowly up the stairs in my socked feet. One sock had candy canes on it and the other had some cartoon animal. Maybe a sloth? No wonder Opal was so quick to get back out of the house.

The silence was complete by the time I made it up to the third floor and all the lights were off. For whatever reason, none of the prickly skin fear from earlier visits was present. Maybe I was getting used to it, after all, or maybe I was just too exhausted. I didn't even bother to turn on the lights. I could see the warm glow of our bedroom beckoning me forward into the hall.

Packing didn't take me long because I wasn't very good at it. I just haphazardly stuffed everything that belonged to me or Dimitri into one of our two bags and sat on each of them to crush everything down while I zipped them. There was a soft knock as I double checked the bathroom for errant toothpastes.

"Yeah?" I called.

Finn appeared at the bathroom door. "Got everything?"

"Yeah, I think so. Have you seen D?"

"Yeah, he's helping Alex carry some stuff from the library out to their car. All those notebooks, I think."

"Oh, shit," I said, slapping my forehead. "I have one of those in the nightstand. I was just...well. I should bring it out to them, you think?"

"Eh, I doubt he'll even notice one is missing. They all look the same."

"I guess..." There was an awkward tension. I needed to tell him we're leaving, like, for real, definitely leaving. "Well, should we call a cab, or are you guys going to head back tonight, too?"

Finn sighed. "I'll see what Lucy thinks. You know I'd rather we all just wait until morning..."

"D isn't waiting till morning." I heaved a bag onto my shoulder and walked out. "Grab the other one?"

He did and followed me to the door. "I think he will if I can just talk to him for a second. He probably had a nightmare or something. I'm sure he's already feeling silly."

I pursed my lips. Dimitri probably *would* feel silly after Finn's patronizing.

Finn dropped the other bag near the door. "Let's just leave these here, okay? We can come back up for them after we talk."

Chapter 12

Perched on the landing, about to trudge back down the stairs, there was the distant sound of the front door being closed.

Finn cocked his head toward the noise. "That must be the Freys leaving. I still don't really understand why they showed up here tonight."

I didn't immediately follow as he began the descent, momentarily frozen at the memory of Opal's creepy smile in the kitchen. Her sinister hints.

Finn turned back to me, only a stair or two down, his eyebrows raised in lazy query.

I'd need to phrase my concerns very carefully, so Finn wouldn't dismiss me again. I noticed that he must have turned the lights on during his trip to the bedrooms and a little twinge of pride bolstered me. Finn felt the need to turn them on. Was he frightened, too, despite all his denial? He stared at me, waiting for me to say whatever it was I needed to say. "They're playing some kind of game with us." As soon as the words passed my lips, I knew it was the wrong tactic.

He laughed, of course. "How do you mean?"

"I mean, Opal knew good and well that there have been freaky things going on while we've been here. She asked about it, and she thought it was funny."

"What, like they're trying to scare us off?" Finn came back up to stand before me. "Hazel, that guy was basically begging me to just sign the paperwork tonight."

My stomach dropped. "Did you?"

He turned away from me again, but I could still see the heat turning the tops of his ears red. "We'll talk about it in a minute when we're all together."

I didn't love the sound of that. Dimitri *said* we were definitely not staying, but how easy would it be for Finn to convince him to change his mind? How easy would *I* be to convince? I didn't know if I trusted myself to not be swayed into something that I was pretty sure was a terrible mistake. I followed Finn down the stairs. What choice did I have?

When we reached the foyer, Finn headed to the front door instead of towards the kitchen and sitting room. "I want to make sure they're gone," he whispered.

I nodded and followed. We were tiptoeing, like Opal might have been hiding behind any decorative ceramic vase on display, waiting to spring out at us with her disapproval. He creaked the door open slowly and peered out into the dark yard. I shivered in the gust of night autumn wind that he allowed in.

The only car in the drive was Lucy's SUV. The Freys weren't there, unless they'd hidden around back...unless they were watching through hidden cameras.

Unless they had ghost spies.

Finn closed the door just as quietly even though there was no one to hide the noise from and suddenly, there was a different noise from down the hall. A high giggle.

It was only Lucy. I recognized her voice, but it carried through to us, dampened and refracting off the antiques made my skin prickle as much as the wind had. I attempted to catch Finn's eye, but he was already heading towards the parlor, apparently not weirded out. Maybe he was just happy she was in a better mood. The better to talk her into staying here, I suppose. I hustled to catch up to him, but walked straight into his back as he stopped dead in the parlor doorway.

I peered around his shoulder and my entire world avalanched. Dimitri and Lucy, arms wrapped around each other on the yellow sofa in front of us. Dimitri's lips pulled away from Lucy's skin with a disgustingly loud slurping sound. My mashed potatoes and cake that should have been long digested rose in my throat. They stared at us. We stared back at them. Their arms were still around each other, their hands still touching each other's skin, buried in each other's clothing.

I pushed down an insistent feeling of embarrassment, like I'd just opened an occupied bathroom stall. Like this was private and *I* was intruding. I grasped around in my head for the appropriate feelings to use as armor. Where was my rage? Where was my pride? They were missing. I settled for pain and maybe nausea.

"What..." I stammered. I swallowed and the act made me almost throw up again. "What the fuck."

A grip like a vice tightened around my arm. I was dragged backward down the hall.

A voice called. Lucy's. "Wait." An embarrassed throat clearing. "Hang on, this isn't..."

But I was already blessedly out of sight.

I looked at the fingers on my arm and recognized them. I turned forward and looked up at the face those fingers belonged to and didn't recognize it at all. It was only rage and complete and utter devastation. Finn had the emotions I'd been searching for. "Finn?" I whispered.

He didn't reply. He just kept dragging me.

"Finn. You're hurting me." My voice was like tissue paper. I might have disappeared. I couldn't handle it. I was disintegrating.

His grip relaxed. We were at the front door. He threw it wide and guided me through, more gently. He pulled his phone out with his free hand.

"Where are we going?" I wanted to ask, *what are we going to do?* but I couldn't. Not right then. I was clinging on to not disappearing.

"We're going home. I'm ordering a cab."

There were a few moments of silence while we walked down the drive. His arm still closed around my wrist, tethering me to the earth. "Finn," I said again.

He didn't look back at me. He might have been crying and didn't want me to know. I didn't want to know. I had an image stuck over my eyeballs that I couldn't get rid of. It was pasted over the darkened driveway like a double exposure. Dimitri. *My* Dimitri. How could he? I stopped and by extension, Finn also stopped. I vomited on the quartz stones. Chocolate cake and mashed potatoes and sour coffee.

"You don't have shoes on," Finn said.

I looked at my sick flecked socks in the moonlight. "Oh."

"Where are you going?" A voice called from the front door. Dimitri's voice. I started to cry then.

"Come on," Finn said. He picked me up and threw me over his shoulder like I was a sack of dog food. Luckily, I had nothing left in my stomach except the dull ache of disbelief. "We'll go down to the road and wait for the car."

I spent the next twenty or so minutes ignoring phone calls from both Dimitri and Lucy and crying silently. Finn was most likely doing the same, sitting next to me on the low curb at the end of the long drive. I didn't look at him. I couldn't.

If I were prettier, more successful, smarter, this wouldn't have been happening. That was all my brain kept saying. If I were as good as Lucy. I kept opening my mouth to apologize to Finn for ruining his life, but I didn't know how to form the words. He was probably furious with me anyway. He must have known it was my fault.

I couldn't help but wonder why they hadn't come down the drive after us. Finn left the car, they could have driven down to where we sat in less than five minutes. They hadn't. What were they doing up there? Packing? Something else? My stomach heaved again, empty but angry.

A sedan rolled slowly up to the curb, and we stood. The driver was already talking as he tilted his head down to see us through the passenger window. "Sorry it took me so long, there's some kind of wreck down the foot of the mountain, no other way around. Hopefully it's cleared up by the time...hey. You two, okay?"

He addressed both of us, but he was staring at me. At my pajamas and socked feet. "We're okay," I said, and my voice was calm. "Just got bad news and we need to get home right away."

Finn opened the back door, and I slid onto the seat. He sat down next me without speaking.

"Going all the way back to the city?" the driver asked, looking at his phone mounted by the steering wheel. "Little bit of a trek. Not that I mind." I caught his grin in the rearview mirror.

"Want to play some music?" I asked dully. "Your choice."

It was code for *we'd rather not talk* and the driver understood.

I leaned my head on Finn's shoulder and had incredibly begun to drift off when he suddenly jerked forward in his seat.

"Holy shit," Finn whispered.

I pushed myself up as well. It was pitch black outside, but flashing blue and red lights bathed the road. The driver crept around two police cars, two ambulances, and a tow truck. The tow truck driver was winching up the smashed remains of a silver car. A convertible, I thought, but an older one. I, of course, knew nothing about cars. I knew nothing about anything.

"That's the Freys' car," Finn said, his voice still low under the music. "Jesus."

"These turns can be tricky at night," the driver said conversationally. "I hope everyone is okay."

A couple of paramedics talked to each other as they slowly closed the doors on one of the ambulances. They didn't seem to be in a hurry.

We were past the scene and Finn sank back down onto the seat. He pulled out his phone, maybe to call Alex Frey, or to check the news, or something. But there were several unread texts from Lucy crowding his home screen and he slid the phone back into his pocket without unlocking it.

We were quiet for most of the ride back. I kept hoping to fall asleep again, to put off feeling all my feelings for just a little longer, but I never got anywhere close to blissful unconsciousness. Maybe my almost doze earlier in the ride was just shock. The superimposed image of Lucy and Dimitri was only gone when I occasionally pictured the smashed-up convertible, and in my memory, I imagined I saw blood on the windshield. It was too dark for me to have seen any such thing. How did everything change so quickly? What would I do?

I turned off my phone when I could no longer stand the constant vibrations of new messages, new calls. I scooted across the seat away from Finn so I could lean my head on the window. After a few minutes, he slid to the middle spot. I briefly wondered if he wanted to sit next to me or if he just felt safer there.

The driver kept making quick eye contact with me in the rearview mirror. I noticed him move the mirror when I moved over. At first, I thought he was being creepy and ignored him, but then I realized he wanted to make sure I was in a safe situation. I was barefoot and in pajamas and he picked us up from the side of the road. I dimly appreciated him, but didn't know what to say.

"Do you want to stay at my house?" Finn asked as we approach his exit.

"I just want to go home," I said, and I started to cry.

The driver was still on high alert. "Let me take you home, ma'am. We'll just drop him off and then I'll take you. No charge."

"No, no." I took a minute to try to collect myself. I desperately scrubbed my cheeks. "My parents." I gestured uselessly.

"Her parents live near me," Finn offered. He swallowed hard. He didn't want to cry in front of this random guy.

I nodded. "It's okay. I'll walk there."

"Ma'am," the driver began again, but Finn cut him off.

"You can borrow..." *Lucy's shoes,* I was sure he almost said. He couldn't say her name. It was as though she were dead. "There're shoes and clothes you can borrow."

I nodded again.

The driver dropped us off and we waved him down the road. "He's going to call the cops on me," Finn said casually. He walked around the side of the house and let us in the gate to the backyard. He never locked the back door to the garage, nor the door from the garage into the house.

While Finn grabbed us each a bottle of water from the fridge and flipped on the kitchen light, I sank shakily to a kitchen chair. I felt like I was about to be interrogated in a cheesy tv crime show.

"What are we going to do?" Finn asked softly.

"They'll be coming home soon," I answered, staring into my water bottle instead of his heart-wrenching face. "They could be here any minute. We're going to have to talk to them." I felt completely numb. I had never even considered the possibility of something like this happening. It was ironic that Dimitri and Lucy had each had their suspicions and jealousy over mine and Finn's closeness, even though Finn and I hadn't shared more than a hug in many years, despite my best efforts before Dimitri. Maybe they bonded over that mistrust. But, *when*?

I wished I could share my sense of detachment with Finn. I floated out of my reverie to find him sobbing, shoulders shaking and head down on the table across from me. "Hey," I said softly. I had to be the strong one this time. It was my turn. "Hey. It's going to be alright. Maybe it's just..."

"Just *what?*" he wailed, not raising his head. The words were liquid, drowned. "You saw them."

I'd seen them. I'd never not see them. "Maybe they made a mistake?" The hope in my voice was pitiful.

Finn did raise his head then stared at me. "Would you forgive him, if he asked you to? Forgive Lucy?"

I tried to consider, looked for the answer in Finn's face. It had been a long time since I'd seen him look that miserable. In fact, it had been just about as long as it has been since we'd shared anything more than a hug. And instead of considering, instead of prodding that open wound in my heart, I said, "Yes. I mean, who doesn't want to kiss Lucy at least once? Have you seen her?"

Finn's jaw fell open, then he rolled his eyes and lets his head flop back to the table. I heard a muffled, "Jesus *Christ,* Hazel." And his shoulders shook again, but he might have been laughing, at least a little. I had to be the strong one, had to make the jokes.

We were quiet for a while, each deep in our private thoughts. I hadn't considered getting up to find clothes and shoes. The need to go to my parents' house had evaporated. If I showed up there, they'd to want to know what happened. They loved Dimitri. I hated myself for thinking it, but I didn't want my parents to stop loving Dimitri. I certainly hadn't, not even a little. Maybe I hated myself for that, too. The heartbreak I felt for the idea of disrupting my relationship, and Finn and Lucy's, was stronger than the heartbreak of the betrayal I'd just witnessed. I didn't want things to change. I'd never understood why people stayed, I thought it was just weakness. Was I weak?

I remembered introducing Dimitri to Finn for the first time. Our relationship had been new at that point, but I'd been crushing pretty hard on Dimitri for a long time before we started *officially* dating, so Finn had heard all about him. The introduction wasn't awkward, we'd gone to an arcade together and most of the talk between the two of them had been straight pop culture. They'd seemed to get on well, better than I could have expected. I remember talking to Finn afterwards, dying to get his opinion, his approval.

"He's too good for you," Finn had said. He was joking, at least he *said* he was. I had brushed the comment off with an easy laugh and I didn't think I'd ever really thought about it again until then, at Finn's kitchen table. "That's the kind of guy that's going to love you forever, don't fuck it up," Finn had said. "He's better than me, and definitely better than you."

He'd completed this assessment by breaking into a chorus of "Movin' on up" and the sincerity of his words had faded into obscurity. How had I messed up this badly?

Finn's phone buzzed in his pocket.

"Give me that," I said.

He shrugged, dug it out, and handed it over. Lucy's picture smiled innocently up from the screen. I answered, "Hi, Lucy."

"Hazel! Please don't hang up." I tried to decide what the tone of Lucy's voice was. I couldn't.

"You've got ten seconds," I said coldly.

"I…" She paused. She didn't know what to say. "Listen."

"I'm listening, Lucy." It was funny, I felt *good*, hearing her fumble. I felt powerful. Righteous. Better than her for the first time.

"Okay. Okay. You know how things were...strange? At the house?" she said quickly, obviously aware that her seconds were ticking away.

"I mean, unexpected, I would say. Devastating? Yes. Strange is low down on the list of adjectives I was feeling at the time." I was so calm. I had the upper hand for the first time since I'd met her. She was the one that needed to grovel, needed to win *my* approval.

"No, no, not that. I mean. Seeing things. Hearing things. You know?"

"The ghosts?" I frowned, forgetting my haughtiness.

"*Yes.* The ghosts." She paused again. "Dimitri and I didn't mean to be doing what we were doing."

"You mean you didn't mean to get caught," I said, my cheeks immediately heating up. Rage that had been absent was finally simmering.

"No! No, I mean. It wasn't *us*." Her voice broke on the last word.

"I fucking *saw* you, Lucy."

"It wasn't like that. I would never. Hazel, listen to me. I would *never* hurt you like that."

Hurt *me*? Would she hurt Finn like that?

"Well, you did. So, that's a lie." I considered hanging up. Her ten seconds were more than over.

"Don't hang up!" She squealed, as though she could see me. See inside my thoughts.

"Hazel." The voice coming through the speaker was suddenly Dimitri's voice and the tears came again, rage instantly extinguished. I couldn't handle it.

"Hazel," Dimitri whispered. "It was like a possession."

I choked on snot. "*What?*" Tears were replaced by outraged laughter. "*That's* what you're going with?" I looked at Finn for the first time since I'd answered the phone and his head was shaking slowly. I couldn't tell if he could hear what was being said on the other end or not, so I told him, "They say they were being possessed."

He obviously couldn't hear, because his face turned from despair to incredulity in about a millisecond. But then, strangely, it read something like comprehension. I raised my eyebrows in question, but he quickly shook his head again and the moment was gone.

"Are you there, Hazel?"

I closed my eyes. "I'm here, D."

"I want to come home. Lucy's driving me. Will you be there? So, we can talk?"

I sighed. "I'll see if Finn will let me borrow his car."

"I love you, Hazel."

I loved him, too, but I disconnected the call without saying so.

Chapter 13

"Look, I really don't know if it's a good idea for you to go home." Finn held his car keys just out of my reach. "Why don't you just stay here until they get back and we can talk it out together."

I shook my head. "No, I need to talk to D alone. I don't want *Lucy* around while we're talking, that'll be a disaster. Just let me go home."

He hesitated, then finally drops the keys into my open palm. "Fine. But..."

I waited what felt like a long time for him to finish that sentence. I'd borrowed a pair of Lucy's shoes, and they were a half size too small. I needed to get home and get out of them. "But?" I urged him.

"Something's weird," he said finally. "Be careful."

If I didn't laugh, I'd definitely cry. "Yeah. Something's weird. I'll call you later probably."

I left without any more preamble. My feet were killing me and I wanted to look at least halfway presentable before Dimitri got home. I wondered vaguely how far away they might be as I tried to remember how to open the door on Finn's car. There was like a button on the window frame or something?

I found the catch finally, and popped the door open. I was feeling okay, focused on the pain of my pinky toe, focused on the minutiae of driving an unfamiliar vehicle. *I'm going to confront my partner about cheating on me with my best friend's wife.* It read like a news crawler on my brain.

Whenever I pictured Dimitri, it was always him on the night I'd met him for the first time in that coffee shop. His dripping hair, his turned-up collar. I tried to picture him then, while I was driving home, but came up blank. That memory refused to surface. I could only see him from today, on the couch, the smack of his lips parting from Lucy. That worried me quite a bit. Would that be what I thought of whenever I pictured him, in the little photo album in my brain that kept all my friends and family safe and eternal? If everything turned out alright, and we ended up married and happy and still in love, would I still try to picture his face and only remember his betrayal?

I told myself not to dwell, to let things be as they were and just drive home safely. My eyes blurred with tears I didn't want to let fall, and it made the safe driving more difficult, but I managed.

My heart skipped a beat when I saw our car parked in our parking spot. Did Dimitri beat me home after all? Then I remembered, he was with Lucy. In Lucy's car. What were they talking about, on their long car ride back together? Were they trying to get their story straight? *Stop.*

That smell of home I never noticed until I had been away too long punched me in the heart as I pushed open the front door. My eyes blurred as I rushed toward our bedroom, mentally rummaging through my outfit and makeup choices. Everything I really liked was left by the door of the room we shared at Lovers' Leap. I'd have to make do with things I didn't like or wear as often. For some reason, looking nice was very important to me for the talk with Dimitri, like he didn't know what I looked like normally, and he might be dazzled if I suddenly put in a little effort.

But our two suitcases greeted me, placed on the end of the bed and waiting patiently to be unpacked. Dimitri had beat me home.

Did I walk right past him in the living room? I turned back to the short hall connecting the two rooms. Yes, there he was, his back to me, sitting in the accent chair I picked up at a garage sale that neither of us ever used. Why didn't he say anything when I walked by? *Because he's dead,* my brain insisted suddenly and most unhelpfully. *He's dead in the chair and you didn't tell him you love him on the phone.*

Now that the idea was present, I couldn't make it leave. And he didn't turn, didn't speak, the TV wasn't on for him to be watching. My heart made itself known by suddenly beating way, *way* too many times. I had to say something. I couldn't make myself. Because what if he didn't respond? What is he just sat there, turned away from me and I had to walk up to him and look into his face and something was wrong? What if this was all a nightmare, and I walk up to him and he *had no face*? What if...

"Are you ready to talk to me, Hazel? It's okay if you want to take your time."

I clapped my hand over my mouth to hold in a scream that immediately dissolved into tears. He didn't turn around when he spoke. After a few seconds of sniffles, I managed to say, "Just...give me a few minutes to change." And I retreated back into the bedroom and locked the door behind me. The click of the lock was embarrassingly loud, I didn't know if I'd ever locked a door within our apartment before. I told myself I just didn't want to be interrupted and reminded myself that I was angry, and hurt, and tired, and, yes, scared, and my feelings were valid.

I was also really hungry. I decided that my next order of business would be to make something for us to eat. I could plan out how I wanted to approach the talk while I cooked, because I certainly hadn't really considered how I wanted it to go with any clarity.

I held up a couple of dresses. Did I want to be sexy? No, smart. Business lady. Practical. I selected an outfit with care. I drew on some spectacularly arched eyebrows and my eyeliner matched first try. I looked good. Ready to win a battle for myself.

But I was afraid to unlock the door. What if he was still sitting there, being weird? I almost texted him to tell him to move. That would have been something I would have done on any other normal day. *Hey, I'm coming out. Get out of that weird little chair, you're freaking me out,* I would say, and I'd hear his laugh a minute later from the other room. I didn't text him though. I just took a fortifying breath and walked out.

He was still sitting there, still resolutely (and creepily) facing away from me. I soldiered on, walked into the room and sat on our couch that we always sit on. I finally made myself look at him.

He didn't look different. I gazed at him as though he were a photograph for a moment. I needed to replace the snapshot next to his name in my head. His freckles. His one dimple that intensified when he smiled, but is always kind of there. His eyelashes. But his face was blank. He didn't look sad or apologetic, or even angry. He blinked twice. He opened his mouth to speak.

I quickly said, "I'm starving. I need to make some food." I stood up. I was only sitting for about five seconds. I turned away from him immediately. I couldn't do it.

"Do you want my help?" Dimitri asked.

Did I? Sometimes we had a great time making dinner together. Getting in each other's way constantly in the tiny kitchen, getting food everywhere, hardly ever making anything truly edible. It would have been nice to do something normal like that. I pulled my phone out and plugged it into the charger on the counter. The screen lit up briefly, reminding me of the dozens of texts, missed calls. "No." I answered.

This really wasn't how I expected this reunion to go. I expected him to grovel. I expected him to immediately tell me what the hell he was thinking, to tell me whatever wild story he needed to in order for me to believe him. I expected him to ache for my forgiveness and to profess his undying devotion to me. I chanced a glance over at him as I selected a pot. He was still staring at the goddamn wall. He hadn't moved.

"So," I said casually. Clattering around enough for him to know this was Angry Cooking. "You going to tell me what you were thinking? Or how long this has been going on? Or what in the actual *fuck*?" I might have been getting less and less casual as the questions went on.

It, at least, did what I needed most. He *moved*. He came into the kitchen, staying about two feet away from me, which I guessed was fair. He was standing kind of oddly though. Maybe he was nervous. "I don't know if you'll believe me," he said.

That was it? He'd stopped talking, so I guessed he wasn't going to elaborate? I'd been filling the pot with water and turned off the faucet as forcefully as I could, then dramatically spun around to face him. I jut out my jaw, I cocked my eyebrow, I crossed my arms, but none of it mattered, because he was looking directly at the floor.

"Let's just say, my mind is wide open right now," I said.

I wished he'd look at me. He shifted his weight slightly from foot to foot.

"Are you going to tell me you were haunted or whatever again?"

He exhaled in a way that might have been a laugh, but no laugh I'd ever heard from him before. "No. Come, sit." He gestured to our table. "I'll help with dinner in a mo...minute."

I eyed him. "This had better be good." I took my usual chair, flopping into it, immediately tying my legs and arms into knots.

He sat down slowly and reached into his jacket pocket. He took out an envelope and pushed it across the small space between us. I didn't even have to open it to know that it was full of cash.

"What's this?" I didn't touch it.

"It's from Lucy," he began, but didn't have time to say more before I shoved the envelope to the floor angrily. He held up a hand to try to quiet me. "Listen, listen. Please."

I bit my lip and stared at the envelope. The money hadn't fallen out, but the clunk it made when it hit the ground...it must have been a lot of bills in there.

"Lucy asked me to do her a very large favor and that's the payment for it. One very expensive kiss."

"*Kiss* is putting it lightly, don't you think?" I scoffed.

"Listen," he said again. I dragged my eyes up from the money to look at him and he was now looking down at the tabletop. "She likes you very much. You're her best friend." He held up a hand to my interjections again. "You're not good for Finn. Finn's not good for you. She asked me to stage this with her so that we could create some distance between you two."

I stared at him, completely nonplussed. "What?"

"She decided she didn't want us to move up there with them. I told her I didn't want us to stay either. We came up with a lie for Finn and Lucy is paying us off to not tell him it was a set up." He finally looked up and held up both arms in a "that's it" gesture.

"So...why are you telling me? Why not give me the lie, too?"

He smiled a small, sad smile. And I realized why. It was because Finn would forgive Lucy, but they didn't think I would forgive Dimitri.

I gazed at Dimitri. Would I have forgiven him? I felt like I was definitely planning on it, wasn't I? "What about the house?" I asked. I felt like I was changing the subject from forgiveness even though it wasn't actually spoken. "Does she even want to move up there after...after all the stuff?"

Dimitri laughed then and there was something different about it. Something forced. "She loves the house! She just didn't love how you and Finn kept sneaking off together in it."

"What? We never..." I tried to think back to the last few days. Did we spend more time without Lucy and Dimitri than with them? If we did, it was purely coincidental. "She's being stupid."

"I know, I know, but..." He gazed down to the floor between us. "It's a lot of money, Hazel."

I squinted at him. Something felt off. *Everything* felt off. A small hiss issued from the stovetop as a droplet of water spit onto it. The water burbled. "I'm going to finish dinner," I murmured and stood slowly. I tried not to look at the money. "You're not off the hook, by the way."

"That's fair," he said and settled back into his chair.

Back at my post over the boiling pot, my neck prickled. Was he just going to...sit there? It was like he'd powered down, staring at the back of my head. I could feel his eyes on me. I turned and stared back. I looked directly into his face for a full three seconds before he gave me a little smile. I didn't return it. "Don't you want to watch tv or something?" I asked desperately.

"No, that's okay."

I stirred the pot, turned down the heat so it didn't boil over (it always boiled over). "Have any emails to catch up on or anything?"

"I don't think so."

I slammed the spoon down to the counter with a clatter, tiny scalding droplets splashing back into my face... "Well, can you at least stop staring at me?"

Dimitri smiled again. "Of course." He turned his head and gazed into the living room.

My heartbeat climbed up into an unhealthy range again. Something was *off*. What was it, what was it? Panic clutched my chest. *What if he has no face?*

It hit me then. He hadn't touched me since I'd been home. He always kissed me when I came home. He always helped with dinner. He always called me "Nut," almost never Hazel.

It's fine, it's fine, he just knows I'm upset, he's keeping his distance.

He hadn't gone out for a cigarette. He didn't take his shoes off at the door. He hadn't checked his phone even once. He didn't even reach out and touch my arm when we were talking.

"Hey, D?" I was afraid to look (*what if he has no face*), so I opened the refrigerator and stared inside aimlessly.

"Yes?"

"Can you set the table?"

"Of course."

I heard him stand. I went back to the stove, stirred the noodles and out of the corner of my eye I watched as he opened the wrong cabinet looking for our dishes. Twice.

Chapter 14

Now

In my dream, I must have been falling. Waking is violent, a thrash into conscious thought that sends all my limbs flailing outward like a marionette and my lungs gasping as though I'd been sleeping underwater.

Before I have a chance to truly panic from whatever nightmare has released me, I'm soothed. I'm in my own car. I'd know its highway noises anywhere, its scent, the cradle of its passenger seat around my back. The seatbelt kept me stationary during my freakout and now I'll be okay.

My heaving breaths settle, and I let my head fall back and roll to my left. There is Dimitri, driving calmly, hands at ten and two. He doesn't look away from the road, but his dimple appears in a smirk.

"Did you sleep well?"

I mean to ask him where we're going—I've forgotten, it certainly must have been a good sleep—and instead a yawn erupts. I push myself up to see out the windshield and fire shoots up my arm, radiating from my palm.

Then I remember everything.

I almost pass out again, my vision gets splotchy, and I can't get enough air. I start to undo my seatbelt, but I'm too dizzy, I can't make my hand do what I want. I throw myself back against the seat. I just need a minute.

"Your friend will be perfectly all right, don't waste your energy worrying about him," the imposter says.

Now I see him, *really* see him. How he doesn't sit like Dimitri, doesn't hold his jaw like Dimitri. How he isn't Dimitri at all. My gaze wanders to the dash, wondering what would be the safest way to crash the car. How many aspects of a car crash could I potentially control from the passenger seat? I've failed this test before, but I might be ready to try again. I hesitate, mostly because whatever this thing next to me is, it's using Dimitri. *My* Dimitri could be in there somewhere. I have to get him back if I can.

Not to mention, the throbbing in my hand is overwhelming almost all of my other thoughts. I have my left hand grasping the right's wrist tight, held over my chest. I don't know if that's what you're supposed to do, I don't know much of anything right now, but I pretend it helps the pain. My whole front is soaked in my own blood. I'm a little to the left of my own body, thick and slow. Am I still dreaming?

"Finn's probably dead by now," I whisper. Tears sting the corners of my eyes. I didn't want to say that, it just fell from my lips, unbidden. True.

"Nonsense," the man says. "Do you want to see a magic trick?"

I don't bother to respond.

"Here," he says. He takes his right hand off of the steering wheel. I can't make myself turn and look at him. My eyes are unfocused and staring at the windshield, or maybe the dark highway in front of us. Whatever.

Suddenly, there's an arm pressed against my face. The pressure shoves my head back against the car seat. My mouth is full of blood, but it's not mine. It's coming from his arm, his wrist. I squirm ineffectually, try to turn my head, but I'm so, so weak.

He keeps my head pinned against the seat for several long seconds, maybe a minute. I think I might throw up. My screams are only choking. The tears that threatened a moment ago are streaming down my face.

"There, now," he says and releases me.

I cough and spit into my own lap and splutter, "What the fuck?!" Because I am very eloquent under pressure. When I wipe my mouth, I unthinkingly press my bad hand to my cheek and scream in pain. I use the left. "What in the actual *fuck* is wrong with you? Who are you?"

He laughs. It's not a loud or a mean laugh. It's mostly just Dimitri's laugh and that pisses me off even more. "Very little is wrong with me, my girl. Very little."

My girl. I manage to spin and stare at him. He's concentrating on the road in front us, back to ten and two, the stolen dimple in sharp relief in the dash light. "Mr. Frey?"

He smiles. "Wonderful, wonderful! But no, not anymore. I am Dimitri Kriska now. Twenty-eight years old. Mother named Vera. One little sister, Alina."

I might throw up. I might pass out. I might just die right here, I don't know. My brain feels like Rice Krispies in milk. It's hissing, crackling. Every snap in it makes me teeter closer to losing my grasp, sinking back into blissful unconsciousness. "How?" I manage.

"We have time," he says casually. "And you are about to start feeling a little sleepy. I promise that I only did what I did to help with your injury, the sleepiness is just a side effect."

I look down slowly at my hand. Is it, maybe, throbbing a little less? Or am I just getting used to the pain?

"I'll tell you anything you'd like to know. I do lose a little sleep over this part of my existence, or at least I would if I were a creature that sleeps. I'd like to make your transition as painless and peaceful as possible, I promise you."

"Transition?" I mumble. My tongue feels heavy and also disgusting, coated in copper. Water would be great. If Lucy were here, she'd have a clean glass rattling with ice cubes for me. If Lucy were...

"Yes," he answers, sadness tingeing his tone. "Unfortunately, yours and Mr. Kriska's appearance the other night put quite a hiccough in our arrangements, I don't mind telling you. Neither of you should have been involved in this at all. I'm very sorry. Next time, we will have to remember to be clearer in our advertisement."

I rub my eyes, forgetting that my hands are covered in blood. It burns. I have no idea what he's talking about. My hand is feeling much better though. I look down at it, flex it, completely distracted by it. "What's... What's happening here?" I ask loudly. I might have cut him off while he was talking, I don't know.

"I possess quite a gift," he says. "I shared a little of it with you to ease your suffering. Finn will have received the same gift from Lucy, don't worry."

"Lucy is...Opal? Opal took Lucy?" Do those words make sense? Will he understand what I'm asking?

"Lucy is Lucy, right now," he says. He's speaking slowly and clearly, the ever patient first grade teacher, or grandfather. "But yes, she *was* Opal, until recently." He hesitates a moment, considering his words, I think. "Soon, she will be you."

"That's stupid," I mumble. I lean my head back against the head rest and let my eyes flutter. "Why would Lucy want to be me?"

He laughs again. With my eyes closed, it could be Dimitri sitting next me. My Dimitri.

"Well, she didn't want to be! It's so ironic you would ask that. You see, there is a ritual that she and I must perform every so often. It's based on the moon cycles, but let's just say it's around every forty-nine years for simplicity's sake."

"Mmhm," I say, like I do when I pretend to be awake while watching a movie and Dimitri asks if I'm paying attention. I'm not.

"Friday, goodness, was it only two nights ago? It was the first night of our ritual (it lasts a full moon cycle, you see), and we had prepared for your friends Finn and Lucy to be our guests of honor. Unfortunately, due to my lackadaisical attitude, it happened to be *you* and Finn that became our esteemed guests."

"Are you vampires?" I ask, rolling my head to the left and cracking open an eye to look at him. I sound like a child.

He doesn't seem perturbed by my interruption, he grins and slaps my knee jovially. I barely feel it. "Very astute! Technically, no. Vampires as you know them don't exist, to my knowledge. But I do believe that we have had some influence on their creation. Quite a *bit* of influence. So, again, for the sake of simplicity, let's just say yes."

"Am I a vampire now?" I close my eyes again. I'm feeling pretty relaxed, pretty comfortable. I could easily sleep.

"No, not yet. Shall I continue?"

I nod. "I'm listening."

"Well," he begins fresh. "Let's start at the beginning, why don't we? Lucy and I are an interesting sort of creature. We are born with our own bodies, maybe a little different from these human ones, but when time inevitably breaks those bodies down, we move on to new, younger bodies and begin again. Sickness does not touch us, and damages are easily and quickly repaired. The only ravage we cannot escape is that of time. We are not immortal. Our kind is usually a fairly solitary sort, and we do not mingle except in certain, and usually grave, circumstances, but Lucy and I..." His voice is dreamy. The man is in love. I've known this since I first saw him doting on Opal. I wish he'd get on with his little story before I fall asleep. I also hate Lucy's name on Dimitri's lips with that inflection. I'm hurting from that little scenario, and this magic blood isn't taking the sting away from that pain.

"We've been together a very, very long time. The inn is named after us, actually."

"You're the lovers leaping?" Isn't that in that Christmas song? Maids a milking, lovers leaping? I'm stupid and groggy. Still dreaming?

"Yes. That was our most fascinating ritual, to date. But I think yours might actually take the cake! We had decided that we should become a wealthy couple that had recently settled in this area. They owned the land where the inn sits now and many acres surrounding. It was a two-part ritual, just like this one has accidentally become. They are very tricky, but we planned the whole thing flawlessly. We first had to dispose of our current bodies (since we had planned this, it was done before the actual ritual night, unlike this time), and procure ones that would make a more heartbreaking tale to become legend. Young people." He nods to himself. "In order to make a splash, as they say. Young lovers mean more to story tellers than sensible older adults. Anyway, we commanded those young selves to leap from the overlook and our new, permanent bodies were there to spread the tale of the tragedy far and wide. We created our own ghosts."

Ghosts. I sit forward and my eyes snap open. "There's ghosts in the bed and breakfast," I say. I still sound stupid, but my brain is beginning to tick back to life. My hand doesn't hurt at all. The joy of discovery has made everything else take a back seat. I'm so excited to divulge what I've just realized. "I saw Opal. I saw the *real* Opal! She's been trying to warn me!" Her face, not creeping in the darkness of the bedroom or screaming at me through a mirror, but sitting, smiling at me in a dream. I *knew* she was familiar.

"So smart," he says. I hate that I feel a little glow of pride at his compliment. "Yes. Our souls, our *essences* replace the ones that originally resided with the bodies we...appropriate." The word seems apt, but he's clearly uncomfortable using it. "We haven't quite figured out how to get them to transcend this plane of reality like they should, there is an unnatural disconnect. They...linger. Usually, they go unnoticed, but they can manifest themselves occasionally, especially in mirrors. We (our kind as a whole), usually don't use mirrors in order to avoid the...reminder, but people seem to find this unacceptable within an inn. We compromise with small mirrors, unlikely to reflect more than the user's own face and also by encouraging ghost enthusiasts." He chuckles.

"Doesn't it bother you?" I ask. "You know they're there. You know what you've done to them."

"You eat meat, do you not? Does it not bother you? This is how we live."

I chew on this for a moment but retort, "Haven't you had plenty of living? It's not really fair. How many lifetimes have you and her had together? And you just go around cutting other couple's lives short? Pretty selfish."

I cross my arms. Checkmate, Dracula.

He avoids my question, redirects. "It doesn't have to be lovers at all, really. It could be any two people. We've just found that couples make the easiest transition, raise minimal suspicion."

"I'd fucking suspect something if Finn and Lucy just never spoke to me again," I argue. "Lots of people must notice their friends and family are suddenly different."

"Would you, though?" He asks, almost dreamily. "Is it that strange for a young married couple to start a new venture, to move away from their family and friends, and then suddenly be too busy to visit? For communication to taper off until it's nonexistent? For them to just become people that you used to know, and you hope they're doing well, and that they might think of you sometimes? It's not that strange at all, and while there might be some tears, no one suspects a thing. It's just how life is sometimes. We grow apart. Even you and your friend Finn have grown apart, though you are trying your best to deny it and cling to him."

I'm quiet for a moment at this. I can't stop thinking of the beautiful young woman I saw screaming in the mirror. It's horrific. "Is...Dimitri there? In the house?"

He doesn't answer right away. He passes a slow moving RV with care. "Dimitri is here. I'm merely borrowing him, as we did the 'lovers' who leapt all those years ago. He is not part of the ritual."

"He's *here*?"

"Yes, you're looking at him, are you not? This body is still his and he still resides within it. I am simply, ah. Attached. He is like a puppet for me."

"Can he hear me?"

"I assume he can. He is present. He's just not in control."

I sit forward, stare at the profile I know so well. "Will he be okay? When you leave?"

"Technically, yes."

The lack of elaboration is deafening. They aren't planning on letting Dimitri or Lucy go, obviously. "Wouldn't it be easier to just get rid of me and Finn? Keep the two you've got? I don't understand."

He sighs. "The ritual is like paperwork. It has been signed. It must be you. Sharing another like I am now is different. Difficult. It requires constant focus. I wish we could have skipped using these two altogether, but Opal deemed it prudent to get control over all four of you. We can't have any more accidents. Every movement in this body is monumental. My senses don't work properly, it's like doing everything with thick gloves on. It's uncomfortable. This is not a permanent state." He looks sideways at me. "Don't get any bright ideas, we've had a lot of practice in these situations. You saw, dear Lucy. You aren't a match for us." He sounds a little sad.

"It bothers you, doesn't it?" I ask. I can't help but ask. It's written all over that familiar face.

He considers his words carefully again. I wonder if he's regretting starting this conversation with me. I've decided that any attempt at escape should probably happen at the house. I'm not going anywhere without my three best friends. A little background information can't hurt.

"It bothers me, yes. I've made something of a hobby of attempting to free the lost souls we must create. The inn is like my laboratory. These talks," He gestures at me. "I'm trying to explain my position to you. So, you can help me, help *you*, when the time comes. Please, when you find yourself on the other side of the looking glass, look for me. Let me help you."

This infuriates me, of course. I try to hold my tongue. "Does Opal share your hobby?"

I've hit a sore spot. He grips the steering wheel tighter for a moment. "*Lucy* finds it trivial. She thinks I have gone a little soft. Luckily for me, she finds it an endearing quirk."

"What's her real name? What's yours?"

"That's very private. It's a rude thing to ask. No one knows our real names, except each other. It's not information that gets shared, even with our own kind."

I rub my hand vigorously on my dress. The dried blood flakes off in a disgusting little shower. Without a thought, I snap the dome light on to examine my wound more closely. The stab has completely healed over, not even a silvery line of scar remains.

"If the ghosts bother you so much," I say, still inspecting my miraculous recovery. "Why don't you just stop? Aren't you bored of staying alive yet?"

"I've had this conversation many, many times," he says, tapping the light back off. "I must say, you seem the most calm. Are you not afraid?"

I grin. "You're avoiding my question."

He sighs, rubs Dimitri's temple. "I think, if I were on my own, I probably would have stopped. But I would never leave her, and she is afraid to die." He pauses. "Don't tell her I told you that."

For some reason, this makes me laugh. It feels strange to laugh, but it bubbles out anyway. Am I scared? No, I realize. I'm not scared yet. I have this idea in the back of my mind that once I'm back with Finn, we can fix this. We can fix anything. I wonder what he's doing now.

"So," I draw out the "o", make it sound like I'm asking for hot gossip. "Tell me about this ritual. What's stopping you from just doing it again? Focus on a couple that aren't going to be such a handful? Kill us all and put up another cute advertisement?"

"If only we could," he says, sighing deeply. "The ritual has already been set in motion, and we can only perform it every so often, like I've already told you. Existing in this puppeteer state for fifty years would be dreadfully tiresome. It *will* be you and Mr. Murphy that we become. It's quite a shame," He looks over to me and smiles. It's a mean smile and it looks foreign on Dimitri's face. "Lucy much prefers her current body."

My cheeks heat up. "Lucy doesn't mean anything without her personality," I spit. "She's being wasted on your snotty wife."

"Well, I must say, *you* will be greatly improved by her. You're very nosy," he replies. It doesn't feel like a barb, just an observation. He also doesn't seem to notice that I'm mad. He's lost his touch with regular people, I think.

Regardless of his intention, his musing hurts. He agrees that Lucy is better than me. I guess everyone does, including me. Including Dimitri?

"So. Dimitri and Lucy...when they were making out on the couch earlier..." Is it important? Probably not in the context of things. But I've got to know. It's important to *me*.

Mr. Frey gives his collar an anxious little tug and clears his throat before answering. "I suppose it would be unfair to pin all the blame on things going so awry on you and Mr. Kriska's arrival."

I wait. He takes his sweet time continuing.

"We decided it would be easiest to dispose of the Freys and secure you and Finn using your partners. It was obvious that none of you had any trust in Mr. or Mrs. Frey and we had outworn our welcomes. None of you ever should have left the house." He clears his throat again. He's obviously embarrassed. "It's been quite a while since Lucy, and I have had younger bodies. We were, er, thrilled to see each other."

I swallow bile. "Why'd you let us go? We waited for a cab for like half an hour."

He's obviously glad to change the subject. "We didn't know how fast the taxi would arrive and the last thing we wanted were authorities involved. We decided to let you go home and work out a new plan. The trouble was, neither of us planned on being in these bodies for more than a few minutes. We haven't practiced. We walk differently, sound differently, know very little about the person we are. It is a truly flimsy disguise. Distance is required for the charade."

I gasp. "You let them talk. On the phone. Oh, my God. You let Dimitri talk to me." I didn't tell him I loved him. It might have been my last chance.

He sighs. "We did. It was risky, of course, and we were sure they would say something similar to what they did. That they were 'possessed'. But we wouldn't have been able to pretend to be them on the phone, not convincingly, and it was imperative that neither you or Finn decided to leave town."

My mouth dries out. Here it is, the info I've been prying for without even knowing what I needed. The weak spot. I need to be careful. "What would happen if the, uh, cycle? What would happen if you didn't get into your contract person before it's over?"

He doesn't answer me. Bingo.

"How long did you say it was? A moon cycle? How long is a moon cycle?"

Still no answer. *Shit.* How long *is* a moon cycle? It's like a whole month or something, isn't it? Could we possibly keep them at bay that long?

I scrape the blood flakes away from my hands as best I can, trying to look at ease. I decide to get him talking again. "Hey, what about the money? Was that really Lucy's idea?"

He still doesn't answer right away, he's staring into the rearview mirror. I turn to look, too, but I see only endless dark. "It was *my* Lucy's idea. I was very worried you'd be more likely to run for it after speaking to me in person. I needed to keep you calm enough to get you in the car and back up to the house. We'd decided it would be best to wait until morning if at all possible. My Lucy thought that a little cash might keep you more interested in sticking around, more willing to make amends."

I wish I hadn't asked. Am I that transparently greedy? Jesus. I wonder what their plan was for keeping Finn around, what story they might have fed him. I'm about to ask, but Mr. Frey says, "Quiet, now."

I don't know why I listen to him, but my mouth clamps shut. A police car flies by us. Its siren isn't on, but the lights are flashing. Mr. Frey squints at the receding taillights and grips the steering wheel a little tighter, ten and two. He's nervous.

I wait a few more minutes before I try talking again. I'm not sure what else I should ask, but the question comes straight from my heart to my mouth, no thinking required.

"Can I talk to Dimitri?"

"He can hear you. He's technically more present than I am."

"Will you let him talk back to me?"

"No."

I let the car sink into silence again. We're getting close to the house, I think. Soon, we'll be taking the exit with the gas station. I think about the man behind the counter, I think about his wife. I hope they have a marvelous time in Italy. I start to cry. I don't want the thing controlling Dimitri to see my tears. I want to seem strong, brave, smart. I don't want to be a baby. But as I think these things, the tears fall harder and faster, and I can't help but sniffle. I don't want Dimitri to die. I don't want any of us to die. Not like this. It's more than unfair. If Lucy had crashed the car on the way to the B&B and we had all died, that would have been a tragedy, sure. But tragedies happen. They're part of life. This is different. We are being stolen. Stolen for selfish love. I'm disgusted, but also, the irony doesn't escape me. *This is* my *hell*, I realize. *Dimitri doesn't deserve this.*

"Dimitri?" I say through my sniffling.

The imposter stays silent. He knows I'm not talking to him. I watch the trees glide past the windows on either side of the narrow road. Most of them are just tangles of darker night, the impression of a tree vaguely drawn black on black. But occasionally, a naked white monstrosity will peek out from the others, reaching out toward the road with its many pale fingers of branches. Whenever the headlights catch these white trees,

I get the impression that the tree has been taken by surprise, paused in its tracks as a deer would. I wonder what nefarious things they might be up to before and after the headlights' glare, when it's just them alone in the dark of the forest.

Animals scamper around out there as well. I see them occasionally, sometimes darting away and sometimes just gazing at the car, curious and unafraid. There are worse things in these woods I suppose. Tall, wicked birches. Ghosts. Vampires.

"D," I start again. I don't look at him. Maybe I can pretend it's just him and me here. "I heard you talking to Finn. About us getting married." I wipe my nose on my disgusting hands. Blood and snot. It's not how I would like him to see me, but I might not have another chance. "I would've just gone to the courthouse. I'm sorry I was so pissy about money all the time. It shouldn't have mattered. I've always been so, so happy with you. You're all I needed. I wanted better for both of us, but you make me very happy. I love you."

I break down completely then, I can't say anything else. The imposter doesn't reply and doesn't let Dimitri reply, but he does reach up and wipe a tear away from his own eyes. I wonder if they're his own, or if Dimitri got through after all.

Chapter 15

"All right now, my dear," Mr. Frey (I can't think of him as anything else. Now that I know, I can't believe I could have ever thought for a second this person was Dimitri) puts the car into park in front of the bed and breakfast. "This could be very difficult for me and very painful for you... Or." He squints severely at me. "You can just do as you're told, and we can be done with this nasty business quickly."

I consider my options. Neither Lucy nor Finn's car are here yet. I'm alone up here with Mr. Frey. Could I take him down by force? Could I somehow talk him into letting Dimitri go before his wife arrives?

I decide I'm more likely to succeed in the second endeavor. Dimitri is about a foot taller than me and strong, and even if I could hurt him, *could* I hurt him? I don't think that I could. "I'm honestly pretty exhausted," I admit. "I don't think I've got much fighting left in me." I sigh, as defeatedly as I can muster. I've got to make him feel sorry for me.

He nods. "That's good. I truly don't want to do you any harm that isn't necessary. You stay put, I'll come around and let you out."

He leaves the car keys in the ignition as he opens his door, and I know immediately he's testing me. If I make a wrong move now, I'm going to end up getting carried inside the house in pieces. I make sure to look at the keys long enough that he sees me looking and then turn my head away defeatedly.

I unclip my seatbelt and wait for him to open my door. When he does, I slide out of the car, and he immediately takes my upper arm in a firm grip and guides me toward the god-awful, beautiful house.

I can't help but notice that I feel excellent. Not only is my headache gone and my hand good as new, but the dizziness and nausea that's been plaguing me on and off all weekend has disappeared. I absently wonder if I actually have had a little stomach bug or something this whole time, and the whole vampire blood trick cleared it right up.

"Did you notice," he casually says as we step into the foyer. "The peculiar bout of weakness that plagued both yourself and Mr. Murphy when you crossed the threshold Friday evening?"

"Yeah," I mutter. "Super 'peculiar'. Why?"

"That was the contract being signed, my girl!" He turns me to face the front door, places a heel on the carpet runner, and drags it to one side. A line of symbols are there, painted in white, all along the bottom edge of the door frame. "It's worked like a charm for many years. The first two bodies to cross my line after the rise of the full moon are opened to us."

"Opened?"

He tips his head from side to side. "It's the best way to phrase it, I think. You are now a waiting vessel. Ingenious, the leaps and bounds our kind have made these last few hundred years. I'm proud to say I've been fairly integral."

I don't know if he's looking for a pat on the back or what, but I'm pretty much out of nice things to say at this point. "You can't figure out the ghost problem, though?"

"I am *so* close." He resumes walking. We're headed up the stairs and his fingers are still tight around my arm. "I just need a little more cooperation on the other side. You will be the one, I think. You're going to help me set you free."

I really, really hope not, but I shrug as best I can. "I don't see what else I'm going to do with eternity, I guess."

"That's the spirit. Ha! Spirit."

I can't believe this is happening.

He leads me upstairs. I assume we're going to some secret room we didn't get a chance to investigate on our house tour. I assume it's full of diabolical medieval machinery that's going to suck my soul out of my body and leave nothing but a me-shaped husk. I assume it's going to hurt. I finally start to feel icy cold tendrils of fear snake up the back up my neck.

We don't go towards a secret room. Instead, he guides me to the library. I'm oddly disappointed. I've been in here, there's nothing strange besides a screechy desk drawer and some errant air currents.

"I'm going to have to tie you up, unfortunately," he says. "No hard feelings, but I assume that your friend Finn might be less cooperative after my dear Lucy's...enthusiasm, earlier this evening. She may require my assistance."

I squint around the room. "I think you forgot rope."

He releases another of Dimitri's charming laughs. "No need. Here, have a seat."

We're at the back of the room, near the gigantic fireplace. He gestures to one of the overstuffed leather armchairs.

I raise an eyebrow. I need to start thinking quickly, I realize we're getting down to the wire here. Time to get him chatty again. "Can I just sit and wait here? I'm honestly kind of intrigued about this whole trapped soul thing. Do you really know how to get the ghosts to pass on? What do I do to get free once I'm, you know..." I roll my eyes up and stick my tongue out in a casual mimicry of my very fast approaching doom.

"Like I've mentioned, others have been quite resistant to volunteer. They'd rather wander around here indefinitely than forward my research at all." He lets out an irritated huff of air. "Like wild animals in a trap, they won't accept my help." He's guiding me towards a chair as he's speaking and gently pushes me down into it. "But in theory, there's little that can really go wrong if you follow my instruction. Matter not being created or destroyed, et cetera. Your soul has to go *somewhere*."

There's a tiny clicking noise and suddenly my left arm is pulled tight against the armrest. Before I can do more than gawk down at it, my other arm has been pressed against the rest on the other side, and I watch in horror as Frey pulls what looks like a seatbelt strap out from under the arm's cushion and snaps it securely to a latch on the other side. He gives each strap a strong tug and I feel the straps bite down against my forearms. I'm stuck.

He looks at me and gives me one of those sad little smiles, and I kick him in the right kneecap as hard as I possibly can. I hear a satisfyingly disgusting snap as his leg buckles underneath him, and he tumbles sideways onto the floor. I take this opportunity to start wriggling ineffectually. I figure I can probably get out of this if I don't mind breaking both my arms and right now, I don't.

"That was unkind, but I suppose I deserve it," Mr. Frey says. His voice is infuriatingly calm.

He stands, favoring the right leg, but I don't think I managed to break anything or maybe it's already healing. I expect him to maybe hurt me in return, and I thrash wildly as he gets closer, but he reaches over my head and pulls down a set of two more seatbelt straps that connect in a "v" shape. He ducks around my flying head and limbs and deftly buckles me in. I'm essentially in a giant child's car seat or maybe ready to ride a rollercoaster. He gives the straps a final tug and I can barely wiggle, though my legs still flap around uselessly, I'm too short to reach the floor.

"Sit tight," he says and chuckling at his own joke, leaves me alone.

Opal, as usual, didn't mess around. Mr. Frey has Finn in a fireman's carry when he reappears in front of me. I couldn't see them enter the room, but I've been hearing Finn scream, both words and just long drawn out howls, for about four minutes. Finn has been essentially hog tied, and I assume it was done before he ever came back to consciousness after the stabbing. I wonder if Opal spoke to him at all during the long drive up here or if she just stuffed him in the trunk and drove in relative silence. Probably the latter. I wonder briefly if she would get car sick if she wasn't driving, now that she's in Lucy's body.

Finn looks absolutely deranged with terror. I feel sorry for him. I want to explain all the things I've learned, just so he has even the faintest clue what's happening to us.

Then, as he's being assisted into another bondage equipped armchair, he starts to speak. I'm the one that's been left in the dark after all.

"No. No, no, no. This isn't..." Finn says. "This isn't how it's supposed to go. We had an agreement!"

Has he lost it completely? I guess everyone handles stressful situations differently, but Finn is acting like they just forgot to mention this in the contract or something. A little footnote forgotten in the house buying process. Does he not realize they mean to kill us all?

"It was supposed to be Hazel. You were supposed to take her."

What?

Frey laughs. "We *are* taking Hazel. Unfortunately, there's been a little snag, Mr. Murphy. The contract had already been signed before you approached me with your silly little threats."

Finn rocks back and forth in the chair, wobbling it a little. "I'll make sure everyone knows what you are."

"Wait." The straps in my shoulders dig as I squirm to see Finn. "You *knew*? How?"

"I don't think we can give him the accolade of *knowing*. He did, however, have some very wild accusations he's been attempting to blackmail us with," Opal says through Lucy's lips. She's standing near the fireplace facing me and Mr. Frey drags over another chair for her to sit in.

This revelation has thrown me. Did Finn deliberately put us all in danger? For what, a *house*? How could it be worth it? I want to ask him, but Opal is grinning that evil, knowing grin, so obviously hers even on Lucy's features. "What?" I snap at her.

"I'm sure you'll be very interested in the conversations your friend has been having with us," she says softly, almost whispering.

"Don't," Finn says, and his struggling momentarily stops. He's looking at Opal, pleading with his eyes.

I look back and forth between the two of them. "What the fuck is going on here?"

Mr. Frey is back with his own chair. He settles across from Finn, humming softly to himself. Apparently, the tense silence doesn't bother him. "Oh!" he says and stands again. "I almost forgot. Ambiance." He flips a switch on the wall and the giant fireplace before me roars to instant life. Must be gas. Or magic, I guess, who the fuck knows anymore. "Now," he says. "Are we ready?"

Opal nods, but I shake my head. "Can you tell me what happened? Please?"

Mr. Frey sighs. "It won't be pleasant for you to hear, my dear. It's best to leave it in the past."

Opal's leering face distracts me from his words. "He tried to sell you to us. A bargaining chip. You *and* your beau."

"What?" I manage.

"It wasn't like that," Finn starts. "It was just a ruse, I never would have let—"

"A ruse?" Opal laughs. "I think the best you can call her is bait, but we know perfectly well you meant for us to take them. He offered his silence and two suitable bodies, in exchange for the house. He thought he was so clever springing it on us upon your arrival the other night. Little did he know." This phrase is in a high sing-song voice. "He sealed his own fate crossing the threshold."

My face is numb. I can't feel my tongue in my mouth to form words.

"It's really too bad that it was you," Mr. Frey says, looking at me. "That entered the house first with Mr. Murphy. If Mrs. Murphy would have crossed, we would have simply let you and Dimitri go home, and that would have been the end of it." Mr. Frey sighs again. "So much messier this way."

"The threshold?" Finn asks stupidly. Nobody bothers to answer him.

I hear Dimitri's throat clear, and I turn back toward the Freys. "Your friend here found us out," Frey says simply. "I suppose through research for his job, he discovered that the Leap changes hands every forty-nine years, yes? From there, it doesn't take too much to realize there's something...odd...at play."

I whip my head back to Finn and he's nodding slowly at the floor.

"He confronted me within minutes of your arrival. Threatened us. And offered us a deal." He shakes his head pityingly. "It's true, my dear. He offered us you and your friend. We would hand over the keys of Lovers' Leap to Finn and his wife, and we would start again somewhere new as Hazel and Dimitri, and he would never tell a soul what he knew."

"You'd have me killed for a *house?*" I gasp, straining more against my straps than ever before. I'm going to get loose and strangle Finn. "What the fuck is wrong with you? How could you?"

Finn sighs and looks up. The fight is momentarily gone from him. "The house was just a bonus, honestly. Plus, you wouldn't exactly be *dead*, right?"

The room goes completely silent. I swear the fire even stops waving, but then I realize that both the Freys are swaying slightly, almost in time with the flames. I've heard the expression "seeing red" before and I always thought it was just that, an expression. But no. I think every blood vessel in my head just violently burst, and now the room swims into a murky red filter. "Why." I whisper. It's all I can manage.

But maybe I know why. Maybe, even though Finn doesn't know my secret, he feels it. While I wait for him to respond, my memory of that day flashes before my eyes like it almost never does any more. I used to see it happening over and over and over, during my road trip. I couldn't get rid of it. Couldn't get rid of the guilt. Until I trained myself to just tweak a few tiny details, nothing really, just minor things. Those little tweaks in a new story let me live my life in peace. I was able to sleep at night, even when I knew Finn was only a few yards away unable to sleep with his own memories. With my new and improved past, his pain was no longer my fault. But now, the truth stings my eyelids in milliseconds. I might be dying tonight. Don't they say you relive your life in the moments you die?

"We're about to have significantly different lives, I think."

It was the day of the accident, though neither of us knew that yet. The morning everything changed.

I laughed, but it was a small, unsure one. I didn't like Finn's tone, his posture. He looked sad and scared.

"Well, of course, we are. We're going to college!" I injected pep I didn't feel into the words.

He pursed his lips. "No, I mean, different lives from each other. I just don't think we'll be able to do it. I think we should just not worry about the whole..." His pause was strained. "The whole *relationship* part of our relationship. We need to make sure our friendship stays intact first and foremost. You're the most important person to me. I don't want to lose you over new school bullshit."

"Hang on," I said slowly. "Are you breaking up with me? Now?" I don't know how to react. I scramble for reasons why he can't do this. "But...our road trip. Our plans? We're supposed to go out for your birthday!"

He let air escape through his nose. It might have been a tiny laugh at my desperation. "I already told you yesterday you aren't coming to dinner tonight. I'm sorry, Hazel."

"No," I said. I heard the whine in my own voice. The panic. "No, you just said it wouldn't be a good idea. But we can talk to your dad, right? About how I'm part of the family? About how we're serious?"

He pinched the bridge of his nose. His father did that when he was irritated. I could see the older man in every one of Finn's features in the gesture. "Let's just take a little break, okay? It'll be good for both of us."

"Did your dad tell you to say that?" I spat.

"Shut up and *listen* for a second." He brought his hand slowly down from his face and looked straight into my eyes, leaning close. "We aren't dating any more. It's not about my dad, okay?

That was just to make you feel better. *I* don't want to date you anymore."

I'd waited until Finn was busy with the dinner time dog walks he did for shit pay. It only left me a tiny window before I had to be at the last minute babysitting gig I'd picked up, but I tried my best to walk casually, carrying my crackling dome of plastic. I had attempted to scrape the price tag from the side, but there was no disguising that I'd purchased this birthday cake from the grocery store. It had elegant chocolate shavings around the rim and white candy roses on top. I didn't think Finn was a rose guy, but I'd needed some way to disguise the hole I'd had to make in the cake when I soaked the sponge with rat poison. I'd tried a tiny taste myself. It was sweet. They wouldn't even notice the difference.

I didn't worry about Finn eating enough of it to actually kill him. He hated chocolate and I was sure he'd be so full after gorging at the steakhouse that if he ate any, it would just be so I didn't feel bad. His mom Matilda was on a constant diet, she probably wouldn't have more than a taste. Frank, though? Finn's dad Frank would go ahead and eat the whole thing and lick up the frosting, if I was lucky.

We (*they*, now that I was no longer invited) were supposed to go to birthday dinner as soon as Finn got home. With any luck, they would eat the cake afterward (it was too bad I wouldn't make it for the post dinner celebration, since I'd picked up a babysitting shift) and we'd all blame the tragedy on the restaurant food. Restaurant kitchens probably had rat poison in them, right? Mistakes could happen.

I pictured all of them falling ill overnight, rushing to the hospital. I'd be there at Finn's bedside to take care of him and his mother, to help them get over the loss of Frank, to join their family.

Frank opened the door and squinted at me. "Finn's not here," he said. He actually started to close the door on me. At my house, Finn could walk in at any hour of the day or night, grab food out of our fridge and start watching our television without anyone batting an eye. Here, this man wouldn't give me the time of day.

I didn't know why he never liked me, just never thought I was good enough for his son. It was definitely his constant stream of nasty comments about me that made Finn finally break down and decide what he did that day. Surely Finn would have never made the decision to leave me without his father whispering in his ear.

I smiled at Frank. "Oh, I'm not here to see him. Did he..." I pouted as prettily as I could muster. "Did he tell you that we've decided to take a break?"

Frank leaned a forearm on the doorframe and dropped just a tiny bit of his standoffishness. "He did. You two are smart kids. You're doing the right thing, focusing on your educations first."

"Thank you," I said, but I couldn't fake too much longer. "Anyway, since I won't be at his dinner tonight:" I thrust the cake at him. "Please tell Finn I say, 'happy birthday' and no hard feelings!"

I skipped back home. Soon, Finn was going to need someone to help him through those trying times and it was going to be his best, oldest friend. His soulmate.

I didn't mean for things to happen like they did, but I can't deny it turned out better for me than I could have hoped. I think that Frank must have disposed of the cake before Finn even got home. He certainly never told Finn I'd stopped by. I tried to tell myself that he'd thrown the whole cake away and that his "medical emergency" during the car accident was just a coincidence. I knew better. Frank probably only threw away a plastic dome, licked clean.

I suppose I was careless. I think if Matilda would have survived, things would have been much different. Losing her was too difficult for Finn and it wasn't good for me either. If she had survived, we would have all leaned on each other for support.

Without Matilda, Finn withdrew into himself until he disappeared, the snake that ate its tail. I don't know this man tied into a chair beside me. He's whatever grew out of the rotting remains of the person Finn used to be. Why did I try to hang on to someone who has been gone for so long?

"You couldn't just leave me alone and let me live my life, Hazel. You've never stopped bothering me since I broke up with you and it's been ten goddamn *years*. And now, you've been in Lucy's ear, you two getting closer and closer and it was getting to the point I thought I'd *never* be rid of you. I know you were the one trying to talk her into adopting all those fucking criminals she pretends to teach. Plus, you're always broke, always needing fifty bucks, a couch to crash on, whatever."

This shakes me more than I'd like to admit. Did he really feel this way? Have all these years, all these double dates, all this *time*, all been one sided? All out of pity? Who is it that plans our times together? Who initiates our phone calls? Who has been putting in the effort?

It's been me, I realize. The reason I was so excited to go to their house for dinner the other night was because Finn had invited *me* for once, not the other way around. The reason I was late to work the other day was because Finn had called me for once, I couldn't ignore it just because I was supposed to be getting ready. *Oh, shit.*

I wonder about Lucy. Did she really want to be my friend? I genuinely thought so. Did she really feel like my sister? Yes. This whole time was she the one that was keeping my connection with Finn open, because *she* needed me? I'd spent all this time perceiving her as some kind of threat and she was the one that cared.

"So," I manage to say. I can't believe that my body can feel all of these emotions at the same time. I can't believe that right now, people are out there, sleeping and shopping and fucking and I'm here, the entire earth imploding on me in front of this gas (or magic) fireplace. "You'd have me killed? What about Dimitri, Finn? Why would you do this to him? *How. How could you do this to him?*" I'm sobbing. I don't even know if that last sentence was comprehensible. "By the way, *Lucy can hear you,* asshole."

He doesn't answer me, but whips his head toward Lucy/Opal, who's been smirking and enjoying this like a tennis match. She deigns to give him a tiny nod of confirmation.

"None of this really matters, anyway." Mr. Frey cuts in. "Dear Lucy and charming Dimitri are about to take a little private vacation to their own unfortunate deaths and the two of you," He points at Finn and I, "are welcome to continue this argument into eternity, right here in this house for as long as it stands and probably after." Almost as an afterthought, he adds, "Unless either of you wants to help me on the most interesting conundrum on how to get you out of here, that is."

Opal laughs from her chair by the fire. "Don't bother. I won't want any mirrors in this house until I'm back out of that *dreadful* body." She sighs, looking at me. She looks almost bored. "It's going to be such a long cycle."

"Aren't they *all* long?" I ask. I hope I keep the desperation out of my voice. I'm really grasping here. I lock eyes with Mr. Frey. "Just day after day after day, doing what? Housekeeping? Are you even enjoying yourself anymore?"

Opal scoffs. "Well, I certainly enjoy myself more than I would being dead. Ask any of these fools skulking around this place how much fun *that* is."

"What's the point, though?" Finn asks, catching hold of the fact that I'm stalling as easily as if I had slipped him a note telling him as much, bless him. "Like, how old are you? What do you have to show for it?"

Mr. Frey's silence is suffocating. Opal turns around in her chair to glare at him. I've never seen Lucy glare before, she looks like a fairy tale evil princess. "Are you ready?"

Dimitri's body twitches with the current of her impatience. "Of course, my love. Say, if you're unhappy with that one," he gestured at me, "we can swap. I don't mind."

Opal stands and approaches Finn, appraising him like a work of art. He does a few halfhearted kicks in her general direction, but we're both good and stuck. He's a raccoon hissing from inside a closed trap. "Hmmm, well...I suppose it might be fun." She runs a perfect white nail along his jaw and my heart breaks for him, despite the fact that this is very much his fault. Seeing Lucy like this is torture. "Okay."

Chapter 16

"Mr. Frey, don't do this. You know you don't want to do this anymore," My heart starts pounding, trying to get out every last beat it can before it's no longer mine to control. I look at him, at Dimitri. "Please."

He's breathing fast and his eyes flick back and forth, like all his options are laid out in front of him and he just needs to reach out and pluck one. He's coming up with a plan. I know he is, because I know that face. I know every blink and twitch and shiver, and even though it's not Dimitri inside, the body reacts the same. Mr. Frey is trying to figure out how to set us free. He wants to end this. Opal should have taken his little hobby more seriously, his guilt has been festering.

Opal sits on the back of Finn's chair. "We should go one at a time, I don't know if I'll be able to handle him without you."

Mr. Frey is still lost in possibilities, Dimitri's face a haze. "Mmhm," he manages, but he's not quite listening.

Opal stands with a dramatic sigh. "These aren't even nice kids, my love. It isn't worth getting yourself upset over. It will be done soon." She reaches up the back of her hand to receive a kiss—

And Mr. Frey snatches her close, trapping her arms against her sides in a bear hug. "She has to go to one of you. One of you two." His eyes move quickly between Finn and myself. "Which one?"

"What? What do you mean, my love? You're hurting me." I can't believe how quickly Opal's voice changes. Instead of her haughty drawl, she suddenly sounds like a sleepy, frightened child. Worse, a caricature of a frightened child. Something that must be protected at all costs. She knows Mr. Frey has had enough.

"Which one of you!" he shouts. He's crying.

Finn screams, "Her, Hazel! Take Hazel!"

Mr. Frey immediately starts dragging a kicking Lucy towards Finn, angry at his cowardice, assuming he's the worst of us. But he doesn't know. None of them know who the worst of us is, except for me. "Yes, me." I surprise myself with how easily it comes. "I'll help you. Afterward."

Mr. Frey chuckles feebly. "I won't be there. You'll have to figure it out on your own."

Opal is shrieking now, like a demon, a banshee. An awful, eardrum bursting wail. She's thrashing so violently I'm afraid she might hurt Lucy. Mr. Frey drags her close to me in two heaving steps and she spits in my face. Mr. Frey places his forehead to her temple and whispers a string of words in a different language, too low for us to hear, too private. Lucy's body sags and he kisses her hair through tears.

This would all be very sweet and very sad, but there's suddenly a shriek vibrating throughout my skull that I can't get away from and can't ignore. It's unintelligible, and the voice is the voice of ancient things. Of graveyards and cobwebs, of sarcophaguses full of beetles. Opal is in my head.

Get out, you idiot girl.

The voice doesn't really say those words, but that's the meaning I comprehend. And suddenly, I *am* out. I'm sitting in the same chair, but I feel my body thrashing, hear it screeching, beneath me. I am jarringly unencumbered by it. I decide to move away and with the decision, there is motion. I find myself at Dimitri's (no, Mr. Frey's, I can't forget) side. He is kneeling in front of my thrashing body, opening weeping, apologizing.

The words sound strange, kind of like I'm underwater. It looks strange, too. Everything seems to have a cottony film over it, edges are blurred and skitter in constant motion. I wave my hand in front of my face, and it leaves a slow streak of movement behind it. I try to focus on Finn, only a few steps away, but he is only a spot of color. I move towards him and see that Lucy is there. She's crying, trying to make her shaking hands undo the shackles around him. She's okay. They're both okay. "Finn?"

He doesn't hear me. That's okay, too.

"She killed your parents, boy!" My body cries triumphantly. "I see it here, in her head! She poisoned your father. Made him sick." Opal laughs a horrendous laugh. Do I sound like that? "A murderer." She whips my head to face Dimitri. "You'll leave me to save this slime? A murderer? *Two* murderers?"

I must not be able to sweat anymore because if I could, I'd definitely be sweating right now. He knows. Finn *knows*. It's possible that I only volunteered a moment ago to die because I would be taking that secret with me. All for nothing. And here I am, maybe dead? Definitely displaced, at least.

"Hey, I never killed anybody," Finn says slowly. "And that's not true, anyway. She would never have..."

"She *did*—"

"Hush, now," Mr. Frey says, standing. I float towards him again accidentally, just by focusing my attention on him. "Listen closely. Soon, I will leave Dimitri's body behind and not assume another's. I don't..." He wipes Dimitri's sweaty hair away from his forehead, something Dimitri would never do. "I don't know what will happen to me then. You'll have to act fast. Leave the house immediately. *Stay away from Hazel.* If you get too close, she could move."

This is all said in a loud, commanding voice. It has to be loud because Opal is tearing my throat open with wild animal snarls and howls. Mr. Frey grabs the chair she (I?) am still attached to, and begins dragging it toward the dancing flames of the fireplace.

"Wait," Lucy says. I'm suddenly beside her, close enough to count her freckles through the hazy air. "We aren't leaving without Hazel. There has to be another way."

My heart breaks. Oh, Lucy. I love you. I wish I could tell you now. I'm ready to say it, too late.

"We've got to go." Finn puts a gentle, newly freed hand on her upper arm, but she shakes him away.

"No." She marches forward, looks Mr. Frey up and down. "You're a smart man, right? A scholar? How do we get her out? There's a way."

Mr. Frey frowns. Opal shrieks, thrashes, breaks my wrists probably. "Well...My notes. I need my notes. They were in the car."

I give a gasp that no one hears. They weren't *all* in the car. I have one, right upstairs in the nightstand. If only I could get through to any of them...but wait! I *told* Finn about the notebook and where it was. Would he remember?

"Finn!" I say, sliding easily around or through Lucy to him. "The notebook! It's upstairs!"

He can't hear me, it's obvious, but something else is obvious, too. He remembers the notebook is up there. I watch him wrestle with himself, trying to decide whether to tell them. I feel my face crumple up, just the used tissue I am. He really wants to be rid of me that badly, even if he doesn't believe I'm responsible for his parents. He really just doesn't like me that much. After an eternity, he sighs defeatedly to the room that would be silent if not for the constant demon yowls coming from my body. "Hazel was looking through one. She left it upstairs, in her nightstand."

"Well, go get it, boy, go on!" Mr. Frey snaps. His nerves are fraying. I don't think it's as easy for him to block out his poor wife as it is for the rest of us. At any moment, he could be swayed back to killing them all. I hope Finn realizes that. I hope he hurries.

"He knows how to free us," A voice, much more close and crystal clear than anyone else's through this underwater veil is right in my ear. I scream. Opal is standing next to me. The *real* Opal, the one from my dream and from the mirror and my bedside. She's dressed casually, comfortable expensive black knits, her little silver cross sparkling. Her face unlined and plump, youthful and carelessly perfect. Her long hair has no trace of silver, dark and straight and luxurious, with no ornament. She is solid and outrageously present. I can feel the weight of her beside me like I've never noticed another person. We're taking up the same space. "He figured it out ages ago. Before me and Alex ever came here."

"Opal!" I say stupidly. "Nice to meet you. I'm sorry Dimitri threw a pillow at you."

She shrugs. "No harm done."

"Wait. You said he *knows*?" For some reason, I'm very offended that Mr. Frey would have lied to me about that. He seemed so earnest. So guilty.

"Yep. He just didn't like the answer, so he's been trying to come up with a different one. We're tied to *them*. Our souls are part of *them*. They've gotta go. Then, we can finally go."

"Aren't you scared?" I whisper. I ask because I'm so, so scared.

"Nah. Well..." She smiles kindly at me and takes my hand. Hers is cool and dry. "Maybe a little, but that's part of moving forward, right?"

I love how relaxed she is. She has a slight southern drawl, slow, easy words. A big, unabashedly toothy smile. Nothing like this wicked witch currently thrashing my body around like a rag doll. "Right."

"Got it," Finn says, slightly out of breath. He holds the yellowing pages over his head, his big trophy. Mr. Frey rushes over.

"Come on," the real Opal whispers and we move closer, putting Finn and the papers in focus. "Maybe you won't come with me after all."

I can hardly dare to hope. We float up high and look over Lucy's head as she dances on tiptoes around the men, trying to see. "Well? Is it here? What do we do?"

"Excellent," Mr. Frey breathes. "It's here. It happened so long ago."

"*What* happened?" asks Lucy.

The witch (it's true, now that I've met this real Opal, I can't think of that old hag as her at all) pauses her tantrum. "Darling?" she says hoarsely.

Mr. Frey scrunches his eyes shut as though he's in pain and doesn't open them as he speaks. "Long ago, when I first began this project, my thinking was too binary. I thought only in absolutes and tried very harsh solutions. One of my first experiments forced me completely out of the body I was inhabiting. No harm done, as its original owner was wandering around somewhere in the basement at the time..."

"*What?!*" My body hisses. "Why didn't you ever tell me about this?"

"Well," Frey nervously fidgets with the pages. "I knew you'd be upset, call me foolish—"

"I *am* upset, and you *are* foolish! You never should have been meddling with our very nature. And now, this. I never would have believed it of you." She forces tears swimming into my eyes, down the cheeks, ruining my careful eyeliner.

"It's time, darling. It's past time," he answers. He looks more wistful than sad, honestly.

"I'm going to gather the others," Opal murmurs beside me. "If she ends up on our side, we might need back up."

"Our side?" I ask.

She shrugs. "She might turn into a ghost or something. I'm not really sure how any of this works, but the more the merrier, right? And anyway," She smirks at me. "Nobody is going to wanna miss this."

I start to say something else, but she's suddenly gone. There was no act of leaving the room, she just disappeared as quickly as she had at my bedside. I wonder if I could do that. If I could just...

"Shit." I'm in the dark, vacant kitchen. *Library,* I think hurriedly and then I'm back with the others. I'll have to be more careful. I can't miss my opportunity to take my body back.

Mr. Frey is attempting to draw careful symbols on the thrashing witch's head, double checking every line with a glance at the math in the binder clipped pages. I wonder when he's going to go about the business of getting the hell out of my partner's body. "Come hold her still, please," he says to Lucy and Finn.

Lucy steps forward, but Finn takes her arm. "Actually, we should probably just go, right?" he says. "We're going to be targets as soon as you're done."

"But what about Hazel and D?"

He presses his lips together. "They're smart, they can take care of themselves. You've been through enough, Lucy. Let's go."

Mr. Frey nods distractedly. "He's right, actually. It'll be safer for you to just head down the mountain. Not much more you can do here anyway." He smears charcoal down my cheek during a particularly viscous snap of my neck. "Shh," he whispers, licking his thumb and trying to wipe it away.

"You go then," Lucy says, tears starting to leak. "If you really don't care, you just go, Finn."

Finn gives an exasperated little grunt and flops back down into his torture chair.

"We're back!" Opal says in my ear and makes me jump and scream all over again.

"Jesus! You should wear a bell or something." I turn, and see that she has other people with her. *Lots* of other people.

"Sorry." She smirks. "Decades of haunting a house will make you a little creepy. Everyone, this is Hazel, Hazel, this is everyone."

I wave awkwardly and count as I make eye contact with each person. There are nineteen new people here, plus Opal. The Freys have been doing this for a long, long time.

"Which one of you is—" I begin, but an anguished scream turns our attention back through the veil. Mr. Frey has finished his spell or whatever he calls it.

"Now's your chance sunshine," Opal says. "Get up close."

Mr. Frey is speaking. "She'll be loose in the room soon, almost like a ghost. I'm going to leave this body and try to hold her back, if that's possible. I don't know."

"What?!" Finn cries. "You don't know?"

Lucy nods and steps forward. "I'm going to be ready to untie her. Hazel!" she calls, and I jump. I didn't think any of them really thought about me being present. "Hazel come on back now, if you're away. Follow the sound of my voice, okay?" She's trembling.

I smile at her. "Thank you, Lucy." I whisper, and *she* jumps.

"I think she's here!" She calls over the screams. "I heard my name, I think!"

Suddenly, my restrained body is completely slack and empty, my head flops forward onto my chest and no more sound comes from it. *She's out.*

But she's not gone. She stands before me, here, in this other place, this in between place. She is everything I imagined she would be, that lifetime ago when I was in the kitchen alone with her.

I suppose, in dim light, if she were wearing a wide brimmed hat...maybe some gloves...sunglasses, she might be able to pass as a very, very old human woman. But here in front of the dancing firelight and adequate reading lights high above, she is atrocious. Her skin hangs off of her in delicate folds, wrinkling over each other like a bulldog puppy, but without any of the sweetness, any of the warmth. It's scaly, papery, dry, and dead grey. Her eye sockets are impossibly deep black pits, and the eyeballs have no white left, no irises, just a piss yellow film. Drool slides out from the formless gash of her mouth, no teeth inside, only glistening darkness. Her fingers taper to black points and I can't tell whether they're sharp like claws or would just flop around like wet cardboard, there's no separation between finger and nail. She is *not* human. Not by a long shot.

"The lady of the hour," Opal says dramatically. "Not looking so hot these days, huh?"

The thing gives a gurgling, bird-like caw and lunges forward.

Opal grabs my elbow. "Go now, Hazel. We'll take care of this. We've been waiting a long time." Jeers and battle cries erupt from all the ghosts.

I feel frozen. I have to see how this plays out. What if they can't hurt her, can't hold her? We won't be safe. We won't ever be safe.

"Hazel?"

I gasp, hand to my chest. It's Dimitri. *My* Dimitri. I know it before I can even spin to see him, before he's even finished speaking my name. It's him and the imposter has left him. I catch the briefest glance of another of the creatures, the one that's been using Dimitri. Frey looks identical to the witch, but he's grabbing her arms, holding her back, whispering to her in a language I don't understand. Their victims descend upon them, all flailing limbs and righteous anger.

"Hazel? She's not back. Where is she?"

I drag my eyes away from the spectacle and back to my friends, who are gathered around my lifeless body. The screams are terrible, and I can hear the creatures crying, too. I just want it to be done.

"Come back, Hazel, please!" Lucy cries.

I sigh and return to myself. As soon as I get close enough to touch my own hand, there's a dizzying snap and I am sitting down. The circulation of air, the hum of lightbulbs, the *whoosh* from the fireplace, all rush back into my ears and make them pop. But the screaming, the crying, the horrible sounds of murder, it's all gone. I open my eyes and stare at the spot where I know the vampires and their ghosts wrestle. There's no indication.

"How will we know?" I ask softly.

The others exclaim, but I guess they aren't sure it's me who has returned, as none of them makes a move to untie me.

Dimitri takes my shoulders and glares into my face. The distrust hurts, even though I understand why it's there. "Hazel?"

I burst into tears. "Are you okay?" There's a hitching sob or two between each word.

He hugs me close. "Oh, my God, yes. Yes. I'm okay. Let's go." He starts undoing the seatbelts.

"Are they gone?" Finn asks, his voice barely a whisper.

"I don't know!" I'm still crying. "The ghosts are like…" I'm unintelligible. "They're. Mr. And Mrs. Frey. They're so horrible. They don't look like people there."

"Where?"

"In the…" I gesture around. "Where the ghosts are. It's."

"Alright, we can talk about this in the car." Finn slaps his thighs like it's time to leave a restaurant.

"Wait, we don't know if…" I begin again.

"Come on." Dimitri picks me up like a sleepy child. "Tell me while we walk."

"Lucy?" I say into Dimitri's shoulder.

"I'm here." I feel her warm hand on mine.

"I didn't see if the ghosts killed them," I finally manage. "The ghosts will be free if the monsters die. We have to make sure they die."

Dimitri sets me down and I fall in step beside him as we reach the sitting area. "Should we just burn the place down?"

"What?" Finn cries, spinning around to face us. "No, why would you want to do that?"

Dimitri shrugs. "Just seems like the kind of thing you do with a house like this."

"The ghosts will get it done. Then it won't be haunted, and it won't have the Freys," Finn says. "Also, I signed the paperwork, it's *my* house. This can still work."

I start to laugh. "*What*?"

Dimitri immediately says, "No."

Lucy sounds exhausted. "We're selling it. We'll split the profit, the four of us. Can I ride home with you two?"

"Hey, Lucy, come on…" Finn whines.

"I just need, I just need a minute, okay? I just need to get my head on straight."

We're coming down the last flight of stairs into the entryway. I'm with Lucy, I feel like I need to recuperate for a week before

I can even start to sort through the feelings I'm having. Finn wanted (wants) me dead. Gone. How am I supposed to cope with that? How am I supposed to even fully appreciate that I'm walking away from that death unscathed? Spite?

"I didn't mean that stuff I said," he's saying now. "Any of it. It just...it got too big, out of hand. You *know* I—"

"I don't know what I know anymore," Lucy answers quietly. She's crying. I should be crying, too, probably. "Can I drive?" This is directed to Dimitri, who's just procured our car keys from his pocket. Mr. Frey must have put them there.

"Sure." Dimitri hands them over, they rattle as his hand shakes.

The two of them pass through the front door and then my fist and nose simultaneously slam against nothing. My hand pulls from Dimitri's grip as he continues walking while I'm stopped short.

"Ow. What the fuck?" *Shit.* Finn is standing beside me, also unable to cross the threshold.

I groan. Of course, it couldn't have been as easy as walking out the front door.

Dimitri turns back, only wondering why I've let go of his hand. I put my palms against the air of the doorway as though it's a window. "We're stuck."

"What?" Dimitri charges back towards me and bounces off the barrier. "Aw, come *on.*"

"We've got to finish this, Finn." I sigh. "We've got to make sure they're gone."

"You don't even know that!" he yells, shoulder checking the space. "You don't know the rules."

"Do you? Was this in one of your super secret contract meetings where you literally *sold my soul*?"

"It wasn't like that! It was a scam. I was *scamming* them."

"Don't quit your day job."

"Hey!" Lucy is standing at the door, hands on hips. "Come on, you two. Time to make up and work together."

"Don't teacher talk us!" I say, but I manage a tiny smile. "Come on, let's get up there and kill some vampires, I guess."

Chapter 17

The library is as silent as we left it.

"Welp." Finn spins around, palms up. "What exactly are we supposed to do in here?"

I sigh and sink onto the arm of a couch. "I actually have no idea. I guess we could get a mirror or something, maybe see what's happening?"

He sits down on the opposite arm, the expanse of the couch stretching between us into infinity. "Even if we saw, what could we do? And I doubt we'll see. They're probably all too occupied to make the effort, right?"

The silence stretches.

"Maybe we should just try a different door. The front door has the symbols."

I feel him shrug more than see it. I'm staring at the floor in front of us. I think he probably is, too.

"Did you really...you know. What she said," he whispers.

Heat creeps up my neck. "Not on purpose. I mean. I don't know what I was thinking would happen. Not what happened, though." It's not really a confession. Not by a long shot, but suddenly, I realize how much weight that secret had been placing on my chest. I breathe a little deeper than I have in many years and then I wait for Finn to kill me. Instead, his voice remains quiet.

"Nothing really seems to have consequences when you're a kid, I guess. Or really, ever. I didn't really think twice about what I was doing, with this place. I just thought...I thought I could...I don't know. It made sense at the time. This is all so fucked up. *We* are fucked up."

"Everybody is, probably," I manage. "I guess we can try to be better. Those two out there deserve better than fuck ups like us. We're gonna have to step up."

He stands. "You're right. You're right. Alright, let's do this. Come on." He holds out a hand to me and I take it without reservation.

"Hey, they can see us," I say suddenly. "The ghosts. They can hear us, too. Hey!" I call to the room at large, breaking away from Finn and waving my hands around. "Anybody in here?"

A lamp falls from one of the desktops.

"Shit!" Finn yelps and jumps away.

"It's okay, that's good. Well, not *good,* they're still here. How do we talk, hmm...Oh!" I pull my cell phone out of my pocket, but leave the screen dark. I can dimly see my reflection in the glass. "Opal? Can you come close? Tell me what's going on?"

I squint into the glass and see a dark shape approaching from behind, growing larger with every step. I don't feel afraid at all, just eager, anxious. I tilt the screen trying to see the advancing shape more clearly.

"Stupid, stupid girl," Finn says from beside me and slaps my arm down. My phone crashes to the floor, face down, one of those face down phone falls that makes you immediately think, *well, that screen is shattered.*

"What is your problem?!" I yell, but then realize, too late, too late. Finn is no longer in control of his body. The witch glares out at me from his face.

"Damn it," I say, surprising myself by being more annoyed than I am terrified. Maybe I've hit my terror limit. "Get out of there, lady."

"He's...he's gone," she says, and Finn's lip trembles. "Gone." She sinks his body to the floor.

"Who's gone, Finn? I'm sure he's around here, some-where...oh. *Oh.*" I crouch down. "You mean, your husband?"

Of all the times I've seen Finn cry today, this is certainly the worst. The witch's sobs rack his entire body and he recoils into a fetal position, face buried between his own knees. "What will I do?"

"Um," I shuffle closer, put a hand on Finn's shoulder. "Do you want to talk about it?"

She doesn't—or can't—answer.

"You know, he loved you very, very much. He told me so in the car." I pause, the crying continues, but there are longer pauses between wails. She's listening. "He also told me that the only reason he managed to keep this up so long was for you. He was so *tired*, you know? Tired and heart sick. We didn't make him go. He needed to go."

Finn sniffles once and manages to peek up at me from the crook of his elbow. "He told you that?"

"He asked me not to tell you. Didn't want to upset you."

She rolls back up into a sitting position, arms linked around knees. "Do you think he's waiting for me?"

"I'd like to think so, but you'd know better than me. I'd never even seen a ghost before this weekend."

"His ghosts are gone," she says with a little huff of a laugh. "All these years trying to set them free, and he finally did it. That's how I got back, they were holding me."

"And your ghosts?"

"They're here. I'd forgotten some of them, honestly. It's been so long."

I take a chance. "You could let them go, too."

Finn's face crumples. "He'd like that, wouldn't he? It's what he wanted."

"Yes."

She sighs, brushes the memory of hair back from ears that don't currently have hair around them. "Well. I guess it's time. Tell your friend Lucy that she is a delight."

Finn gives a gasp that belongs to him and there is the sound of feet pounding down the hall runner. Dimitri and Lucy skid in through the open doors at a run.

"Broke a window." Dimitri wheezes as he tries to catch his breath. "But the front door's working again, Lucy walked right through while I was cutting myself up. Are you two...?"

"We're us," I answer quickly, heaving Finn to his feet. "I think it's over."

"It's over. Opal says bye." Finn gazes at the empty room around us. I'm sure he's looking for the traces of the people he was just talking to.

"Let's talk and walk, please?" Lucy grabs both mine and Finn's hands and pulls us forward. "No more coming back."

As we reach the front door and successfully cross to the front lawn, Dimitri says, "Just a sec." and dashes back inside. We only wait for a couple of minutes before he's joined us, and we head towards the cars.

"What did you do?" I ask him as we both tumble into the backseat of Lucy's car. Lucy will drive and Finn flops into the passenger. We'll worry about our car some other day. Right now, we all just want to be together.

"Nothing," Dimitri says, too casually.

I turn to face the house as the curtains in the windows framing the front door are glittering with bright flames. They aren't LED.

Chapter 18

Three weeks later

"You are *so* beautiful," Lucy whispers and wipes a delicate tear from the corner of her eye.

We're in a Sunday school classroom of my parents' church they hardly ever attend. Lucy is supposed to be helping me with my makeup, but we both know that I'll be doing that myself so that I don't look like a stranger on my own wedding day. She's mostly helping by handing me things from my bag on the floor I can't reach while constricted in my dress and reminding me how perfect Dimitri and I are for each other. I don't need the reminders, but I'm grateful she's here with me all the same.

I've decided it's time to start saying things when I feel them. "I'm so glad you're here," I tell her and lean close to the mirror she's set up on a kinetic sand table (luckily the sand is nowhere to be found) to apply mascara.

She grins at me through the mirror. "I have something for you, for luck. I'll be right back. Do *not* leave this room, I don't want you to ruin the surprise for D."

I roll my eyes. She's big on the tradition of the bride and groom not seeing each other before the ceremony and we're humoring her, even though neither Dimitri or I care. I actually feel mostly lonely without him around all day. I wish he was in here.

I also wish Finn was here. I don't think he's coming. Lucy has been carefully avoiding talking about him at all, to stay happy for me. They're taking "a break," as she calls it, though she hasn't once mentioned the d-word. Finn took the attempt to burn down Lovers' Leap pretty hard and hasn't spoken to Dimitri since, not that Dimitri minds.

Dimitri has apologized over and over to me for his actions, not that he thinks he made a mistake, but for the wedge it placed between Finn and I, and even Finn and Lucy. Dimitri had no idea how upset Finn would get over it. Finn's been mostly staying up at the house, overseeing repairs. Lucy says he hasn't slept at home once since we escaped.

She's upset with him for other reasons, mostly the things he said about me and her students that day. She doesn't know how to work through it, at least not while he's insisting on being so distant. Lucy doesn't want to move up to the house at all anymore, but Finn won't let it go.

I sigh and accidentally blob my cheek with mascara. "Shit." My corset makes me creak like I'm nothing more than a skeleton as I bend and dig for a makeup wipe.

I don't even really care about the things said that day. I just want my best friend back. He never returns my calls and his texts are short, like I'm bothering him. I truly don't even know if he'll show up today, even though he said he'd "try" to be here. I wedge myself and my massive dress back into the child sized desk chair, squint into the mirror for the offending mascara smudge. And like a magic trick, there Finn is, standing just a few feet behind me.

I smile, but try to act like it's no big deal that he's here. I can't let him know that his absence would have made my most magical day so much less so. "Hey," I say. "Decide to show up after all?"

He's not really dressed for a wedding, even if we're keeping things really casual. I assume my dad will be wearing his cleanest blue jeans, but that'll be the extent of the fancy dress outside of my own ridiculous outfit my mother insisted on buying. But Finn's wearing an old t-shirt. Joggers. What he'd usually wear as pajamas. Finn never leaves the house looking like that and he always gives me a hard time for doing so.

I can't make myself care. I'm just glad he's here. Honesty hour part two. "I'm really glad you came," I say to him through the glass as I attempt to salvage my face. "It wouldn't have been right without you."

The corner of his mouth twitches upward, but he doesn't say anything right away. I think he might have tears sparkling in his eyes. Maybe I am beautiful today.

The door flies open, and Lucy bounds back inside, ending our little moment. "Ta-da!" She gestures at the doorway like Vanna White. I raise an eyebrow, waiting for her to notice her surprise has already found his way into the room. But there, between her flourishing hands, from the dimly lit hall, strolls...Finn. Dressed in appropriate wedding guest attire, a chilly smile on his face.

I drop my mascara wand into my lap and twist around as much as the dress will allow to look directly at the man behind me, with his rumpled nightclothes and wistful eyes.

But, of course, he isn't there. He remains only in reflections.

CHECK OUT THESE OTHER GREAT READS FROM ROWAN PROSE:

Rikki Goodwin is a professional body piercer by day and a horror/thriller author by night. She owns a successful piercing and tattoo studio. "Lovers' Leap" is her debut book. She resides in North Carolina.